I0658045

AUCTUS

SAM CHEEVER

ELECTRIC PROSE PUBLICATIONS

Auctus...Augment: A portal protector and her baby gargoyle, a guardian daemon, a hellhound, and a witch. Together, they must survive in a strange land filled with unknown monsters. Combined they must be strong enough to defy an elite group of magical terrorists. They are Auctus, augmenting the magic flowing through her world...but will they be enough?

I'm Glynn Forester. I'm Magis. More. Recently, in an attempt to save my friends and home from the Body, a group of elite magical terrorists, I accidentally dragged them all through the portal I'm charged with protecting. We ended up in a place where monsters thrive and nothing is familiar. Survival is our first order of business. I need to figure out how to provide food, clothing, and shelter to the people I brought with me.

Though the power of this new place sings through my veins, filling me with magical purpose, I'm in way over my head. I don't know how to take care of so many people. I was barely scraping by just taking care of myself and Boyle, my baby gargoyle.

And then there's Hawk, a powerful daemon guardian whose touch turns my bones to goo. And Nicht, his faithful Hellhound, who is fierce and deadly, unless he's giving a certain baby gargoyle horsey-back rides across my living room.

How am I going to keep my people safe? How will I save my friends who we were forced to leave behind? What will I do about the Body? And the portal? And Grams? And...so much more?

One thing is clear. My relatively safe, slightly boring little world is gone, gone, gone. And I am up to my eyeballs in challenges I have no idea how to meet.

This should be interesting.

STAY IN TOUCH

Sam doesn't give away a lot of books. But she values her readers and, to show it, she's gifting you a copy of a fun book just for signing up for her newsletter!

SIGN UP FOR SAM'S NEWSLETTER!

https://samcheever.com/newsletter/

1

The land that stretched out in front of me was a patchwork of different types of plants, all sown in perfect rectangular gardens with strange rock formations on every corner. In the farthest field, an enormous horse pulled a metal contraption through the gray soil. A tall man rode the back of it, standing on a small metal platform as the horse furrowed the fields.

I lay on my belly beneath the soft, overarching branches of a bush, a pair of special field glasses pressed to my eyes. With those glasses, I could see the small patch of white hairs on the horse's back, probably regrowth after an old injury. I could also see the determined set of her taskmaster's jaw and the hard glint in his pale eyes.

A bird trilled several yards from where I lay, and my gaze jerked in that direction. Tiny pieces of a nearby sandstone tree fluttered down around my head. I sneezed as the granular wisps of bark that gave the tree its name got sucked into my nostrils.

The man on the plow tensed and a hostile gaze slid unerringly in my direction. I hunkered down with a mumbled swear.

"Don't swear, Glynnie," said a soft, chastising voice. "It'th not nithe."

Setting down the field glasses, I rolled onto my back and looked up at the baby gargoyle. "If somebody didn't keep throwing bark dust at my face, I wouldn't be worried about getting caught, and I wouldn't accidentally say an admittedly unfriendly word."

Boyle tsked me clumsily, his tongue not accustomed to the gymnastics needed for the sound. "Don't make 'scuses for your bad behavior, Glynnie."

I frowned, but there was nothing behind it. He was just too darn cute. Even if he was becoming a bossy boy since his Aunt Sissy had decided we were barbarians and started teaching us both manners. "We have to stay really quiet, baby boy. I told you that. If the man over there saw us spying on him..."

"He'd be really angry," said a deep, rusty voice from a few feet away.

Boyle's head shot up, his turquoise gaze went wide, and he covered his mouth with a long-fingered hand.

I rolled and leaped to my feet in a single move,

the knife I kept in a sheath on my thigh hitting my palm before my mind even had time to register that I'd gone for it.

The man standing on the gray-green grass five feet away from me crossed tanned, muscular arms over his chest and lifted shaggy silver brows skyward. "First, you trespass on my land and now you're going to stab me with a knife?"

I moved to stand between him and the baby, who was climbing down the tree with the ease of a monkey or a...well...a gargoyle. "When you put it that way," I said. "It sounds unfriendly."

I couldn't be sure, but I thought his lips twitched slightly at that.

His gaze slid to Boyle as the baby clasped my hand in his warm grip. "Don't be mean to Glynnie. She's not treespassin'. She only mostly passed bushes ta come here. Not trees."

I pressed my lips together to keep from smiling.

The man in front of me cleared his throat. He looked down at his muddy boots. "Well, if you're sure she's good people, I won't yell."

Boyle's little face lit up in a smile. He bounced up and down, jerking me along with the energy of his jumps. "See Glynnie, he nice. We don't have ta be quiet no more." Boyle kept bouncing like he had an invisible jump rope, his energy off the charts from too many recent days stuck inside Victoria. Apparently, we'd landed in Outvald just before the rainy season. And, so far it had been a doozy.

The man's eyes sparkled, his steel-gray eyes warming. "He sure is a springy little thing."

I nodded, sliding the knife back into its sheath. "He's been cooped up too much lately."

The man looked out over his fields, grimacing. "It's all I can do to plow this year. The mud's just about to do old Bessie in."

As if responding to his statement. The enormous horse blew through its nostrils and dipped its head. The short tail swished at a bug and her head whipped around, big teeth snapping at something that pestered her. I'd noticed the bugs in Outvald were downright scary. At least twice as big as anything I'd ever seen at home.

The man extended a work-roughened hand. He looked at it and grimaced, pulling it back. "Name's Shane. You have to be Belle's granddaughter, Glynn."

Belle was a nickname Grams had used, a name from her past. "I am. How'd you guess?"

"She had long brown hair just the same color as yours, with the sun glinting copper off the strands. And you have her eyes. A brown as dark as night." He tilted his head. "You're taller than Belle though, what are you about five-ten?"

"Five eleven," I told him, feeling self-conscious about my size. I wasn't only taller than most women, but I wasn't small-boned either. I was a big woman, not meaty, but strong. Not a woman who men felt like they had to tuck away and protect.

"Belle was a strong woman too. She always gave as good as she got." He stared toward my land, his expression seeming to reflect good memories rather than bad.

Hearing him call Grams Belle was a little disconcerting. I knew Grams had been called different names by different people. She'd liked to compartmentalize the segments of her world. But to me, she'd always just been Grams.

Belle had been a special name. She'd told me a little bit about the time when she'd used it. And I'd seen the fond memories dance across her face as she had. It was a name from her youth. So, it made sense she would have gotten the name on Outvald. She'd spent her youth there. "I haven't heard that name for a while," I told him, laughing. "Except as it pertained to that stupid car."

It was his turn to look surprised. "She still has that old Chevy? Goddess, that thing has to be as old as I am."

"We still have it, yes." I gave him a searching look. "You knew Grams passed, right?"

His gaze slid to the horizon toward Victoria, and sadness filled his expression. "I didn't know for sure. But I thought she had." He stared hard at the rolling hills and oddly shaped trees in the distance as if he could picture Victoria's weathered peaks and chipped paint from there. "I'll tell you a little secret, Glynn, your Grams was never far from Outvald, even when she went through the portal that last time." He thumped his chest with his fist. "She stayed here. In the hearts of all the people she touched." His eyes glistened and he blinked, looking away with embarrassment. Sniffing, he turned to Boyle with a forced smile. "And who is this handsome young man?"

"I'm Boyle," the baby said proudly. He drew himself up to his full height of twenty-eight inches and a smidge, as Sissy liked to say to make him giggle.

"Boyle's my son," I told Shane. My gaze held his for a beat, looking for any kind of judgment that would make it impossible for us to be friends.

But he only inclined his head in a quick nod and crouched down to speak to Boyle. "I'll bet you've never ridden a horse."

Boyle's eyes almost popped out of his head. He started bouncing again, his fingers clutching at my shirt as his eyes went wide. "Can I, Glynnie? Can I? Can I?"

I grabbed his hands to keep him from ripping my shirt and looked at Shane. "Are you sure it'll be okay?" I nodded toward Bessie, who was contentedly ripping gray-green grass out of the ground with her powerful teeth.

"Absolutely. Old Bessie loves kids, don't ya girl?"

The horse lifted her head and nickered softly, her ears twitching toward Boyle and then swiveling away, unconcerned.

"Then, I'm sure he'd love it. Thank you," I told him warmly.

He held my gaze a beat and I saw the truth in his words when he said, "It's my pleasure, Glynn. It truly is."

———

I sat at the base of the tree Boyle had been climbing and laughed at the baby's antics. He was in heaven. But I wasn't sure Bessie would ever be the same again. To her credit, she took his leaping and kicking and caterwauling in stride. It probably didn't hurt that he was like a gnat against her massive bulk. His short legs barely even reached across her wide back.

I lay my head back against the warm bark and sighed. The usual weariness nagged at me, but it was a pleasant nagging. We'd worked hard over the weeks since we'd entered Outvald, trying to forge our place in the untamed and low-technology place.

It had been hard work. Backbreaking work at times. But it had been a labor of love. And I'd been surrounded by people I cared deeply about, so that made it all worthwhile.

"Taking a nap in the middle of the day?" A deep voice accused from way too close.

I jolted, my back coming off the warm bark as I reached for my knife.

Hawk chuckled, throwing up his hands. "I come in peace."

I pulled air in and let it out slowly, my heart slowing. "You're going to come in pieces if you keep sneaking up on me like that."

His chuckle made my belly tighten pleasantly. He glanced toward Boyle again, and I allowed myself to give him a thorough once over while he was distracted. I admired the new highlights in his dark blond hair from working in the sun and the bristle of whiskers peppering his lean jaw. His lips were full and kissable, his cheekbones were high, and his nose was ruthlessly straight. Adding a piercing hazel gaze surrounded by a thick fan of dark lashes, he was a beautiful man in every respect.

Beside him, Nicht was looking perplexed. He cocked his head one way and then the other, trying to figure out what the big creature in the field was doing with a bouncy, Boyle-shaped growth on its back. He whined softly.

"It's okay," I told the oversized guard dog. "He's riding the horse. You know, like cowboys and Indians?"

Nicht skimmed me a quick look and then jerked

his gaze back to the horse, which had turned and was heading back our way. Boyle was invisible behind the mare's big head, except when he bounced off her back and flew up into the air, long arms flailing.

"I hate to break it to the kid, but I've never seen cowboys or Indians flopping around like that. They'd be laughed off the ranch or the reservation if they did."

Nicht gave a little growl and started panting, clearly stressed at the sight.

I twisted a grin, feeling disloyal for wanting to smile. "He has his own, unique style."

"That he does."

Shane stopped the plow at the end of the row and walked over to give Boyle a hand down. The baby grabbed both the older man's hands and jumped, landing on Shane's chest with a squeal. Our neighbor managed the awkward dismount with more skill and grace than I would have been able to do. He was laughing good-naturedly when he settled Boyle to the ground.

Nicht barked happily as Boyle raced toward us. If it weren't for his small wings and tiny horns, Boyle's slender tail and bent legs would have made him look a little bit like a monkey as he ran.

Nicht loped over to meet him, snuffling his belly and his face until he dissolved into helpless laughter.

"So, you met the neighbor." Hawk observed unnecessarily. His expression was tense.

I nudged him with my elbow. "We did. He's nice. He knew Grams and that wretched old car way back when."

Hawke's brows lifted. "Really? Does he know how to deal with that metal monster?"

"That's what he said."

Shane walked in our direction, his strides slow and strong. The older man took the enormous hellhound in stride, but he eyed Hawk just as warily as the guardian eyed him, pulling off his sweat-stained hat as he approached. Shane inclined his head. "Guardian. I'm surprised to see one of your kind around here."

Hawk stiffened just enough to let me know he'd been caught off guard. I guessed not many people recognized what he was. He offered Shane his hand and they shook... two quick, hard pumps.

"I'm here to keep Glynn and the boy safe."

Shane's jaw tightened as if he took that statement as a personal insult. Then he nodded. "That's good. Belle would want them to be well protected."

When Hawk frowned, I laughed. "He's not talking about the car. That's what he calls Grams."

Hawk nodded. "Ah. Well, I wouldn't be surprised to hear that old pile of scrap metal had opinions. It's certainly been resisting my charms."

"She always was difficult, that car," Shane said.

"Belle used her own special mix of magic and elbow grease to keep her running. If you'd like, I'll take a look at her. I used to know quite a bit about making her work."

I hid a smile, not sure if he was talking about Grams or the car.

"Thanks. I'll keep that in mind," Hawk said.

I offered Shane my hand. "Thanks for letting Boyle ride Bessie. You made his year."

Shane nodded. "Tell ya the truth, he made the work go faster. I was so fascinated watching his gyrations, I forgot to be bored."

I didn't doubt that.

"We'll see you around," I told him.

Shane inclined his head.

"Come on, sweet boy!" I called to Boyle. A moment later, Nicht loped out of the trees, Boyle clinging to his ruff and waving an arm in the air.

"Ah," Shane said, "That explains a lot."

We waved goodbye and headed back to Victoria, Boyle, and Nicht running around in front of us like lunatics. I got the impression the big hellhound was trying to compete with Boyle's horseback ride.

Hawk and I fell into a pleasant silence. It was a rare moment of peace in a world that had become hectic and unsure. There was always so much to do around Victoria and the new "apartments" we were building for everyone. I'd left Hawk and my brother atop the oversized outbuilding we were turning into homes for several of the people who'd made the trip to Outvald with us. The two men had been trying to figure out how to add skylights that would let in light but wouldn't leak.

I looked at Hawk. "Did you need something?"

"What?" He turned a relaxed gaze on me.

"You came looking for me. Did you need help with something?"

"Oh. Yeah. But I'm sure it can wait. Tell ya the truth, I was just making sure you were okay."

I'd made it a personal goal to scout out the neighbors on every side of our property, figuring that would be a good place to start making relationships that would hopefully lead to bartering arrangements. There were no grocery stores in Outvald. At least not that we'd seen within walking distance. But, though the plot of land that came with the house encompassed over a hundred acres, I'd come to realize there must be other homesteads along our borders.

Shane had been the second such neighbor I'd scoped out. The first one we'd placed squarely into the "Do Not Disturb" category.

My forays to the edge of the property were really the only times I was away from the rest of the group for any length of time. I enjoyed them. Boyle and I so rarely got to spend time alone anymore. But not everybody liked it when we put space between us.

Hawk, in particular, seemed to want to always

know where everybody was. I chalked it up to him being a guardian.

"We were fine. It's a beautiful day for a walk."

He nodded and returned to his thoughts.

"You should take Shane up on his offer to help with Belle."

Hawk didn't respond. For some reason, he didn't trust the older man. I'd give him time to come to grips with the idea, and then I'd push it some more. Shane had a good garden. He might have milk for Boyle. We could maybe offer him some of the meat Hawk and the guys had hunted in exchange for some vegetables and milk. It would be a good trade.

"You should ask your Grams about him," Hawk said. He lifted his head and settled his hazel gaze on me. "See what she says."

It wasn't a bad idea. In fact, I should ask her about all the neighbors. "I will."

He nodded. "Good."

2

When we'd been forced to run from our home in the Earth dimension, we'd been under attack by the Magical Body, a corrupt organization that sought to control all the people under its thumb, magic and non-magic users alike. The street where I'd lived was in a tiny country town about an hour from Magical Indianapolis. Render had been a mix of magic users and non-magic people, all trying to live their lives the way we chose, all keeping mostly to ourselves under fear of drawing the notice of the Body.

Several years ago, on the Earthly plane, a corrupt few magic users had gotten it into their heads that they should control everyone and everything. Through coercion and promises of power, those few had managed to convince many other magic users to join them.

That was the beginning of the time we called the Disruption.

In the beginning, the Disruption had mostly focused on drawing all magical energy into the cities, where it was thought the close proximity would create an axis of power that people without magic would be reluctant to take on.

It quickly became an Us against Them struggle, where non-magic humans were cast as the villains and deemed dangerous to those who had magic.

But, true to human nature, a little dominance proved not to be enough. Those who were trying to consolidate their power soon decided that all magic users needed to comply with their edict to relocate to the cities.

Anyone who didn't favor being told how to live their lives became just as much the enemy as those who, by nature of their limited or non-existent magical abilities, were considered intrinsically hostile.

The Disruption had started in Magical Indy, but like any good contagion, it quickly spread across the country, infecting many of the larger cities in most of the states. Millions of the non-magic ran into the countryside, hiding in caves and abandoned buildings. These independent souls preferred to eke out a meager existence of their own design rather than be forced into slavery by magic users.

Despite the greater world's assumption that all

the magic had been pulled into the cities, the resi-
dents of Render knew better. In our small, forgotten
place in the universe, we held our magic close,
hiding it from the few non-magic humans who still
resided in the dusty, broken town.

And from those who would try to bend it to their
will beyond the small town.

Those of us who'd wanted to remain in Render
had either gone deep underground until the focus
left our unprepossessing little town and we'd all
been forgotten, or had fled deeper into the countryside to make a new kind of home amid the skeletal
remains of towns that barely clung to life along the
ribs of the country's battle-scarred rural zones.

Those months had been terrifying and painful
for me as a portal protector. I'd had Victoria to
protect, a not-quite-sentient but definitely magical
Victorian-style home that I'd inherited from
Grams...or rather my brother had inherited and
hadn't wanted, but that was a much larger story. And
I'd had Victoria's oh-so-dangerous portal. So I'd had
to stay close enough to do my job while keeping out
of the eye of the roving bands of Magical Indy
soldiers.

My best friend, Sissy had put a spell on Victoria
to make her look like a fallen-down corpse of a
building. Empty and uninhabitable. And I'd warded
myself into the basement, leaving only rarely, when
my stores of food and water had been depleted.

After a while, the soldiers lost interest in Render. And those of us who'd stayed behind had slowly come out of our mouseholes and reestablished our lives. Unfortunately, the event had scarred us. Deeply. We were a private bunch. Suspicious and borderline unfriendly.

But we were living under our own directives. Surviving under our own rules. And for most of us, that was enough.

And then the Body had discovered us. Or, rather, it had discovered Victoria and the portal. And it wanted her portal in the worst way. Hawk had been sent to Render to keep an eye on us and report back. But the guardian had had other ideas. He and a bunch of like-minded Indy cops had watched us with an eye for something entirely different—protection from the Body.

They probably never expected that protection to include being pulled through Victoria's powerful portal into an entirely different dimension.

I hadn't expected it either. Though I thanked the goddess every single day that they'd been dragged into our adventure with us.

Victoria came into view in the distance, sitting atop a wide hill and surrounded by a proud stand of the local trees, whose massive trunks and arrow-head-shaped tops speared toward a cloudless turquoise sky, straight and unberding. Mixed with the strange-looking Outvald trees were several trees that could have, and in some cases had, been transplanted from Render, including the big old oak tree from my old front yard.

We came upon the single bleached wood cross in the grassy meadow at the bottom of the hill and stopped, taking a moment to say a prayer for everlasting peace at the grave of the seventeen-year-old son of one of our transplants who'd been killed in the Body's initial attack on their home. They'd fled to Victoria to put themselves under Hawk's and my protection, carrying their dead son with them. We'd buried young Devon Kraft on Victoria's land and turned our healing efforts to his distraught family. Devon left behind his parents, Trudy and Pen, and a seven-year-old sister named Emma.

Thoughts of their grief tugged some of the warmth from the day. I blinked tears away before turning once again toward home. Desperate to drag my thoughts away from the painful memories, I turned to Hawk. "Tell me what's happening with the construction."

"Everything is on schedule. With no major disruptions, we should have Barracks One completed by the end of the week and Barracks Two shortly after that."

In the interests of space and for practical purposes, we were putting the three men from Hawk's team together in one housing unit, which we were calling barracks because the sleeping arrangements consisted mainly of three narrow beds in one large room. The second barracks would house Alina, the one female soldier, with room for two more if we bring on more security at a later date.

Given that we had no idea what we were up against security-wise in Outvald, we'd decided to let everybody go with their strengths. Which meant that Hawk and the other ex-Magical Indy cops would initially perform security ops on the property for their room and board, with salary to come at a future date once we figured out how to finance it.

Hawk had a room in Victoria and he was in charge of keeping everyone in the house safe.

My brother Art and best friend Sissy were also staying in Victoria.

The rest of our transplanted crew, which consisted of Sissy's neighbor Micah Blunt; the Krafts; the Tellsons, a young married couple who spent most of their free time alone somewhere on the property; and Kara Blanchette, a forty-something single woman who rarely spoke and barely interacted with anyone in the house, would all eventually live in the Annex.

Unlike the others, Kara seemed aware when Grams appeared nearby, which I found interesting since nobody except me seemed to hear or see the ghost.

I jerked myself from my thoughts and looked at Hawk. He'd apparently been answering my question while I gathered wool.

"...the walls up and stuffed with sound dampening and insulating materials, and we're hoping to mud them up over the next few days."

"Will there be enough materials?" I asked, pretending I hadn't missed a word.

The grin he gave me made me flush and look away. As always, he seemed to know when I was listening and when I wasn't. "Fortunately, your Grams had enough plaster in the building to do most of the walls. We're using old newspapers and magazines as sound dampeners and insulation. She had enough of that to insulate all of the exterior and a few interior walls. There was plenty of lumber to frame the walls, but we're going to cut a few of the native trees to finish them. We'll also use that lumber to make cabinets and furniture." He frowned as if ticking off his mental to-do list.

"Is that decent wood?"

"It's not too hard, which makes it perfect for our purposes, and it has a nice grain. There's enough of the stain left over in the garage to treat it, especially since none of that wood will get weather." He shook his head. "That woman was a serious pack rat."

I laughed. "She was. I'm starting to think she knew she'd be supplying this effort one day." As far as I knew, Grams hadn't been prescient. But the amount of useful stuff she'd left us in the big outbuilding made me wonder. "I'm really glad I never got around to throwing it all away."

Hawk nodded, his expression serious. "I don't know if you heard me..." He lifted his brows and I flushed again. "But the guys locked all of the stuff from your Grams' spell work in the storage area. It's as secure as we can make it. But you might want to go through it soon and bring anything that requires extra protection into the house."

I nodded, knowing he was right. I'd avoided that particular task because Grams had been a powerful sorceress who'd been known to dabble in seriously scary magic. I didn't have the power in my entire body that Grams had in her little finger. But Hawk was right. Whether I intended to use the stuff or not, some of it was too dangerous to leave lying around. And Sissy, who was a witch, would probably have some use for it. "I'll do that tomorrow."

I wanted to sigh. The tasks just kept piling up. I'd planned to set out for the north end of the property, where I'd spotted a large grove of trees bearing some kind of fruit. I intended to harvest some of it and bring it home, where I was going to put the Tellsons to work testing recipes with it. The young couple had made their living selling baked goods to shops in Magical Indy.

Then, I'd wanted to go over the plans for bringing running water to the Annex with my brother Art. He had a strong engineering mind and some ideas for how we could carry water from the stream that ran diagonally across the property through pipes into the Annex.

As far as I could tell from speaking to Grams, Victoria was on a neverending well which, though neverending, apparently wasn't ever-expandible. We couldn't find a way to share the water from it with the Annex.

After that, I'd planned to check out the neighbor to our east, who I suspected might work with metal. My initial plan was to barter fruit and baked goods for some handy items like pipes, knobs, gates, and bathing tubs for the Annex.

I'd have to push some of that off until the next day. But it couldn't be helped.

"I saw a plume of smoke coming from the south this morning," Hawk told me.

I gave him a startled glance. "Really? But I thought that homestead was empty." Our neighbors to the south had apparently moved away. Their home, a large cabin built of wood and stone, could be seen from the road. On one of our forays to see what kinds of conveniences might exist in our immediate area, we'd noticed the house. It had a decidedly deserted appearance, up to and including a front door that flapped in the wind and a broken-down well in the front yard. The driveway had old ruts in the mud from some kind of vehicle, but it was clear by the condition of the drive and the age of the ruts that nobody had driven on it for quite a while.

Hawk shrugged. "Maybe someone moved in. I thought I'd walk down there after dinner. I'd like you to join me if you're interested."

I nodded absently. It would be great if someone moved into the cabin. We could use another potential barter partner. And a populated boundary was a protected one. We were currently blind on that side, which made patrolling the grounds more complicated than it might have otherwise been. "Who's on patrol tonight?"

Hawk and his guys took turns doing night duty since they spent several hours each day working on the Annex. "Alina. She'll come with us."

"Sounds good." We neared Victoria, and the delicious scent of something cooking wafted out to us. My stomach grumbled loudly.

I turned to Nicht and Boyle, who crouching over something on the ground. Whatever it was, Boyle was watching it as if it were the best television program he'd ever seen. I grinned. The little gargoyle hadn't even missed things like TV since we'd been upended into another dimension. With a child's overactive imagination, every day was a living adventure to Boyle. I envied him the pure enjoyment he brought to every encounter. "Hey, Cowboy Boyle.

I'll race you home. It smells like Sissy has dinner ready."

With a squeal and an excited bounce, he was off. And despite the fact that I had about a ten-foot lead on him, that little stinker still beat me into the house.

3

My older brother, Artur Forester, stood in front of the window in the library, which had also been Grams' office where she'd been alive. The room was dark and dusty despite my best efforts and cluttered to the point of claustrophobia.

And I loved it.

The claustrophobia was book-induced, coming from two full walls of built-in wood shelves that were full of every kind of book. Magical reference books butted up against romance novels and human anatomy tomes nestled against essays on mathematical equations and physics.

Behind Art, on the big old scarred wood desk, lay the drawings he'd been creating to address our piping issue in bringing water to the Annex. Next to the drawings was an engineering text on practical water management.

I inhaled deeply as I entered the dimly-lit room, scenting Grams on the air. Her scent still clung to the ratty old couch that dominated the center of the space and infused the old robe she'd kept hanging on a hook behind the door.

"Hey," I said, breaking through my brother's thoughts.

He turned as if he hadn't known I was there, a smile breaking across his face. "Hey. I heard we might have a barter-buddy on the south side?"

I was only mildly surprised at how quickly he'd heard the news. Our little group had all the signs of becoming like any small gathering of people who were searching for the comfort of familiarity and shared knowledge. Gossip was rife among us.

I dropped onto the couch, pulling the fuzzy green afghan over to hug as I dropped my head back with a weary sigh. "His name's Shane. He farms. And he knew Grams."

Art's eyes widened, and he finally turned away from the window. "Really? Maybe he can dish some dirt on her wild past."

I laughed. Peering past his shoulder, I spotted the object of his avid attention through the window. Alina was pushing the swing the guys had hung from the big oak, sending little Emma so high into the branches she emerged with a handful of leaves, delighted laughter accompanying her descent.

Art caught me looking and flushed. He'd made

no secret of the fact that he was interested in the scary cop, but it still seemed to embarrass him. I wondered if he was afraid she wouldn't be interested back. I'd have to try to pick Hawk's brain on that. Maybe he'd have some insights.

"I'm not sure I want to know about Grams' love life," I told him, grimacing.

"Ew!" He agreed. "I just meant her adventures. From what I heard at the Body, Grams was quite the magical adventurer in her day. She made an impression on the Magistrate and other members of the Bench." The Regnant Bench consisted of the thirteen most powerful members of the Body. They were the ruling elites of the city.

By habit, I watched him for signs of his feelings about the organization. My brother had spent nearly half of his life at the Body, first as an intern and then working his way up to becoming one of the Magistrate's most trusted assistants. He'd lived and breathed politics and had told himself that he was working for the public good. But then, one day, he'd started to see a different side to the Body. An ugly side. And his confusion at his part in it all had brought him to Render—back to family. He'd come with the hopes of sorting out his feelings and making decisions about his future.

But he hadn't been given time to decide what he wanted to do. The Body had come to Render and had tried to destroy everything there. Everything except for Victoria. Magistrate Cole Martin had a lust for dominance. Victoria's portal offered him inroads toward total domination.

If I hadn't managed to bring us through the portal to Outvald, I shuddered to think what the evil Magistrate would have done with all of Victoria's available power.

"Glynn?"

I blinked, pulled out of my thoughts, and found Art watching me. "Woolgathering again?"

I plucked at the afghan. "Sorry. I'm tired. I always drift into my thoughts when I'm tired."

"I said," he repeated, "I asked Sissy about taking the tattoo off now that we're in Outvald."

I tensed. Sissy specialized in magical ink that obfuscated and muffled magical energy. She'd placed a muffling tat on Art because we'd discovered he'd been being influenced by the Magistrate, and he didn't have any control over it. Recently, she and I had decided that it was still too dangerous for my brother to go unprotected. We had no idea how far the Magistrate's power reached. We certainly didn't want to inadvertently provide him with information on our location and activities in Outvald.

"It's not a good idea," I told him, bracing for an angry reaction.

He scowled down at the plans he'd so painstakingly created but didn't respond.

"I'm sorry."

He shook his head. "Maybe one day you'll trust me again."

"It isn't *you* who we don't trust."

He lifted a hand. "Save it, Glynn. I'll see you later. I have work to do."

The door opened and Sissy's tousled blonde head poked into the room. "Dinner's ready."

I stood up and dropped the blanket back onto the couch. "It smells great, Sis."

She grinned. "Mystery stew again. Boyle's favorite."

I tried not to grimace. Since we'd been transplanted to Outvald, we were pretty much stuck eating whatever we could hunt. Some of it was just too ugly to eat, but we'd found some favorites, even though we had no idea what we were eating half the time.

I stopped at the door and looked back at Art. "Coming?"

"You go ahead," he said, avoiding my gaze. "I'll eat later."

Sis and I shared a look as I closed the door behind me. She frowned, tucking a strand of wavy blonde hair behind her ear. Her hair had grown a couple of inches since we'd come to Outvald. Mine probably had too. It made me realize we were going to have to find someone to barter grooming services with soon. I sighed. Or else, one of *us* would have to figure it out.

Sissy's gray eyes narrowed on the door. "What's he got stuck in his craw?"

I wrapped an arm around her shoulders, tugging her close. Sissy was only five feet two inches to my five-eleven, and she was curvy where I was solid. She felt even tinier than she was as I pulled her down the hall so we'd be out of Art's earshot. "He's mad about the tattoo."

She sighed. "I know. He talked to me about it. I told him to give it time. We need to settle in and figure stuff out before I try to tackle that."

"Tackle what? Do you have a plan?"

She twisted her lips, looking like a pretty, perplexed pixie. "I didn't figure we'd leave the block on indefinitely. He can't use his magic with the tattoo. I know from personal experience how hard it is when you can't use your magic."

She certainly did. Sissy had been hiding her magic all her life. First, from her parents, who would have expected her to stay in Magical Indy with them if they'd known. And then from the Body for the same reason. She had no interest in having her life and her magic controlled and managed by a bunch of snobby elites who only cared about their own dominance.

She was right to be concerned. We'd already lost a couple of our friends to the Body's rabid quest for control and power.

"I need to find a way to twist a block around only

the usurping magic and leave his own untethered. It's going to be a tricky operation to perform. But first, I have to come up with an even trickier spell to lay the groundwork." She sighed. "He's being a brat. We're all dealing with stuff. He just needs to suck it down."

I nodded. I knew she was right. I did feel bad for my brother. But even if I could send him back to Render so he could go back to his own life, I wasn't sure I'd trust that the control the Magistrate had over him wouldn't be used to find us in Outvald.

"He'll figure it out."

Boyle was bouncing around on his chair when we came into the kitchen. "Boyle, sit!" I barked out without thinking. "You're going to fall and hurt yourself."

"Yeth, Glynnie," he said with apparent docility. I wasn't buying it, though. I caught Alina winking at him.

The baby giggled.

Hawk was at the sink washing up. Micah was dishing some kind of stew into big bowls. Sissy smacked her handsome ex-neighbor on the butt to get him to move to the side. He laughed and slid sideways so she could pull two fat, golden loaves of bread out of the oven.

I closed my eyes and breathed deeply, letting the delicious aroma infuse my senses. "I'll mourn the loss of flour above all things."

Sissy set the pan down and retrieved a dish of butter from the fridge. "I have enough for a month or more. We'll find a substitute by then."

Finding a wheat substitute was one of the tasks the Tellsons had been given since their main job would be baking items for us to eat and barter. They'd been carting nuts and grains into the kitchen for weeks, trying to find something that ground up like flour. There were a couple of promising possibilities so far, but nothing quite as good.

I looked around. "Where is everybody?" The kitchen table could seat as many as eight people if we scrunched. But when everybody was eating together, we ate in the dining room, where the table was twelve feet long. A ridiculously large table that we'd rarely used in all my years living at Victoria.

Alina flicked a tiny ball of paper at Boyle, and he succumbed to shrieking laughter when it bounced off his nose. "The guys are eating at the barracks. They installed a fire pit today and wanted to test it out with the beast they killed last night."

I grimaced. I'd seen the beast. It was beyond ugly. A bumpy misshapen thing with green fur and bulgy eyes. It had teeth like a rat and a tail like an opossum. "Better them than me," I murmured.

Alina nodded. "They're good test subjects. They'll eat just about anything."

Hawk set napkins in a single pile at the center of the table. I reached for them and placed one next to every plate, skipping Boyle. Since Alina had instigated their new "game," I was pretty sure his napkin would end up in a dozen tiny paper balls flying around the kitchen. I threw the gorgeous mercenary a glare which she answered with a smirk. In reality, I could forgive her for stirring up the baby. Despite Alina's deadly nature, she loved kids and mostly thought like one. It was like having a nearly six-foot-tall playmate slash babysitter who could slice off a potential kidnapper's head. Almost a perfect creature. Except for the fact that, like the child whose mentality she mirrored, she had no idea about limits. As she carved a sliver of butter off with her fork and prepared to flick it at Boyle, I grabbed the fork and smacked her hand. "Bad Alina!"

Boyle giggled and Alina gave him a fake pout and another wink.

Micah placed bowls in front of Boyle, Alina, and me and went to get the rest. I watched him move around Sissy, not missing the way he watched her. I realized in a flash of intuition that Micah always managed to touch her whenever she was near. A hand in the small of her back...a finger swiping a random strand of hair off her cheek. Oh yeah, there was something building there. I smiled.

"So, the guys are at the barracks, Art's in the office, where's everybody else?"

Alina frowned. "Is he still working on those plans?"

I nodded. "He said he'd be in later."

She grabbed a second dish and threw a hunk of bread into each bowl, shoving to her feet. "I'll take him his food. Maybe he could use another brain to think things through."

"Great, thanks," I told her.

Micah sat next to Boyle and proceeded to butter a piece of bread for him. "The Tellsons are still in the fields. They found a promising grain they wanted to check out."

Sissy sat down next to Micah. "The Krafts ate earlier and they were going for a walk. Emma's playing with the baby raccoons in the yard. And Kara's in her room. She said she wasn't hungry."

Sissy and I shared a look.

"This smells delicious, Sis," I told my friend.

Micah nodded, swallowing his first bite. "Is this that chicken thing we found out by the pond?"

She nodded. "It's good. Tastes like a mix between a chicken and a turkey."

"Mmm." I gave her a thumbs up. The conversation flowed into normal, domestic-type things and, for a while anyway, I felt at home in my own skin.

Until Victoria's lights suddenly flickered, and the night beyond her glass shifted in movements that didn't seem natural.

We were shoving our chairs out to investigate when the first screams sliced through the night.

4

Victoria's outside lights flared on as we plunged through the front door. It bathed the area around the house, well past the giant oak tree. The little black cat shot past us as we came outside, disappearing into the safety of the house.

I stared out at the nightmare standing thirty yards away and felt my blood turn to ice.

I was dimly aware of the others sliding to a halt around me as we all took the measure of the monster in the yard.

It stood on its hind legs, the enormous claws of its forelegs slicing the air in front of it like Godzilla smacking away airplanes.

It appeared to be close to twenty feet tall standing upright, and had the basic form and musculature of an enormous bear. But we weren't in Kansas anymore, and the bear-shaped monster

wasn't a normal predator. It stared at us through eyes
that glowed a putrid green color. Its maw, open and
snarling, had fangs that curved down and around its
bottom jaw and horns on its head like a longhorn
cow.

Blood dripped from the creature's slashing claws.
It didn't take me long to figure out where the blood
had come from. One of Hawk's guys lay across the
ground at the creature's feet, his body flayed like a
fish, and the ground around him dark and glistening
with blood.

There was so much blood I couldn't tell which of
the guys had gone down.

The creature snarled and circled its victim,
showing us a back full of spears that didn't appear to
be slowing it down much. Our people didn't use
spears. Which made me wonder how long those
things had been embedded there.

"What is that thing?" Sissy asked from
beside me.

I didn't know, but I knew we needed to do something. I looked at Hawk. "We have to distract it away
from the guy on the ground..."

"Rian Pierce," Hawk said, his expression
unhappy.

I swore silently. Rian was the nicest one of the ex-
cops. He was a truly good guy.

A soft sobbing came to us beneath the angry

sounds the creature was making, and our gazes slid slowly upward.

A small, pale face peeked at us from between the branches of the oak. "It's Emma," I breathed, my chest tight with horror. *No, no, no, no, no!* I'd stepped down from the porch and was striding toward the monster before I even realized I'd moved. Magic swirled around my hands, sizzling and potent.

Heavy footsteps sounded behind me. I didn't look to see who'd joined me. I was pulling even more energy from the air and forming it into a sword that I hoped would do a better job of killing that thing than the spears had. The monster saw me coming and dropped to all fours, running at me so fast I nearly didn't get my energy sword up in time to hold it off.

I quickly realized my mistake. The thing's legs were longer than my sword, and the first swipe of those claws sliced through my shirt and burned tracks along my flesh before I could spin away.

"Down!" screamed somebody. I hit the ground and light flared as an energy pistol was discharged into the beast.

The energy smacked into the creature and flared up, yellow flame creating a bloom of destruction on its furry chest. It reared up with a roar of pain, paws smacking the air around the flames.

Without warning, the thing's huge frame shivered and transformed, becoming something reptilian, with scaly green skin covered in a greasy gloss that immediately extinguished the fire. It had a long snout filled with layers of triangular teeth that snapped the air as it swung its powerful tail and tried to take our legs out from under us.

The same spears that had been in the bear creature's back stuck up like porcupine spines along the reptilian form.

I slashed at the thing's scaly leg, my energy blade barely scoring the flesh through the hard, green plates.

"In the face!" Hawk yelled as he slashed the creature with first one and then the second of his long blades. Green blood arced into the night as he severed the hood rising up behind the reptile thing's head.

"Down!" Alina's voice barked and Hawk grabbed my arm, yanking me toward the ground.

Energy lit up the night, exploding in several dense streams that combined into one massive blast to pound the creature backward. It hit the monster right in the snout, consuming its entire head in a wash of brilliant energy that should have melted its flesh into goo.

But as the blast ended, the creature clawed at its singed eyes and magic flared over them, regenerating the flesh as if it had never been damaged.

Hawk and I leaped back into battle. We were joined by the three remaining ex-cops, all bearing large, deadly-looking blades. Like Hawk, Alina had a blade in each hand, and she was deadly fast, spinning toward the creature, slicing one-two, and then gliding back out before it could retaliate.

The other two men carried broadswords, their well-polished blades glittering with energy that crackled and burned against the monster's skin. We surrounded it, all attacking at once and dividing the creature's focus until we started to make inroads in our attack. The thing was bleeding everywhere, and one of its legs had nearly been severed.

We'd managed to move the creature far enough away from Rian that Micah and Sissy were able to tug him closer to the house. There, Sissy attempted a healing spell, trying to save him.

The monster's body shimmied again and it started to change form.

"It's changing!" Hawk yelled, and I threw a quick look at the little girl in the tree, seeing Emma's eyes, the size of golf balls in her pale face.

"It's got wings!" one of the guys yelled.

Terror sliced through my chest. *Wings*! I couldn't let that thing fly up and grab Emma.

The monster grew until it was ten-feet-tall from its three-toed, clawed feet to the leathery tip of its pointed head. It threw back its head and shrieked, the sound too much like the call of an ancient dinosaur for my comfort.

The wings, thirty to forty feet wide if they were

an inch, unfolded in leathery bands from bony frames that had lethal-looking claws at the joints and tips.

I looked at Hawk and he went very still. "No, Glynn," he said, starting toward me.

I shook my head and shrugged. "Wish me luck."

"No!" he yelled.

But, I was already running, my hands swirling with energy as I slammed a foot into the side of the monster and launched myself onto its body. The creature beat its leathery wings and started to rise off the ground, my weight throwing it sideways enough that I started to slide back down.

In a desperate attempt to keep from falling as the monster rose into the sky, I grabbed at a spear and used it to pull myself onto its back.

The attack from below had stopped. The guys couldn't use the energy pistols with me on board. It would be up to me to deal with the monster on my own.

The pterodactyl-like creature pounded its wings, lifting higher into the sky with every stroke. I needed to work fast, or I was quickly going to find myself too high to retreat.

I crawled up the creature's body, wedging myself between the spears and using them to keep my seat as the creature rolled from side to side in an attempt to displace me.

I wrapped my arms around its neck and took a

deep breath, pulling my siphoning energy from my core and tearing into the creature's magic as it screeched its rage.

There was no time for subtlety. So, instead of easing the creature's energy away from it, I yanked, ripped, and tore at the sweet magic infusing the terrifying creature. It came to me in fits and starts at first, an uneven rush of power that slammed into my system like bullets from an old-fashioned gun.

I was nearly blown off the monster's back as it bucked and rolled, fighting the siphoning of its magical energy nearly as hard as it was fighting to displace me. The energy I consumed didn't burn. It wasn't putrid and sour like I'd expected from a creature whose wish had been to make a meal of a small child.

I jerked in shock, realizing I'd read its intent through my connection. Worse, the thought hadn't burned my psyche like the caustic substance it was. As before, when I'd thrown myself so completely into siphoning a monster, I was becoming the creature...seeing through its eyes as a leaden night sky rose up around us, spinning dizzily as we rolled beneath the clouds. My wings whipped outward, stretching to catch a rampant stream of air that would give us the lift to unseat our enemy, and then, as the current flowed away, allowed us to plunge back toward the ground in a dizzying rush of controlled but violent descent.

Our skin recoiled from our enemy's touch. Our organs burned under the too- rapid loss of magic.

Then, with a joyful cry that scraped delightfully through our throat, we spotted the child. Our stomach twisted with hunger. Our eyes glowed with anticipation. And we lifted our wings, pulling out of the dive to control our flight. Aiming directly for the terrified child in the tree.

I screamed, shaking my head to remove the essence staining my brain. The sound came out sounding like the bellow of the monster I rode, my essence already merging with his. The creature's energy boiled through me, a siren call that horrified even as it eluded my attempts to drain and kill.

Far below us, a cry went up as the people scurrying across the earth realized where we were going.

The creature threw back its head and screeched in victory, its beak already clacking together with delighted anticipation of its meal.

Something inside me rebelled. I had to get rid of the magic before it pulled...

The child's eyes widened, fear burning deep within them. She scrabbled backward on the branch, her scent sour with fear.

We bellowed our hunger to the sky. A silvery projectile flew through the night and I dipped sideways, allowing it to glide harmlessly past.

The tree flew up to meet us. Twenty yards. Fifteen. Ten...

In a desperate final attempt to yank free of the monster, I dug for the last of the magic from its veins, fighting the pull to merge, to become one monster instead of two.

Below us, a strident scream ripped me in half. Part of me cherished the sound, embracing it like seasoning for our meal. Part of me was horrified by my hunger.

Screaming again, I knew I'd run out of time. Desperate to stop the monster from reaching its target, I pulled the tainted magic from my core and flung it toward the wings. I wrapped the leathery projections with shimmery golden lassos and tugged them hard, losing my seat as the magic ripped the wings downward. My weight threw the monster off course, sending it spiraling toward the ground.

I hung beneath the monster, tethered to it only by the energy of the lassos I'd wrapped around its wings. I was free and clear but heading quickly toward a hard landing no matter how the current situation ended.

"Now!" I screamed, praying Hawk and the others caught my intent. And then closed my eyes as the ground whirled up to meet us.

Arrows whipped past me, sinking into the creature's thick hide. Energy from the guns flared over it, sizzling away great hunks of its flesh.

The monster screamed again, fighting my

control, and I sent more of its own magic into the lassos, feeling it burn against my fingers.

The ground flew up and smacked me hard.

Energy blasted us as we skated just above the hard-pack earth, and the skin on my back ripped painfully against rock and root.

"Let go!" Hawk screamed as an enormous knife flew past me and buried itself into the monster's throat.

I tried to release the energy lassos. My fingers wouldn't unclench. The monster rose higher, slamming me into a tree and then whipping sideways as its body convulsed into another form. The bear snapped into existence and started to plummet, its wings gone.

The energy ripped from my fingers, taking skin with it, and I fell, slamming into the ground.

The bear crashed down next to me, its convulsing claws barely missing taking a chunk out of my middle before I used the last of my energy to roll away from it.

I lay there, coughing and throbbing in pain, my body battered and painful.

A shout rose from the darkness. Footsteps pounded toward me as, unbelievably, the bear stirred.

And started to rise.

5

Hard hands grabbed for me and yanked me off the ground as the monstrous bear straightened to its full height, the massive maw spreading around its enormous fangs. It gripped the knife Hawk had embedded in its chest between its paws and, unbelievably, yanked it free.

The blade clattered to the ground and the bearthing rounded on us.

Hawk released me, shoving me behind him as he pulled another knife from a sheath at his calf. He had to be running out of blades soon.

I really wanted to know where he hid them all.

I pulled energy from my core, happy to find I still had some stores. The power answered my need, filling my cells with more energy than I'd ever felt. It throbbed beneath my skin, almost painful in its ferocity, and the flesh of my arms rippled in a way that felt a lot like bugs crawling over my skin. Pain burned in my fingers and they cramped, curving and twisting as I stared in horror.

Claws sprang from my fingertips; long, curved, and razor-sharp.

The bear hit the ground on all fours and charged.

Three arrows flashed through the air and embedded themselves into its hide, joining the spears that still quivered along its back.

With a growl of his own, Hawk attacked, blade flashing so quickly I barely saw him move. A line of blood spilled from a wound the width of the monster's chest. The bear roared, slashing at Hawk.

The guardian moved too quickly for the eye to follow, and he was suddenly standing on the bear thing's back, the blade repeatedly slicing through the quivering flesh.

The bear rose up on its hind legs, forepaws carving the air and teeth snapping helplessly as Hawk shredded its back.

Then the thing was suddenly gone, and Hawk hit the ground with an "umph".

Almost before I could blink, it was back, and it was a lizard again.

To my horror, it rose above Hawk and smacked him hard with a long, muscular tail. He flew sideways and crashed into the tree where Emma hid.

The thing's snout rose, its tongue snapping out to

taste the air, and the tiny wings on its back fluttered around the embedded spears.

That was the point where I lost my patience.

Pulling on the energy saturating the grounds and Victoria, I wrapped myself in as much magic as I could siphon and held it within my shimmering, malformed frame. Strength imbued my muscles, thickening my legs and lengthening my face. My skin scaled before my eyes. Wings flapped above and behind me, their muscular feel both foreign and delightful at once.

The lizard creature started to climb the tree, its snakelike body twisting agilely up the wide trunk before I had time to drag in a breath.

I was out of time.

I looked up into the chalky face of the trapped seven-year-old, her eyes wide pools of terror, and I released all semblance of my humanity, whittling it down into a single purpose, an all-consuming goal.

With a thought, I was airborne, my leathery wings meeting the pressure of the air and lifting me toward the branches high above my head.

The lizard thing was nearly there. Ten feet. Eight feet. Five feet.

I reached out and grabbed it in my claws, pounding my wings to yank it off the tree. With a supreme effort that nearly broke my remaining reserves, I fought weariness to rise above the tree with my thrashing burden. I continued to siphon its energy as I rose higher and higher into the sky.

The monster changed to the bear, then to the birdlike thing I was currently mimicking, then to the lizard and back.

Bear, bird, lizard, bear, bird, lizard.

Each transformation grew progressively slower, taking longer to happen, until the monster hung limply in my claws, wearing its lizard form.

I looked down into its face and saw the whitish film glazing its eyes, the slackened jaw.

Beneath my siphoning magic, the monster's skin began to slough, its body to shrink, until I was certain enough of its death that I could release the monumental control it was taking to keep me in the sky.

Then, with a final, exhausted shriek, I dropped my burden and watched it fall, and fall, and fall, hitting the ground with a concussive sound that trembled on the air.

My body rebelled against the sheer amount of magic I'd asked it to assimilate. Charcoal crept along the edges of my vision. The wings above me wavered, weakened, and started to thin.

My leathery chest fought to drag air into over-burdened lungs.

My limbs weakened, thinning down to human size, and the scales gave way to skin. The ground rushed at me, a final, relentless enemy.

I knew I was going to come down hard.

But I was too weak to do anything about it.

I had nothing left.

When the last of the magic sifted away, I closed my eyes and hoped for a quick death.

I didn't get my wish.

A beat later, I was jerked to an abrupt, painless stop. My eyes jerked open with surprise. I was hanging above the grass, two feet in the air.

Hawk was suddenly there, easing me the rest of the way to the ground.

My brain was muzzy. "What..." I licked dry lips, my vision drifting as I tried to refocus my eyes. "What just happened?"

Hawk pulled me half into his lap and ran his hands over me, checking me for broken bones.

I grabbed his arm, finally focusing my gaze on his. "Why am I not dead?"

His handsome expression tightened. Slowly, he lifted his gaze toward Victoria.

I followed his gaze and gasped.

Artur stood in front of the house. His arms were outstretched, palms upward, and his eyes were...

"His eyes," I said, horrified.

Hawk made an unhappy sound. "I don't know who that is behind them," His arms tightened around me as if fearing for my safety. "But it's not Artur." Our gazes linked, a shared horror living behind them. "That's not your brother, Glynn."

Goddess in galoshes!

Sissy appeared behind Art, a silvery spell woven on the air around her hands. Her lips were moving and her fingers danced lightly along the edges of her spell, growing it, increasing its complexity.

The light dimmed in Artur's eyes, and his hands lowered. He started to turn as if sensing Sissy there.

My best friend looked him in the eyes as he turned, and she smiled. "Hey, Art." Then she smacked him on the forehead with the flat of her hand.

The spell slammed into him, shimmered brightly for a couple of beats, and then sank below his skin. Artur went limp, folding toward the ground.

Micah stepped out of the shadows and caught my brother before he hit the ground. The big man threw Art over his shoulder and carried him into Victoria.

I started to stand, to follow, but my legs gave out on me. I crashed back down onto Hawk's lap.

"How about I carry you inside?" he asked with a grin.

I hated it. But I didn't really have any choice unless I wanted to crawl. And there wasn't much dignity in that. Then I remembered, "Emma?"

"She's safe. Tomas took her inside, and Nicht's watching over her and Boyle."

Relief filled me. "That explains why Nicht wasn't out here with us."

Hawk frowned. "I told him to stay with Boyle. I thought that would be your choice."

I nodded. "You're right. Thanks."

He carried me into Victoria and sat me on the couch. Almost immediately Victoria's healing magic started its work on me.

Sissy came out of Art's room, her expression grim.

"Sis?" She glanced my way and came over. "How's Rian?" I asked.

Sissy took a deep breath and blew it out. "I did what I could. Maybe you can give him some of Victoria's healing energy when you're feeling better. He was pretty ripped up."

Anger filled me. That thing was the first monster that had dared, or been able, to cross our wards since we'd arrived in Outvald. Had we just been lucky? Or had the creature been uniquely suited to passing our wards? I looked at Hawk. "We need to figure out how that thing got in."

"Alina's already on that. She and Grodan are doing a perimeter check. They're looking for fractures in the ward."

Normally they wouldn't be able to see a break in Victoria's wards, but we'd imbued the protections with special energy that showed bright green where a breach had occurred. Since our security force wasn't magically tied to Victoria, it had been a necessary precaution.

I laid my head back for a moment, enjoying the healing touch of Victoria's energy.

Trudy and Pen Kraft hurried over and Trudy bent down to give me a hug. "Thank you so much, Glynn," she said in her high-pitched voice. Her dark blue gaze was shiny with tears and her curly brown hair was a mess, as if she'd been running her fingers through it. "You saved her life."

I hugged her back, giving Pen Kraft a smile over her shoulder. He scraped a shaky hand over his bearded face, tears sliding from his gray eyes.

"Where is she?" I asked.

"In the kitchen. She and Boyle are getting ready to bake." Pen laughed. "We thought it would be good to distract her."

I nodded. "Watching Boyle bake would distract anybody."

Pen sniffed, laughing wetly. "Bless you." He looked at Hawk. "All of you. We can't tell you how much what you did means..." His voice trailed off and his chin quivered as he looked away.

Hawk reached out and clasped the man's shoulder.

"Do we know where the Tellsons are?" Sissy asked.

I glanced at Hawk.

A deep voice responded instead. Micah came into the room and stood next to the couch. "They're in their room. Everyone's accounted for."

We'd created makeshift sleeping quarters for everyone until the Annex was complete. Like most Victorian structures, Victoria was a rabbit's warren of small, sometimes oddly shaped rooms. We'd divvied those rooms up and spread them out as much as possible, allowing everyone to have at least the illusion of privacy. The Krafts were on the second floor. The Tellsons were down the hall from them. My room was also on the second floor.

Hawk had turned one of the small rooms on the first floor into his space. Alina took another.

Boyle was in his attic room on the third floor since gargoyles loved high spots. That also gave him direct access to the roof when he felt the need to climb around out there. There had been a small storage room on the third too, and Kara Blanchette had taken that. We'd cleaned it out, put odds and ends of furniture in it from around the house, and she'd announced it perfect. She spent most of her time in that room, and she seemed content.

As if my thoughts had conjured her up, I heard Kara's soft-spoken voice coming from the kitchen, followed by the high-pitched giggles of the children. I arched my brows at Sissy.

"They're making cookies. Kara thought it might help them forget the trauma."

I nodded. "That was really nice of her."

"Yeah." Sissy slid a look toward Art's room. "It was."

"Tell me," I said in low enough tones that only those in the room could hear.

She sighed. "I'm not sure. It seems like his magic rider is sneaking past the ward somehow."

"I didn't think that was possible," Hawk said, his voice also low.

"It shouldn't be," Sissy agreed. "I need to think on it for a bit. I'm perplexed."

And I needed to speak to Grams. She'd been a powerful sorceress when she'd been alive. She might be able to suggest something that would help us rid my brother of his unwelcome guest.

"Is he safe?" Hawk asked. He threw me a slightly guilty look. "I'm worried he might be a danger to us."

I bristled at the question, but I knew he was right to ask it. The Body had been the reason we'd fled to Outvald. If the Magistrate was somehow keeping tabs on us through my brother, that was bad. He might even use the situation to figure out how to get to us. I was under no illusions about the leader of the Regnant Bench. The Magistrate wanted to tap into the power of Outvald, to use it for his own unscrupulous purposes. He'd wanted Victoria's portal for that reason, but I'd removed that option for him. If he could use my brother to get what he wanted, I had little doubt he'd do it. "Locking that down has to be our first priority," I told them. "Until we do, nobody's safe here. Including my brother."

I received a chorus of nods for that sentiment.

"I'll talk to Grams," I told Sissy. "Maybe she'll have a suggestion."

"Good. I'm going back to him. Right now, we have him in restraints. He's going to be ticked when he wakes up. So we either need to keep him under for a while or find an alternative."

"Personally, I don't care if he's ticked," Micah growled. "He brought this on himself."

Sissy's jaw tightened. She'd known my brother all her life, and she'd always had a soft spot for him. I suspected she'd had a crush on Art when we were much younger.

"We're a family," Hawk said, surprising me. "We stick together." He leveled a look on Micah. "And we give each other the benefit of the doubt. It's the only way this is going to work."

Micah didn't look pleased, but he didn't say anything else. When Sissy headed back to Art's room, he went with her.

The Krafts left too, leaving Hawk and me alone.

Hawk looked at me, his gaze narrowing. "Are you going to be okay? That was pretty..." He seemed to struggle with the right words for what he'd witnessed out there.

It hit me suddenly, what I'd done. I'd actually become the monster I'd siphoned. I'd never done that before. Yeah, I'd come close once, taking on the thoughts and even a couple of the traits of my victim, as well as seeing through its eyes. But I hadn't fully transformed. That was a new one for me.

I shoved uncomfortable memories of the experience aside. Having almost gone too far into the change...thinking of Emma as food...it suddenly hit me how dangerous it had all been. "I guess my magic works better here, in Outvald."

He laughed shortly. I was pretty sure he was thinking what a giant understatement that was. "You're probably pretty sore, huh?"

"A little, yeah. But the house will heal me."

He nodded. "I'm going to go meet up with Alina and Grodan. We need to find that breach and get it sealed up fast. Will you be able to help with that once we locate it?"

"Sure. I'm going to talk to Grams and then I'm all yours."

He squeezed my shoulder and turned toward the door. Stopping with his hand on the knob, Hawk turned back to me. "You know you saved Emma. If you hadn't done what you did..." He frowned. "I don't think we could have killed that thing without you."

He left before I could come up with an adequate response, leaving me victim to my thoughts. I glanced toward Art's door, fear and worry twisting my gut as I realized he'd saved my life. Whatever was going on with his magic rider, my brother had been the one to stop my fall.

I realized it would be up to me to save Art. Sissy could do a lot, but I suspected what we were dealing with was a family sensitivity to the magic in Outvald. Art and I might never have lived there, but our genetics were attuned to the energy in the place.

With a soft groan, I pushed to my feet and headed toward the stairs. Hopefully, Grams could help me figure out how to help Art. Because if she and I couldn't figure it out. He was a danger to all of us, including himself.

6

"Grams?"

Back before we'd relocated to Outvald, I'd had to do a whole thing to reach the ghost of my dead grandmother. But since returning to her childhood home, Grams had been much more "alive" and present than before. Her spirit had always infused Victoria, her magic forming the basis for the enchanted home's power. But, though she was more available to me in Outvald, she'd been conspicuously absent over the last couple of days. A fact that I just realized when I'd decided to speak to her.

"Are you here?"

I stood in the center of her office, a room that still held her familiar lilac scent, despite the fact that she'd been gone five years. I closed my eyes and reached for her, sensing her smoky magic before I felt her.

The air in front of the window thickened and gained weight and color. Finally, Grams stood there, her back to me and her gaze on the horizon. She wore a dress that might have come from her time in Outvald, a plain, cotton dress with long, tight sleeves and a bunched hem that reached just to her ankles. Saggy gray socks covered the flesh below the dress, and her boots were plain black leather, rising to just above her ankles. Her dense cloud of gray hair had been braided and wound in a thick plait at the back of her head, the front pouffed around her face. Despite the ugly clothing, she looked beautiful. Grams had never lost her girlish figure and had stayed youthful until the day of her death.

I watched her for a moment, feeling a sadness that worried me. Since we'd returned to Outvald, Grams had been upbeat, excited about being back. She'd been immeasurably helpful and a great resource for how to survive in the harsh environment.

But, sometime over the last couple of days, she seemed to have fallen into a funk.

I joined her at the window, staring out over the hilltop the house stood on, to the wide, flat land where Devon Kraft was buried. I frowned. We needed to put a fence around that spot, protecting it from predators and designating it as a special place.

In the distance, I saw a narrow column of pale smoke rising into the sky. Shane's home? It was likely. I needed to take him a pie or something and pick his brain. Like Grams, he'd be a great source of information about Outvald and our neighbors.

"We met one of our neighbors today," I told her. "Shane. Do you remember him?"

Gram seemed to jolt out of her thoughts and turned to me with a smile. "You met Shane?"

I nodded, grinning. "He let Boyle ride his plow horse."

Gram's face was alight. She laughed. "Bessie? I'll bet that was interesting."

Good Goddess! How old was that horse? "You have no idea. Shane told me he was so distracted by Boyle's antics he forgot to be bored with the work."

Her laughter warmed my heart, and I couldn't help laughing with her.

Grams shook her head. "That man has never been bored a minute when he was working his fields." Her gaze turned soft, and she looked out over the land again. "His power comes from the soil and its power from him. They're a magical harmony. A balanced pair."

An interesting choice of phrase. "Magical harmony," I repeated. "I like that."

She grasped my hands, giving them a squeeze. Her skin was cool and calloused, as it had been in life. Grams had never been sedentary or introspective. She'd moved through her life like a whirlwind, hungry to learn, and do, and grow.

I liked to believe she'd infected me with that same spirit. But I wasn't so sure it wasn't wishful thinking on my part.

Grams moved away from the window, her step light. A weight of some kind seemed to have lifted from her narrow shoulders. "What can I help you with, child?"

So many things, I thought. I didn't know where to begin. I decided to start with the most pressing. "You're aware that Art was spelled when he was at the Body?"

She frowned, lowering herself onto the couch and clasping her hands. "Nasty stuff, that spell. It will be hard to remove. It's not a surface spell, adhering to his magical core. It's actually woven into the boy's brain."

I blanched. "Into his brain?" I sank dejectedly onto the couch beside her. "That's terrifying."

Grams nodded. "It won't be something we can extract from him. It wouldn't be possible to excise the spell without damaging his mind."

I fell back on the couch, feeling as if she'd smacked me upside the head. Tears burned in my eyes. If we couldn't remove the Magistrate's spy magic from Artur, how were we going to live with it? With him? And poor Artur. How would he live with himself? I couldn't imagine how horrifying it would be to have another presence intruding on my every thought and action. "What are we going to do?" I murmured to myself.

Grams patted my knee. "We'll think of something. I have a couple of ideas."

Hope flared in the desolate place inside me. "I'll help in any way I can."

Grams observed me for a moment, lines of worry denting the space between her brows. She placed a cool palm on my forehead and sent questing fingers into my mind. The invasion was gentle, careful, but disconcerting none-the-less. Her frown deepened. "You must take care, child. Transmogrification is serious business. You've been ill-trained for the practice."

"I didn't actually do it on purpose. It just happened when I siphoned." I tilted my head at her in question. "Could you teach me to siphon without transmogrifying?"

"Siphon to the death?" Something in her gaze warned me I was on shaky ground with her.

"Really just to the point where we can subdue. I didn't set out to kill that thing. I was only trying to stop it from taking Emma."

At my mention of the little girl, Grams pursed her lips. "Yes, the child must be protected at all costs. Like the gargoyle, they are important to our future."

I wondered what she meant by that but pushed it aside for another day. I had enough things to ask her about at that moment. "I don't know how that thing got through the wards."

Grams thought about it for a moment. "Variabilis Bestia. It is a foul creature. Unfortunately, its chameleonic form makes it almost impossible to ward against."

Alarm tightened my chest. "Are there a lot of those things in Outvald?"

"A few, yes. Have young Sissy frame a spell tied to the chameleon. That should take care of this type of creature." She shook her head. "Victoria's basic protective wards should have at least warned you it had come through. The fact that they didn't is worrisome. Unless..." Her gaze lifted to mine. "Was the creature able to fly?"

"Yes."

She nodded. "That's it then. We must add air wards to the mix." She patted my knee. "Give me a bit of time to work on that."

"Thanks, Grams."

"Of course, child. Now..." She eyed me carefully. "What did you really come to see me about?"

"You know I've been observing the neighboring homes?"

She inclined her chin.

"I'm looking for opportunities to barter. That's how we met Shane. I was hoping I could get some information from you about the people around us?"

"Is there a specific neighbor you wanted to know about?"

"All of them, really. But I realize that will take some time." I actually didn't realize that until Grams paled beyond even her ghostly white color. "Um...for now, what can you tell me about the people near the road. The cabin on the southern border?"

"Ah, yes. David Bernes. He was a university professor on Earth. He studied species and their variants."

Well, that surprised me on a couple of fronts. "He's from Earth?"

"Yes, child. Many in Outvald are."

"How'd he get here?"

"Through a portal, of course." She shrugged as if people passed from one dimension to another through portals as an everyday occurrence.

"Well, knock me over with a feather."

She grinned. "No, thank you. Anyway, David is a good man, if a little rough around the edges. That's probably due to his genetics."

"What's wrong with his genetics?" I asked, worry starting to filter through the curiosity.

"Nothing at all."

I arched my brows, wondering if she was being difficult on purpose or if it just came naturally to her.

The twitching of her lips gave me my answer. It was on purpose.

"Grams," I said in a warning tone. "I've got people out there looking for a ward breach. If there's something we need to know about this David…"

"Pshaw!" she flipped a dismissive hand. "He won't hurt them. He can't. The wards won't let him in."

I raised my brows again, giving her a disbelieving look.

"Oh. Right," she said. "The breach. Okay, then I would approach him with caution. He's not always amenable to visitors. Occasionally, he'll be involved in a tricky transformation and he can be downright crotchety."

I bit back a sigh. "Grams, in three words or less, tell me what David Bernes is."

Her face lit with pleasure. "Oh, a game! I love it. Okay, let me think. Three words or less…" She cocked her head and narrowed her gaze on me, then nodded. "He's a shifter."

I swallowed hard. "What does he shift into?"

"Just a wolf."

Okay, a wolf shifter. Got it. Not perfect. And we wouldn't be bartering meat to him. But he might be good for a security role. I'd just have to figure out what we could do for him in return. "That's not too bad."

"No," Grams agreed. "Not at all. He's relatively harmless."

I felt better. "Okay, I'd better get going. Hawk needs my help with something."

"I'll work on the air warding," she told me. "Oh, and Glynnie."

I stopped with my hand on the knob. "Mm-hm?"

"Take care around David's place. His guests can often prove to be deadly."

7

Goddess guild a gourd! The woman could be so infuriating.

My face must have shown my irritation. When Sissy emerged from Art's room and met me at the base of the stairs, she took one look and asked, "What happened? You look ready to throttle someone."

"Grams happened. I'm starting to think death has rattled her brains."

Sissy snorted out a laugh. "Or her chains."

"Ghost jokes, har," I said grumpily.

Sissy's expression turned serious. "Did she have any ideas about Art?"

"Yeah." I frowned.

"That great, huh?"

"She's going to work on something, but..." I sighed. "It's not good. Grams believes the spell is woven into his brain. It's going to take delicate work to remove. If it's even possible at all."

Sissy frowned. "Not the news I was hoping to hear."

"Yeah." I wrapped an arm around her shoulders and gave her a hug.

"Glynnie, Glynnie, Glynnie!" Boyle called excitedly. He came bounding out of the kitchen.

I turned to look at him and burst out laughing.

Little Emma ran up behind him, and she was beaming. "Do you like our pretty faces? I'm a kitty princess. Boyle's a tiger."

Yes. He. Was. "Um. Is that frosting?" Boyle had painted his face with orange frosting and scored lines over the cheeks with his fingertips. I knew this because the tips of his long fingers were covered in frosting, and he was currently painting his shirt with it. Frosting was also globbed onto the thatch of hair between his ears and clumping his lashes together.

Emma's paint job was similar, except her frosting was pink, with dots of some kind of sparkly stuff all over it. She also had frosting globbed in her dancing brown locks and mounded up in front of her nose. Her fingers played with her hair, leaving fresh smears of the stuff in the strands. Her mother was going to kill us. But she no longer had the haunted look on her face, so in my book, it was well worth it.

Kara hurried out of the kitchen, a worried look on her handsome face. She was kneading a towel between water-roughened hands. "I'm so sorry, Glynn. I just turned away for a few minutes to pull cookies out of the oven and wash the bowls." She fixed a horrified look on the two kids. "I should have known when I heard the giggling."

"It's fine. They look beautiful."

The kids bounced up and down, giggling happily.

Micah came out of Art's room, his hazel eyes going wide. "Okay. There's that."

Emma hopped excitedly. "Aren't we pretty?" Tiny flecks of frosting fluttered down from her animated face, littering the floor beneath her.

"You're..." Micah tucked a strand of his wavy black hair behind one ear, clearly unsure exactly what they were.

Sissy saved the day. "Come on, you two. We'll get you cleaned up and see if there's any frosting left for those delicious cookies I smell."

The kids turned on their heels and skipped after her, leaving chunks of frosting on the floor behind them.

I grabbed Kara's hand, giving it a squeeze. "Thank you. Emma doesn't look like a scared little mouse anymore."

Kara's gaze fell to the floor and she flushed, carefully extracting her hand from mine and rubbing it with her other hand. "I'll just go clean up."

I watched her retreat, my heart heavy. What had

happened to that poor woman that made her so timid and so leery of human touch? Whatever it had been. I probably needed to know some details if I was going to help pull her out of it.

"Where's Nicht when you need him?" Micah asked, his eyes glittering with humor as they tracked the frosting trail.

"Don't let him hear you say that. He'll bite you. Nicht isn't a dog, and he refuses to be treated like one."

"I beg to differ, Micah said, "Hell*hound*." He raised his brows. "Plus, I've seen you feeding him table scraps."

I put a finger to my smiling lips. "Our little secret."

He laughed.

"How's my brother doing?"

Micah's smile fell away. "He's still out. Between you and me, I'm not comfortable with this new development. It's like having a spy from the Body living with us."

Yeah, I thought. It was *exactly* like that. "We'll figure it out. Thanks for helping Sissy with him."

Micah's gaze slid toward the kitchen, and his expression warmed. "It's my pleasure." He seemed to pull his attention from the happy voices in the kitchen with an effort, narrowing his gaze on me. "How did that thing get onto the property?"

"According to Grams, we have a hole in our wards. We neglected to ward for flight."

"Ah." He nodded. "Makes sense. Is that something Victoria can fix?"

"With a little help from her friends," I said, smiling.

The front door opened. Hawk strode inside, looking harried. "Glynn, are you up to coming out with us?"

I nodded. "Absolutely."

Hawk glanced at Micah. "You're on point for house security. Lock 'em up and don't let anybody in who Victoria doesn't recognize."

Micah performed a crisp salute, causing Hawk to roll his eyes.

I moved past him, grateful to be getting out of the house for a while. "Hopefully, you haven't found any more of those chameleon things?"

He closed the door and waited while the locks slid home. "No. But we've definitely found something."

There was a tone in his voice that made my stomach twist with concern. "What?"

Nicht flew out of the darkness, tongue lolling. His eyes blazed red, a sure sign that he was on the job. "Stay here and guard the house," Hawk told him.

With a quick butt of his head against my hip, the

big hellhound bounded past me and headed for Victoria. I expected him to drop into his favorite spot on the porch, where Boyle had placed a big pillow for him, but he disappeared around the corner instead.

"Nicht's doing a perimeter check of the house? Is there something I should be worried about?"

Hawk gave me a quick glance and then broke into a jog. "Just being paranoid after what happened tonight."

Yeah. I knew how he felt. "So tell me what I'm walking into." My voice wobbled a bit as I ran. I wished I could run as effortlessly as Hawk and his people. But then, I wasn't trained for movement. I was more a watch and occasionally adjust the portal type gal.

"We found the breach. It's close to the road."

A chill ran up my spine, despite the fact that I was starting to sweat from the running. "Near the neighbor's house?"

"Yep. Like in his back yard."

Okay, that wasn't good. I couldn't help thinking about what Grams had said. Could it have been one of David Bernes' guests? "How big is it? We probably should have brought Sissy out."

Hawk spared me a glance. "I don't think you want Sissy here right now."

About a quarter-mile in front of us, the visible line of warding glowed softly through the night. It wasn't supposed to be visible, but there was one circumstance when it came to light.

"The warding was like this when we arrived. That's why it was so easy to see that."

I looked to where he was pointing. There was a wide, ragged opening in the magical wall. The breach was dark like the night, the edges of the ward hanging like the two sides of a torn piece of fabric. Overgrown bushes and too-long grass showed through the opening, as did Bernes' home, which was only half an acre away. On either side of the break, the ward pulsed in blues and reds and angry yellows from the ground to well above the trees.

A magical ward kept working even when there was a fissure. It worked everywhere except where the break occurred. But the break in continuity caused the magic to skew. That skew resulted in what we were seeing—the pulsing visibility of the magic.

"This way," Hawk said, leading the way through the breach.

I followed him around to the front of the home, my nose crinkling as a putrid stench met us. The smell grew stronger as Hawk led me across the yard.

Alina and Grodan Lance were standing next to an abandoned car. As we approached, not only did the stench of rotting meat grow, but I also couldn't miss the bloody claw marks that had all but ripped the vehicle into shreds.

But it was the body, sprawled half in and half out of the trunk, that really painted my spine with ice.

I put a hand over my mouth and tried not to breathe. "Who is it?"

Alina held up a leather object, offering it to me.

I took it and grimaced. The surface was stained with something that felt slimy against my fingers. Very gingerly, I opened the wallet, looking at an old photo of a man who'd been ruggedly handsome when the picture was taken. It was a driver's license from Chicago. "David Bernes." My heart sank. The man who was draped so ungracefully over the old rust bucket of a car had been my neighbor.

Grodan reached into the trunk and lifted one of Bernes' arms, showing me a clawed hand covered in fur all the way up to the man's elbow. "It looks like he was trying to go furry when he was attacked."

I forced my feet to move closer. Magic stung my skin and I jolted to a stop, glancing around.

"What's wrong?" Hawk asked.

I frowned. "I'm not sure." My gaze slid back to Bernes. "We're sure he's dead?"

The three cops lifted their brows.

I made a face. "Yeah. Stupid question."

"Why do you ask?" Alina cocked her head, her expression curious.

"I felt magic when I moved closer."

"Is it still there?" Hawk asked, his posture stiffening as his hazel gaze scanned the area.

"No." I rubbed my arms. "It's gone."

The three of them relaxed only slightly.

I looked the corpse over, grimacing. "Something tore him to pieces."

"Could it have been that thing we just fought at Victoria?" Grodan asked.

The claw marks were deep, scoring his back all the way down his legs. One arm was almost completely severed.

I pointed to his throat. "Whatever it was, ripped his throat out. That's something a wolf would do," I told them, rubbing my arms against a new array of goose pimples. "The claw marks are deep, but you saw the claws on the chameleon, right? Those claws would have done more damage than this."

Alina nodded. "I agree. I'd say we're looking for some kind of shifter."

Grodan pointed to the clawed hand he still held. "Judging by the blood on these claws, I'd say he got his licks in before he died."

I couldn't help thinking about what Grams had told me. "Grams said Bernes sometimes had guests that might or might not be dangerous. maybe we should start there."

Hawk glanced at the house. "I'm going to have a look around inside."

Alina indicated the grounds around the house. "I'll see what I can find out here."

Nodding, I opened the car doors, wincing as the

bent and rusted metal screeched into the night. I siphoned energy from the air, surprised at the ease with which my body assimilated it, and consolidated it into a circle of light so I could see. The front seat of the old car looked about like you'd expect. The dashboard was coated in dust, the leather seats cracked and faded with time and heavy use. I was surprised to see a set of keys dangling from the ignition. "He was getting ready to go somewhere," I told Grodan.

The cop had his head in the trunk and was searching around the body. I grimaced. The guy was made of sterner stuff than I was.

Refocusing on my task, I carefully removed a metal cup from the center console and sniffed it. Herbal tea. Very civilized. There was nothing in the front except dust and some kind of sticky residue, which didn't seem to have a magic signature.

I moved to the back, searching the seat, the space in front of the window, and the floor.

I found a sheet of paper on the floor. It was pushed far enough forward that it might have been dropped from the front seat. I tugged it out and stared at it, not knowing what I was looking at.

"Live Auction. By invitation only. Bidders responsible for transport."

I backed out of the car. "Hey, Grodan, does this mean anything to you?"

He took the flyer, frowning. "No, but I'm not getting warm feelings from it."

"Why?"

He pointed to some markings above the main heading. I'd scanned past them initially, thinking they were just a random design. But looking more carefully, I noticed the pattern. Pawprints and claw prints of all kinds fit together to make a pattern that suddenly made my stomach clench. "Is this what I think it is?"

"What is it?" Alina asked, coming up to the car.

I handed the flyer to her. She looked at it for a beat and then started scowling. "Where is this?"

I took the page back from her. "I don't know, but we need to find out."

And I knew just the person I could ask.

8

The house was little more than a rough shed inside. The floors were unfinished wood, coated in years-worth of dirt and grime. The walls were unpainted, the once-white boards that were nailed across the framing blotched with what looked like food and other less palatable things. Gouges in all shapes and sizes marred the surface.

The ceiling was open, the joists exposed. And the vents were rusted and badly seated in the wood.

The bulk of the house appeared to comprise one room. Tucked against one wall of the main space, a sink, a few cabinets, an icebox, and a wood-burning stove represented the kitchen part of the house. The rest of the large, open space was a living area. The furniture was all rough too. It looked handmade, and there wasn't a cushion or anything representing a soft surface to be seen.

The room smelled like wet fur and backed-up sewer pipes.

Hopefully, it hadn't been like that when Bernes was alive.

As I stood rooted to the spot just inside the front door, another jolt of stinging magic found me. I twitched from the feel of it against my skin. As before, it didn't give me a threatening vibe, but it was definitely something I hadn't experienced before.

I shook it off and went looking for Hawk.

It didn't take me long to find him.

He was standing in a doorway off the main room of the house, his body tense. His arms hung at his sides, and his hands were fisted.

"Hawk?"

He didn't appear to have heard me.

I walked closer and reached to touch his shoulder. "Hawk?"

He spun around and grabbed my wrist, his grip tight enough to be uncomfortable. His expression was filled with rage. Almost feral. His hazel eyes had darkened to the point where they looked black, and his jaw was tight enough I was afraid he'd fracture a tooth. He didn't seem to recognize me.

I held very still, afraid to speak or move.

The magic I'd felt briefly in the outer room washed over me, its energy so rich and overwhelming it sucked the air right out of my lungs. It no longer stung my skin. It sank into it, a probing force that threatened to overwhelm my natural magic.

I panicked, clawing at my chest and making little mewling noises as the invading energy dug its way inexorably beneath my flesh.

I was helpless against it.

The room was saturated with the invading magic. I didn't dare try to use it myself. Not that I'd know what to use it against.

Hawk?

He wasn't my enemy. Was he?

I fixed a terrified look on him and forced words through my tightly clenched jaw. "Help...me."

A feral red glow blossomed in his eyes, the color swirling from the palest red, almost pink, to deep burgundy—the color of oxygenated blood.

His upper lip quivered, and a throaty growl emerged. The sound vibrated against my flesh, calling out an answering rage.

Without warning, my hand shot out and wrapped around his throat.

He moved, the growl deepening. His muscles bulged with sudden power.

I didn't even think about what I was doing. I grabbed the invading magic and summoned it to my use. The energy shot out of my palm and my fingers curved, elongated. Blood beaded beneath my...claws?

I gave a little scream, the shock of what I was

seeing wrenching my hand from Hawk's throat and sending me scuttling back. Horror made it hard to breathe.

Hawk coughed, the sound broken and weak, and fell to one knee.

I backpedaled into the main room, putting as much distance between us as I could.

I was panting, my vision thready and unfocused, and pain seared through my head.

The door opened too loudly. My head shot up and I growled before I could stop myself.

Hawk rose to his feet.

Alina took one look at him and then me and slowly backed outside.

Good choice.

I forced my clenched fingers to unclench. My palms were bloody where I'd pierced them with my claws. My chest heaved.

I could hear Hawk breathing heavily a dozen yards away from me.

For a long moment, neither of us spoke.

Then a face appeared in the window above the sink. Alina widened her eyes in an exaggerated way. "Is it safe to come in now?"

I frowned at her for a long moment, and she lifted a brow.

Inexplicably, I laughed, and the tension broke. I glanced at Hawk. His color was better and his iron control seemed to have relaxed a bit. "What just happened?" I asked him.

He stalked down the hall toward me, his big body moving with the grace of a large predator. "I have no idea. But it didn't feel natural. And it didn't feel healthy."

I couldn't argue with that. In the back of my mind, I wondered if somebody had used the poisonous magic we'd just experienced to create a murderer. My mind replayed the deep scoring along David Bernes' back and legs.

"Let's get out of here," Hawk said.

There was no way I was going to argue. Without further prompting, I headed for the door.

W e buried David Bernes near where Devon Kraft was buried. As the last clump of dirt was pressed into place, I made a promise to myself that we'd build a fence around the graveyard as soon as the Annex was complete.

Sissy, Tomas, and Micah came with us to help with the burial. Working together, it didn't take us long to mound rocks over the entire grave.

The moon was high in the sky and full, as it always was in Outvald, painting our little party in a silvery glow as we headed wearily for home.

"What happened out there?" Sissy asked as we climbed the hill.

My calves ached from the climb, reminding me more than anything that it had already been a long day, and we still had work to do.

"David Bernes was killed. Somehow it's tied to the rupture in the ward. But I don't know how, yet."

Sissy thought about that for a minute. "Do you think that chameleon thing might have killed him?"

"Maybe. But the others didn't think so. The claw marks seemed to have been done by something smaller. Not small," I clarified with a weary smile. "Definitely something we need to worry about, but smaller than that thing we fought."

Her silence told me she was considering the information.

A soft chittering noise caught my attention. I glanced toward a nearby bush. It was an Outvaldian bush, purple with almost circular leaves on white-barked branches that were heavy with tiny, bright red berries.

A small creature stood next to the bush, peering through the dark at me with glittering black eyes. It sat on its haunches, tiny nose twitching, and its small forelegs curled near its chest. In the darkness, the creature looked pale gray, with a white star on its chest and white fur sprouting from the tips of its ears. A wide tail, like a beaver's only covered in fur, brushed the dust behind it.

The creature watched us pass on by, seemingly unafraid.

"So cute," Sissy said, making smoochie noises at the little animal.

I smiled. It *was* cute.

When we hit the front yard, Sissy mumbled something about grabbing her spell basket and headed inside. Micah stayed with Alina, Tomas, Grodan, and Hawk. Apparently, he intended to go with us. "Someone should stay here to protect the house," I said.

Behind the cops and Micah, Victoria's porch lights flared and slowly died back to black, her way of telling me that she didn't need a babysitter.

I ignored her, knowing she was probably right. But the events of the evening had me spooked, so she'd just have to deal.

"I'll stay," Grodan said. "And Nicht's here."

"Actually," Hawk told him. "I want Nicht with us." He slid a look toward me, and I nodded. If we were dealing with teeth and claws, Nicht was better suited to handling it than any of us were.

Grodan headed inside and, a moment later, Sissy and Nicht joined us on the lawn. I pulled air into my lungs and squared my shoulders, hoping to get a second wind for what we needed to do. I briefly considered telling the others I'd stay at the house. They didn't need me out there. I could insert Victoria's magic into the ward from the house. I really wanted to talk to Grams about what had happened inside David Bernes' home.

A family of raccoons trotted toward the house from the big oak tree. The mother chittered unhappily when she saw us and then waddled off into the taller grass beyond the light. Her three babies waddled after her, looking adorable.

"What's going on with the critters?" Micah asked.

Even as he asked the question, the little black cat that had come with us through the portal bumped against my calf, purring as it rubbed its little face against my leg.

I shrugged. "My energy draws wildlife. It always has." Grams had once told me I had a special connection to the animal world. I realized that might be part of why I kept transmogrifying when I siphoned too deeply. I reached down to give the little cat a scratch between the ears. "Hey, Buddy."

"If he's going to hang around," Sissy said. "He needs a name."

I didn't respond. I'd think about that another day. When my mind wasn't already running in twelve different directions. "Before we go to the breach, I need to look in on Rian."

I glanced at Hawk. He nodded. "We'll gather up supplies to board up Bernes' place."

"Good idea," I said. If he didn't live so close to the road, it wouldn't be such a big deal. But as it was, the house would be subject to squatters. Until I found out if he had family, it probably wasn't a good idea to let that happen.

I headed into Victoria with Sissy. She filled me in on Rian's condition as we walked.

"I was able to help him start the healing process. His smaller wounds have mostly healed, and his lungs are working again." She frowned. "But that thing must have had poison on its claws or something. He's not healing like he should."

I nodded. "Maybe Grams can have a look at him."

Sissy's pretty pixie face got that wistful look it always got when I mentioned Grams. A couple of times over the last few years, Grams had been strong enough to be visible to my friend. Sissy had loved talking to the powerful sorceress about magic. She'd been disappointed when those instances had been so few and far between. It bothered her that she couldn't always see Grams. I'd secretly hoped that would change when we came to Outvald, where Grams' energies were so much stronger. But Sissy hadn't seen Grams once since we'd arrived.

Sissy stopped in front of the door to the window-less central room on the lower floor where Rian, Tomas, and Grodan had made their temporary quarters until the barracks were done. There were three single beds pushed up against the walls of the octagonal room. The arrangement didn't leave a lot of extra space in the center. The two empty beds were made up with military precision, everything smoothed and tucked. The men's few belongings were hanging from hooks inside a single closet and folded neatly on the shelves. Several pairs of boots were flung haphazardly on the floor of the closet as if they'd used up all their soldierly neatness in the other areas and couldn't be bothered to keep their footwear tidy.

Rian lay perfectly still on top of the covers of his bed. His limbs were straight and rigid, fists clenched as if he were fighting great pain. By contrast, his eyes were closed and his expression appeared peaceful. No doubt the result of a spell by Sissy.

I sat down on the edge of the bed and touched the arm nearest my hip. It was cool, the skin like stone. I gave it a gentle pinch, but the flesh was fixed, as unmalleable as bone. I glanced at Sissy. She gave me a worried pinch of her eyes and mouth.

Rian's chest was rising and falling, but just barely. His breaths were shallow and slow. His color was gray, with no hint of his normal healthy tan.

I pulled energy from Victoria and felt her concern in the ready offering of her healing magic. The energy flowed easily to me and from my hands into the unconscious man. Golden light slipped from my palms, spreading over his body as I smoothed my palm from his head to his feet.

I felt no resistance. The magic eased beneath his

skin, but I saw no change in his condition from my efforts.

"See? There's something there that's blocking the energy."

I nodded. Lifting my head, I called out, "Grams? We could really use your help."

Sissy's hopeful gaze scanned the room.

The light flickered above our heads, and the air at the end of the bed thickened. Soon, Grams was standing there, her familiar face filled with concern. She looked at me and shook her head. "This young man is gravely ill," she told me.

Sissy stared hopefully toward the spot where I was looking. "Is she here?"

I nodded.

Grams observed my friend a moment, something warm filling her gaze. Then she reached out and wrapped a hand around Sissy's slender arm, giving it a squeeze.

Sissy jumped, her eyes going wide. Then she smiled and placed a hand over the spot where she'd felt Grams' touch. "Grams?"

"Yes, child. I'm with you."

Sissy's gaze slid to mine, filling with tears. "I can hear her!"

"Grams? Any ideas what we can do to help him?"

She pursed her lips a moment, keeping her hand on Sissy's arm. "There's a plant. Shane grows it on his land. It's black, with purple fuzz over its leaves.

The Outvaldians call it Easy Death. It is indeed a poison, causing a painless, quick death if used incorrectly. But if you make a mash from the roots of the plant and the soil around it, then place it over his wounds, it might be enough to draw out the poison the chameleon left behind."

Sissy nodded. "An extraction poultice."

"Yes, child. But take care in the making of the poultice. If you handle the leaves directly, it will poison and likely kill you."

Sissy paled. "I understand."

"I guess we're going to see Shane in the morning," I told Sissy. "Thanks, Grams..." I started to say. But when I looked up, she was gone.

"Alrighty then," I muttered. Apparently, she had other things to do.

Ten minutes later, after a long drink of water and a quick snack for energy, we were on our way back to the rupture in the ward.

Sissy and Micah, unscarred by previous events at Bernes' house, chatted easily as we moved through the darkness.

Hawk and the other security force members carried lumber and tools and walked in silence.

I kept my own silence, my mind playing over the events of the night. A sudden realization brought my head around, and I caught Hawk's eye. "We need to go to that auction."

He didn't even hesitate. He'd clearly been

thinking the same thing. "Yes. We do." But he didn't look happy about it. "Just so you know, I'm going to ask Shane to join us."

I thought about that for a beat and nodded. "That makes sense. He knows his way around Outvald."

"Good. Then it's settled. We'll go as soon as we get Belle on the road."

Oh. Ugh. I grimaced. "Hm. Hopefully, there will be other auctions."

Hawk looked offended. "You don't think I can make that old boat seaworthy?"

Alina snickered. "Good analogy. The best thing for all involved might be if you found a large body of water and drove that piece of junk into it."

The guys snickered.

Hawk glowered at Alina.

Proving she was indeed a warrior. She laughed it off.

I hid my smile. "Belle isn't just a car. She runs on magic as much as mechanics and fuel. We just need to find the right spell."

"That's why I'm going to take your new bestie up on his offer to help. He claims he's gotten her running before. I'm going to test the veracity of his claims."

"Word of the day, kids," Grodan said. "Veracity. It means the level of lyingness."

Hawk inclined his head. "Yep. That's exactly

what it means."

We all shared a laugh, which was sliced off at the sound of Nicht growling in the darkness ahead.

Without a thought, I yanked energy from the air, drawing heavily on Victoria's defensive magics. Lumber and supplies hit the ground in a clatter of sound, and Hawk and crew were suddenly holding weapons. The men had oversized knives in each hand. Alina gripped two energy guns, her weapons of choice.

We crouched low and moved toward the sound, Micah and Sissy staying behind. I noticed Micah held a blade too, and Sissy was spinning a spell on the air.

Nicht was standing in a patch of moonlight near the rupture in the ward. His mouth was open, the terrifying sight of his enormous teeth flashing in the silvery light. His hair stood on end, making him look twice his normal size. His eyes glowed red, the color swirling with agitation as he faced off with the creature standing twenty feet away. Nicht's growl was a constant, unnerving pulse through an otherwise quiet night.

The thing he was growling at stood in silence, the rangy body taut with anticipation. Its eyes glowed too, a fierce golden color that stood out against the midnight black of its long body. It stood upright, looking like a combination between the Big Foot of human myth and a wolf. Its big head was surrounded by a thick fringe, its face had a long muzzle, wider than a wolf's, and its ears were short and pointed, high on its head. The mouth was open, showing perfect white teeth with oversized canines. It simply stared at us without apparent aggression.

Magic bit against my skin and the monster twitched, its gaze blinking away for a beat and then glowing even brighter than before.

With a jolt of awareness and newfound fear, I realized the creature was staring right at me.

Nicht snarled and lunged. The monster lifted a hand and showed the hellhound its palm.

I stilled. It was such a human gesture, meant to calm and immobilize.

I looked at Hawk. He was frowning.

Nicht whined softly, his tail drooping.

We all waited, the atmosphere filled with expectation that had no form. I didn't know what I thought would happen, but I was unwilling to do anything to engage whatever it was.

A low rumble rolled through the quiet night, and I realized it had come from the wolfman-like creature. The glow of its eyes dimmed. A human-looking gaze found mine.

I jerked in surprise. But that was nothing compared to what came next.

The monster opened his mouth and said. "Avenge him." Then his body seemed to flex, and he melted into the night.

9

W e stood in shocked silence for a beat. Then someone whistled.

"Well, that just happened," I said.

Someone else chuckled.

"What was that thing?" Sissy asked.

Hawk was still frowning. He didn't seem inclined to speculate.

I had no idea what anything was in that goddess-forsaken place, so I didn't comment either. But the fact that I'd heard human speech was beyond disturbing. I fully intended to find out what we'd just seen at the earliest possible opportunity. In the meantime... "Let's get this breach repaired and get home. I'm tired."

There were several mumbled agreements.

Hawk looked at Sissy. "How long will it take you to repair the break?"

She glanced at me and I shrugged. "I'm ready when you are." I'd have to provide Victoria's native magic to the ward to make it work. Sissy was just building the framework.

"A half-hour?"

He nodded. "That should work." He headed for the break in the warding, and the others followed. "Look alive," he told his people, "We don't know where that thing went or if there are others like it around here."

I was starting to think there probably were. Grams' warning about watching out for David Bernes' "guests" had taken on new meaning.

Avenge him.

The words played through my mind, the odd, feral intonation giving them more meaning than the words themselves offered. Who did that thing want me to avenge? Bernes? Or had there been someone else at the house when Bernes was killed? I was so caught up in my thoughts I jolted in surprise when Sissy spoke a while later.

"Okay, will you go get them? I'm ready to close this thing."

I pushed wearily to my feet, "Sure."

As soon as I stepped through the rift in the warding, I felt the new magic sliding over my skin. It still chewed on my nerve endings, but it had ceased to shock except for the surprise engendered when I realized that I was growing used to it.

I headed toward the sound of pounding at the front of the house, my head on a swivel.

I couldn't shake the feeling that something was watching me. The night felt unnaturally dark, and the quiet I'd noted earlier was lost behind a wash of movement that swished over leaves and scraped against bark. Somewhere out there, beyond my ability to see, air soughed through lungs and nails scratched flesh.

A breeze slipped over me and something touched my hair.

I ducked, making a small sound that I hoped none of the others heard. My tough girl image would take a hit if they saw me cowering in the darkness because of a bat.

I watched the little creature dip and soar, snatching bugs out of the air. It was oblivious to me and my little fears.

I laughed softly. "You're jumping at nothing, Glynn," I scolded myself.

"Something wrong?" Sissy called out to me, impatience in her tone.

I lifted a hand to tell her I was fine and started forward again.

Swish!

I jolted to a stop. My eyes searched the shadowy vegetation around the house.

I didn't see anything.

I turned toward the front of the house.

Whoosh!

I stilled.

Scritch!

Okay, that was it. "Whoever's out there, show yourself."

Sissy said, "Huh?"

Then silence. Even the pounding stopped. I sighed. I was losing my mind.

In the space of a blink, the night around me lit up with a hundred pairs of glowing eyes.

"Glynn?"

Jumping several inches into the air, I whipped around to find Hawk staring at me, looking perplexed.

"What's wrong?" he asked, frowning.

"I..." I swallowed hard, a lump in my throat the size of my fist. Pointing toward the bushes at the edge of the yard, I asked, "Did you see that?"

He scanned the area visually and shrugged. "See what?"

Soft laughter wafted toward me through the air. Ice clawed across my skin. "Did you hear that?"

Hawk was frowning. "Glynn, I think that chameleon's poison left you with residual effects. We should get you home."

Grodan, Tomas, and Alina came around the corner of the house, laughing. Tomas had the claw of his hammer resting across his fingers, swinging it as if he was very comfortable around tools. Alina had slipped hers through a belt loop on her jeans, and Grodan carried a small bag that I knew contained nails. Grams had, inexplicably, kept a bucket full of all kinds of nails in the outbuilding she'd used as a garage back in Render.

"Sissy's ready to close the ward," I told them.

Still eyeing me, Hawk said, "Good. Let's get it done."

They filed toward the gap in the visible magic energy. I hung back for a moment, my gaze sliding once again toward the shadowed trees.

Hundreds of eyes glowed out of the vegetation. One pair was familiar. As I looked into the fiery gaze of the big wolf-like creature, it inclined its head.

And I scurried away before he could talk to me again.

I was truly losing my mind.

After much consideration, I decided to bring Boyle along on our visit to Shane the next morning. Hawk insisted on coming, and that made sense because he needed to talk to him about Belle.

I'd brought some cake and bread the Tellsons had made to barter for Shane's help.

There was a light drizzle as we walked toward the humble white farmhouse in the distance. Boyle and Nicht were unnaturally subdued once we crossed from my property to Shane's.

I didn't know if they thought they were protecting us or if we were supposed to protect them.

The thought made me smile. Neither the hell-hound nor the kid had enough sense to understand their own mortality. They were protecting us.

A knicker greeted us as we rounded the paddock of the barn complex.

Boyle jumped up and down on Nicht when he spotted Bessie.

"Glynnie, Glynnie, Glynnie! Can I ride the horsie again? Pleathe?"

I shook my head. "She doesn't belong to us, sweet boy."

"I can ask Shane," he said, his expression without guile. A careful examination of his face proved what I suspected. His bright turquoise gaze sparkled with cunning.

Hawk and I shared a grin. "We'll ride the horse another time," Hawk told the little gargoyle. "We have important business today."

Boyle sat taller on Nicht's back. "I do important bidness."

"Yes," I agreed. "You're very important to our business."

"Stop right there!"

We jolted to a stop at the unmistakable sound of a shotgun being racked.

The woman looked to be about my age—around thirty. She was slender almost to the point of being too thin, and her plain cotton gown fit her snugly, highlighting the roundness of her breasts and the faint curve of her hips. It fell almost to her ankles, and she wore loose brown stockings beneath it and scuffed brown leather boots on her small feet. The woman's green eyes were filled with distrust as she moved around where we could see her, never lowering the gun. "Who are you, and why do you think you have a right to just march across our property?"

She addressed Hawk, dismissing me as if I wasn't important.

"We met Shane yesterday," I told her. "We wanted to talk to him." I held up the bag with the baked goods. "We brought you gifts."

The hostile glare finally slid away from Hawk and scanned quickly over the canvas bag. "Who are you?"

"Neighbors," Hawk said, a smile finding his handsome face. "I'm Hawk. This is Glynn and Boyle and Nicht."

The gun lowered a fraction of an inch as she took in Boyle and his "horse". Something that looked like amusement softened her features when Boyle wiggled his long fingers at her. "Hello. I Boyle. Dis my horse, Nicht."

Her lips tightened, and I realized she was holding back a smile. "That's a mighty fine horse you've got there, Cowboy Boyle."

The baby 'goyle grinned at being called a cowboy. "He's a bunkin bronto."

She gave up on trying not to smile. "Is that so? I'll bet he goes really fast."

Eyes wide, Boyle nodded with a solemnity only a child can manage. "And he jumps over trees real good."

"Really well," I corrected automatically. I offered the woman my hand. "We live on the neighboring property. I'm Glynn Forester. It's nice to meet you...?"

After a beat, she lowered the gun and took my offering. "Kate. Grampa told me about you." Her eyes sparkled. "He said the kid here was quite a horseback rider."

Boyle perked and preened like a peacock.

"Yeah," Hawk laughed. "He's got a very enthusiastic horse."

As if insulted, Nicht sat abruptly, causing his rider to slide ungracefully to the ground.

We laughed.

"Come on, Gramps is at the house." She ran her forearm over a glistening forehead. "We've been canning since three this morning. We have to get it done before the heat gets too bad."

Holding the shotgun across her middle in both arms, she turned toward the farmhouse.

Shane came out as we approached, the screen door slamming behind him. He pulled a hankie from the pocket of his jeans and scrubbed his forehead with it. His shirt was damp around the neckline and under the arms, and his white hair was dark with sweat. "Glynn Forester." He smiled and inclined his head toward Hawk. "Mr. Hawk." Shane grinned at Boyle, who was trotting alongside Nicht, one arm lifted to drape over the hound's back.

Nicht was keeping a leery red gaze on the house, as if he thought monsters were going to leap on us from the upper windows.

Even outside on the grass, I could smell the sweet and savory scent of something cooking. "It smells delicious out here."

"Range beans," Shane said, taking the gun from his granddaughter. "They're a staple around here. Filling, full of protein, and tasty. We cook them up with a little Ormix meat and they're an easy meal." He looked at Kate. "Katie girl, why don't you pack some jars up for them to take home."

"I can do that. Cold tea?"

He nodded his agreement. "Out here on the porch, please. It's too hot in that dang house."

"I can help," I offered. But Kate shook her head. "I've got it. But thanks."

I held out the bag. "Bread and cake. We're lucky

enough to have a couple of talented bakers living with us."

Shane closed his eyes. "Sweets...we haven't had sugar for years. We'll surely cherish your gift. Thank you."

I nodded, pleased. "I hope you don't mind our just stopping by like this?"

He laughed. "Unless you understand smoke signals, there's really no other way around here." He looked thoughtful for a minute. "I do miss the phone, though."

"You had a phone?" Hawk asked.

"Still do. But it's dead as a hunk of hair. Has been for three years. I'm not sure why. This entire area lost our communications about the same time."

Hawk nodded. "Glynn's brother is pretty good at engineering stuff. Maybe he'll be able to come up with something."

Shane's eyes went wide. "You do that, and you'll never have to barter around here again. People would pay just about anything to be able to contact each other. Especially in an emergency."

Well, that was certainly food for thought. I filed it away for later when I could talk about it with Art.

The screen door opened and Kate came out carrying an oversized tray that was laden with a big pitcher of iced tea and several glasses.

"I apologize," Kate said. "We don't have any sugar for the tea." She glanced at Boyle. "There's a special glass of fruit juice there for Cowboy Boyle. It's full of sweet energy to help him fight off bad guys."

Boyle jumped up and down, clapping his hands.

I smiled at Kate. "You understand how he thinks."

She shrugged. "I like kids." She handed the baby 'goyle a glass of red juice and he tasted it, his bright blue eyes going wide. "Yummy!"

"You'll have to tell me how you made that," I told her. "I don't have any juice for him. We also need milk. Do you know where I can get some?"

Shane nodded. "We have milk cows. I'll give you a quart today and anytime you want more, just bring me some of that cake." He grinned.

"You got it." I was pleased with the result of that little bargain.

"You have Arboro trees on your property, I believe," Kate said. "The fruit is long and slender, looks like an orange banana?"

I nodded. "We do have those."

Nodding, Kate said. "That juice I gave him is just pulped and strained Arboro. I use the pulp to make a dense bread pudding. It's not as sweet as real pudding, but it's not bad."

I made a mental note to pass that information on to the Tellsons.

She handed the glasses around and then sliced into the cake I'd brought, offering it to everyone. Boyle took a slice and Shane took two, groaning with pleasure as he bit into it. Hawk and I declined slices, wanting Kate and Shane to have it.

When Shane had eaten his fill and drained his tea. He fixed his gaze on me. "What can I help you with today?"

"Grams told me you might have something growing on your property called Easy Death?" I said.

He inclined his head. "We do, yes." He narrowed his gaze. "Why would you be needing a poison?"

"We were attacked by a chameleon monster last night. One of our guys was pretty torn up. We were told that a mash of this plant will help him heal," Hawk said.

Shane looked at his granddaughter.

She nodded. "I'll get you some before you leave. I have some mash prepared. We don't get visits from those changeable critters very often, but we've learned to be prepared."

Relief made me smile. "Thank you. One day soon, if you wouldn't mind, would you come for a visit and walk the grounds with me? I'd like to know what resources I have. And I'm betting we have stuff on our property that you'd find useful. If we do, we'll be happy to share."

Kate's smile was eager. "I'll take you up on that."

Shane leaned forward in his chair. "So, what's the real reason for your visit?"

"We need to take a road trip," Hawk said. "But we can't get that confounded car to run. I was wondering if I could take you up on your offer to help?"

Shane nodded. "I'd be glad to help with that. Especially since it will get me out of some of this infernal canning."

Kate snorted out a laugh. "Where are you headed?"

Hawk and I shared a look. We hadn't really wanted to get into that, but I had a feeling our new friends would be offended and ultimately less friendly if we didn't tell them.

"Last night, we found David Bernes dead," I told them.

Shane jerked in surprise, his face paling beneath the tan. "Dead? By what means?"

"Murdered," Hawk said, throwing an apologetic glance at Kate for his brutal response. "Pretty badly torn up. Any idea who or what might have wanted the man dead?"

Shane's expression turned angry. "I told him to have a care. He was messin' in things that he had no business messin' in."

"Like what kinds of things?" Hawk asked.

Kate and Shane kept their gazes down for a long moment. Neither of them appeared to want to share what they were thinking. Finally, Kate said, "David was a good man. He tried to help. But some people saw his help as interference. He'd ruffled a lot of feathers with his work."

"What work?" I asked. "What exactly did he do?"

Shane shook his head. "Best to stay well out of that, Glynn. Your grandmother wouldn't thank me for getting you mixed up in that ugliness."

"We're going to get to the bottom of it, Shane," I told him. "I have people to protect on my land, and we've already been affected by whatever David Bernes was doing. As I told you, we were attacked last night. One of our guys is in really bad shape."

Shane bristled. I held his gaze, hoping he'd read between the lines of what I was telling him. If we were being attacked, he was in line for trouble too.

"The chameleon?" Kate asked, her voice soft.

Hawk nodded. "We nearly couldn't stop it from getting to a seven-year-old girl."

Kate sucked in a breath. I watched horror sweep over her face, but it was slowly replaced by pleasure. "You have a little girl at your place?" There was longing in her voice.

"Yes. Her name's Emma."

"Emma'th my fwiend," Boyle said, licking frosting off his thin, gray lips.

Kate slammed her mouth closed as she remembered we had little ears listening. She forced a bright smile. "Boyle, would you like to come inside and help me for a bit?"

He jumped up and ran to me, grabbing my arm and tugging it as he hopped from one oversized foot to another. "Can I Glynnie? Pleathe, pleathe, pleathe?"

"Of course. You be good and do what you're told."

He hurried over and grabbed Kate's hand, turning his little face up to her. "I be a good boy."

Nicht climbed to his feet and trotted after them.

Kate didn't even blink. She just held the door open for the big hound and they disappeared into the house amid Boyle's happy chattering.

"Tell me what you're planning," Shane said, his voice no longer conversational.

"We found this in the car near the body," Hawk told the older man. He handed Shane the flyer.

Shane stared at it a long moment, his jaw going tight. Then he sighed. "That's what I was afraid of." He looked up and handed the page back to Hawk. "You won't find that auction without me. But here's the deal. I want Kate kept safe. She'll stay at Victoria while we're gone. And you'll assign someone to escort her back and forth to tend the house and the animals."

"Agreed," Hawk said without hesitation.

"I'm not done," Shane said. "If..." He shook his head. "If I don't make it back here. You'll promise to look after my granddaughter."

"Of course," I said softly. "We'll do whatever we need to do to keep Kate safe. You have my word."

Shane inclined his head. "We'll leave in the

morning. It will take us two days minimum to get there from here. Three if we run into any trouble. And we'll want to get there before the auction starts. We can't just march in there with our heads up our butts. This will need to be done delicately."

He climbed to his feet. "Give me an hour to pull my stuff together, and I'll head your way to take a look at that car."

"Thank you," I told Shane.

He turned a hard glare on me. "Don't thank me. I'm starting to wonder if I'm glad you came back to Outvald, Glynn Forester. You might just be the death of us all."

His words sliced me in half. I felt my face heat and knew it had flushed with guilt.

He reached for the screen door, but Hawk put out a big hand, stopping it from opening. "We need to be clear on one thing, old man. Glynn didn't bring this trouble to your doorstep. She didn't kill David Bernes or make him do whatever he did to cause his death. She's only trying to protect the people who are counting on her for their safety. The same as you. I won't have you making her feel bad for doing what she believes is right."

Shane and Hawk held dueling gazes for a long moment. Finally, Shane looked away. "Point taken. Now you understand this...I swore to Katie's mama that I'd keep her safe to my dying day. And now it looks like that day is gonna come sooner than I expected. And at the moment, you two are the only ones I have at hand to blame for it."

With that, he yanked the screen door open and went inside, leaving Hawk and me to stew in his displeasure.

10

I'd had many ideas in my head about how Outvald would look. Most of them, I realized, were fanciful and based generally on my fears. Where I'd expected a wild and wooly wilderness, filled with every conceivable kind of monster, we mostly just saw an endless ribbon of dusty road, surrounded by a tangle of untamed vegetation. The road was broken and unkempt, the recalcitrant Belle puttering unhappily along and occasionally dropping noisily into a rut that her big tires had no trouble pulling her out of.

For the entire first hour, I sat in tense silence in the front seat, certain the old gal was going to drop into pieces beneath my butt at any moment. My fear wasn't based on any physical deformities in the car. Belle was actually in decent shape for her age. But mechanically, to put it mildly, she was not cooperatively inclined. For that reason, I was happy we'd brought Shane along. He hadn't been kidding when he said he had a way with the old gal. She seemed to purr beneath his attentions.

It was just the rest of us she didn't like.

Shane had driven for the first several hours. Hawk had taken over after a potty break performed behind scrub brushes in a surprisingly flat and open area alongside the road.

Despite his angry words when we'd asked him to help, Shane had settled in behind Belle's oversized steering wheel with a relaxed and even contented air. He drove with a slight smile on his face. Watching him, I wondered what his relationship with Grams had actually been. He certainly seemed very comfortable driving her car.

I'd have asked her that very question. Except she'd avoided me for the half-day it had taken to pack up our stuff, get everybody organized and settled on their roles and responsibilities while we were gone, and set off amid tears and lamentations.

The former had been mine. Watching Boyle's sad little face get smaller as we drove away nearly did me in. He and I hadn't been separated for more than a few hours since we'd found each other.

This would be the first time we'd spent several days apart.

I was determined to make it the last.

The lamentations had come from Tomas,

Grodan, and even Rian, who seemed to be doing much better after Grams' and Sissy's careful ministrations, and had already been getting antsy to be back on his feet. The guys thought they should be able to come with us. They seemed to think, in the way of cops and men everywhere, that we couldn't possibly survive without them.

Maybe they were right. I didn't know whether Shane's magic had any defensive use, but we had Hawk, Nicht, and Alina. I'd put our odds of surviving our 'seek and assess' mission at higher than fifty percent.

Not bad.

"What do you know about this auction?" Alina asked Shane. He turned away from the window. Since giving the driving over to Hawk, the old man had been staring into the forbidding landscape with a faraway look on his grizzled face.

He didn't speak for a bit. I turned in my seat, and Alina and I shared a look.

Nicht, who was draped across the center of the bench seat, stretched to put his big head on Shane's lap, whacking him with a paw as if trying to nudge him into talking.

Shane's rough fingers dug into Nicht's thick fur. "The ability of living creatures to abuse each other never ceases to astound me."

His words made my stomach twist with dread. "The auction is pretty bad, huh?"

Shane frowned. "Bad? I guess that depends on your perspective. The owner is a monster. She should have been put down years ago. But the people who run the place aren't all horrible. I actually know a couple of them. They believe they're doing the right thing by finding responsible solutions for some of the creatures they auction off. But many of those critters shouldn't be there in the first place."

"Will they talk to us about Bernes?" Hawk asked.

Shane turned to look at Hawk. The big guardian's gaze was locked onto the rearview mirror, caught in Shane's unhappy stare.

"They won't be happy about it, no."

"Why not?" Alina asked.

Shane turned his unhappiness in her direction. "Would you like to speak about the person who, by his very existence, highlighted your hypocrisy and cold-bloodedness?"

The car was silent for a beat. Then Alina, ever the warrior, took the bull by the horns. "How did David Bernes do that?"

"He took as many of those unfortunate creatures away from that place as he could. Then he tried to help them fit better into the world so they could live independently."

"That explained the laboratory I saw in his house," Hawk said, his tone angry.

Shane nodded.

I turned to look at Hawk. I suddenly realized what he'd been looking at when we'd both succumbed to the angry energy in that house—no wonder he'd been so affected. In our world, laboratories and monsters were rarely a positive mix.

"David was a scientist before he came to Outvald," Shane explained.

When he'd lived in the Earth dimension, I added inside my head. I had a sudden urge to tell him about the strange magic around Bernes' home. "When Hawk and I were inside David's house..." Hawk's gaze slid to mine and, for a moment, I thought he was going to ask me not to talk about it. But then he returned his attention to the road—only a tightness around his mouth giving away his unhappiness at the subject.

"We were affected by a kind of magic I've never felt before. Do you have any idea what that was?"

Shane nodded. "David called it the feral flu. Many of the creatures he rescued arrived with it. One of the things he used to do was to treat them through the process of kicking it off."

I frowned. "So, it's some kind of virus?"

"In a way. But it's not from nature. The feral flu is completely man-made."

"What did it do?" Hawk asked.

"Like the name implies, it brings out the enraged beast in everyone it touches. The more you're exposed, the worse the result—nasty stuff. Many of the animals at the auction were infected with it, so they could be sold as fighters or protectors. My understanding is that it drastically shortened their life spans." Shane shook his head.

"Was David successful in eradicating it in the creatures he rescued?" I asked.

"In most cases." He frowned. "Not always. When you described how he died, I couldn't help wondering if one of his rescues succumbed to the flu and killed him."

Grams' words flitted through my mind again. *His guests can often prove to be deadly.*

We sat in silence for a long moment, listening to the sound of Belle's big tires crunching over the broken road.

I finally decided it was time for a change of subject. "You said David came here through a portal."

Shane nodded. "That's right."

"Where are these portals? And how easy is it to gain passage to them?"

Hawk turned to me, his expression telling me he understood what I was thinking. If it was easy to get to Outvald from other dimensions, what was keeping the Body from finding us?

"You should know," Shane said. "You live in one."

"Yes, but I have control over Victoria's portal and only her portal. I'm talking about portals others might use."

He nodded. "They're very limited, and access is strictly controlled. For most people, it takes three things to gain passage through one. Connections, money, and a darn good reason."

I wished that made me feel better. But none of those things would slow the Body down. "Does somebody keep a record of who comes through?"

"Including the private ones?"

I frowned at that. I hadn't even considered that somebody might have monitored our passage into Outvald. "I guess so, yes."

"Theoretically, the University has all of that information. But Professor Guwalt, the man who's in charge of portals, is a bit of a scatterbrain. I'm not confident he'd have what you're looking for."

I thought about that for a moment. Then I looked at Hawk. "We need to pay a visit to this Professor Guwalt."

"I agree."

And with that decided, we fell into silence for the next hundred miles.

"Wow, there are actually some people here," someone said. I was half asleep and the sound jerked me awake. I sat up, blinking and yawning.

"Yes, we've reached a population zone," Shane

said. "We should be able to find a place to stay for the night."

I straightened in the seat, my eyes widening as I took in the strange sight. It wasn't like any city I'd ever seen. Or, really, like any place where people should live, even in sparsely populated areas.

The road was slightly less decrepit, the land marginally less wild, but the "homes" we saw were really just mud huts. They had no windows and what looked like curtains flapping over the arched doorways instead of actual doors.

"What's with the huts?" Alina asked. She was in the front seat where I'd been, and Shane was driving again. We'd switched seats after one of our stops to stretch our legs and dump more fuel into Belle from the cans we'd brought. I'd spent the last hundred miles with a big hellhound head in my lap, and I was pretty sure I had a large drool spot on my jeans where he'd been.

Nicht stretched his long legs and yawned widely, but he didn't lift his head off my leg. He was worse than a dog. Apparently, the big hound kicked Hawk in a sensitive spot when he stretched, earning a smack to the butt that resulted in a low growl and not much more.

I grinned at Hawk. "You've lost control of your sidekick."

He snorted, "That happened years ago."

"This is a poor part of Outvald and the weather's

mild, so they make use of natural materials to build their homes and take advantage of the breezes with the open doors. You can't see them from here, but each of those huts has a second door in the back for airflow," Shane said in answer to Alina's question.

Alina wrinkled her nose. "I thought you said we'd find a place to stay. I'm not seeing any vacancy signs on the mud huts."

He chuckled. "There will be a vacancy."

I blinked in surprise. Was he seriously suggesting we spend the night in one of those huts? I was pretty sure I'd rather sleep under the stars.

"What about security?" Hawk asked. "They don't look very secure."

"Physically, no. But magically, they're virtually impenetrable. There's magic woven into the mud. The Outvaldian Brotherhood has deep roots in the natural magical energy of Outvald."

"Natural magical energy?" I asked.

Shane nodded, his gaze sliding over the crooked line of huts. I noticed a few people dressed in plain, roughly-made robes walking between them or sitting together in small clusters on the ground. Their darkly serious gazes watched us drive slowly past.

The people looked as if they were from the same big family. They all had smallish dark eyes with heavy black eyebrows, bald heads, wide flat noses, and oversized, almost fishlike mouths. The ones I could see all appeared to be men, and the tallest one was probably only about five foot six.

"Like all dimensions," Shane said. "Outvald has a natural energy that people who use magic can tap into. But unlike the Earthly dimension, for example, the energy here is strong. Really strong. It's the reason we have such a wide variety of magical creatures, humanoid and other. The Brotherhood taps into the deepest core of the available mystical energy. They embody the energy, assimilate it into their very essence and shape it to their own purposes. They're not *of* magic, they *are* magic."

Looking at the severe, unflinching faces we passed, I could believe they were secure in their imperviousness. "So this isn't just a poor area, is it?"

"Not even close. They're poor in monetary ways, but these people fear nothing and no one. They are some of the most powerful creatures you'll ever encounter in any dimension."

Shane slowed Belle and, before I knew what he had in mind, he'd turned onto the dirt in front of a hut that looked much like the rest. A man stood near the hut, hands folded and unfathomable gaze locked on Belle.

Curiosity finally got the best of me. "Are there any women? Children?"

"The brotherhood are an asexual people. They don't procreate. And they have no known sexual proclivities."

Alina's eyes went wide. "No sex?"

I hid a smile behind my hand. The unshakeable warrior had finally found something that shook her to the very core.

"They are above the needs of the physical form," Shane said in a slightly smug tone.

Alina snorted out a laugh. "No wonder they look so crabby."

Glaring across the car at her, Shane turned the key. Belle's magically-enhanced engine sputtered to an ungainly stop, a gust of black smoke belching from her tailpipe before she went still.

"Wait here," he told us and then climbed out to speak to the creature waiting in front of the hut. Several harshly barked statements in a language I couldn't understand later, Shane gave the creature a shallow bow and returned to the car.

Without a word, he climbed back inside and started the engine.

"No vacancy?" Hawk asked, his tone dry.

"We have been instructed to pull around behind this hut. Accommodations will be provided to us."

"Really?" I laughed, disbelieving. "What's the cost?"

Shane flushed and avoided looking at anyone. "I'll take care of the price for tonight's lodgings."

Hawk, Alina, and I shared a look.

Hawk shrugged. Alina peered carefully at Shane as if trying to see inside his brain for the truth.

I just sat back and watched the "brothers" as we circled through their camp. It wasn't Shane's responsibility to account for our lodgings. He'd come along as a favor to us. But, whatever was going on, he was clearly embarrassed to talk about it. So, I'd talk to him later, away from the others, and find out what was going on.

With that decision made, I applied myself to taking in everything I was seeing around us. Memorizing it so I could tell Sissy all about it when we got back.

We stopped in front of a mud hut that was bigger than the rest. The entrance had a tunnel-like affair, even more like an igloo than the others, and the mud had been painted a dusty white.

Two of the Brothers crouched near a large firepit, barely looking up at us as Shane parked the big, noisy car, and we climbed out.

One of them came out of the shadows of a nearby hut and walked along Belle's side, running a hand over one of her sharp fins and mumbling under his breath.

Like static electricity, magic rose in the air and pulled the hairs up along my arms. A chill caused me to shiver and look around. "What's happening?" I asked no one in particular.

Hawk glanced my way, his expression wary. "I don't know. But I'm not feeling very welcome."

Alina had a hand on each of her weapons and

her eyes held a hostile glint. "I vote we get back into that fuel-guzzling monstrosity and keep on keepin' on down the road."

Shane stood with the two men who'd been tending the fire. The three of them were in a conversation that had hard edges and was accompanied by brusque hand gestures.

He finally bowed, his expression grim as he strode back to us. Shane pointed to the larger hut. "We'll stay here."

"What was all that about?" Alina asked. Her unhappy gaze still scoured the men in the camp, who watched us with what felt like hostile gazes. They stood near other huts, converged in small groups, and crouched near firepits similar to the one in front of us.

"I'm not feelin' the love," Hawk told the older man.

Shane sighed. "No love. But they'll keep their word."

"About what?" I asked.

"I got them to agree that, as long as we follow the rules, they won't open up the ground and bury us alive in it."

11

"Say what?" I asked. "I'm pretty sure I didn't hear you right."

Shane's gaze landed on the two men standing before the hut. "You heard me right. The Brothers aren't fond of travelers. Let's just say they've been burned a time or two."

"And yet this is where you brought us to spend the night?" Alina said. Despite her lowered brows, there was a suspicious twitch in her lips that made me think she was amused by our situation.

I wished I felt the same.

"I'll agree it's not perfect," Shane said.

Hawk barked out a laugh. In a blink, several of the brothers had weapons in their hands.

We went very still, eyeing their weapons.

"Are those...?"

Alina's slender fingers caressed the handles of

her guns. "Blades made of stone. Interesting choice of weapon."

"Don't underestimate those blades," Shane said, absently rubbing a shoulder. "They hone them until they're impossibly sharp. And they can split a mosquito from forty yards with one of those things."

"Let's take a vote. Everybody who wants to move on," I said, raising a hand.

Alina raised her hand too. When she saw Hawk hadn't raised his, she lifted her other one. "I'm voting for two."

I snorted out a laugh. A man stepped from the shadow of a smaller black hut. He held his blade low at his side, balanced between two fingertips. His expression didn't show any emotion, but even from a distance of fifteen feet, I could tell he was tensed to throw the knife.

"Shane," I murmured, pulling energy from the air. I gasped as the magic rushed to fill my core, thick and rich and vibrant with expectant power. I absorbed so much and so quickly that it shot to my hands, swirling in thick rust-colored clouds that filled the air around us with static electricity.

Every hair on my body stood at attention. Beside me, Alina sucked air and laughed with genuine humor. I turned to find her touching the ends of her hair that were floating around her head.

"What the...?" Shane rubbed the hair on his arms back into place, only to have it rise again.

I looked at Hawk. He looked back, his dark blond hair drifting around his face like an aura. He arched a single brow, making no attempt to tame his flyaway locks. That made me smile.

"I guess now we know why they all shave their heads," Alina said.

"Um...look alive," Shane mumbled, moving away from us and extending his hands as if preparing to fight.

That was when I realized every Brother in the camp was holding at least one blade. Several of them held a weapon in each hand.

And the air around us had become so saturated with magic it was almost impossible to draw breath.

We were going to die.

Belle's door creaked as something shoved it open.

We didn't dare turn to look at Nicht as he dropped lightly to the ground. A beat later, I heard him yawn, a long, theatrical affair that usually involved exposing a lot of big white teeth.

I risked a look and almost laughed. He looked like a giant black puffball. All of his fur stood at attention from the static.

Like a cold summer rain, the hellhound's appearance doused the building hostility in the camp.

Blades slipped out of sight without any apparent movement. Backs went ramrod straight.

And before I knew what was happening, every

single Brother had dropped to his knees and lowered his forehead to the ground.

We all looked at Shane. He shook his head. "I have no idea. But the dog seems to have caused a break in the hostilities, so I say we go for it."

His comment was met with a low, extended growl, followed by another doggy yawn.

"What's the point in staying?" I asked Shane. "Other than watching the hound get the royal treatment." My lips curved upward as Nicht took a morsel of something from a Brother's fingers and rolled onto his back, legs awkwardly splayed to offer his belly.

Another man in robes scurried over, some kind of brush in one hand, and began carefully grooming the hellhound's wide belly.

"Yeesh!" Alina said. She'd found a discarded stone blade inside the hut where we'd be spending the night and was honing it on another rock. "That's disgusting."

Nicht rolled a big red eye in her direction and grinned, his wide tongue sliding out of the side of his mouth.

He looked about as far from scary as he could be.

"In answer to your question," Shane said, ignoring the hound worship, "The camp is heavily protected magically and by reputation. We'll be able to sleep well here. If we set up camp out in the open, we'd have to post sentries and sleep with one eye open. I'm too old for that. I need my handsome sleep."

I blew a raspberry. "Yeah, you're downright decrepit." I wasn't falling for Shane's act anymore. He might have some years on him, but he was strong enough to muscle Belle and fling enormous rocks around in the field. His protestations of age were just another weapon in his arsenal. One which I was sure would come in handy before our quest was over.

Shane waved a dismissive hand. "Regardless, we'll need our rest to deal with what we're going to encounter tomorrow."

Since I had no idea what we were going to encounter, I had nothing to say to that.

We sat staring at the flames for a beat. I was enjoying the sweet scent of burning wood and the soft crackle of the fire. It was mesmerizing. I felt my muscles turning soft and my lids drifting lower.

A pebble snicked against the stones surrounding the firepit and I jolted awake, my gaze rising to find one of the Brotherhood staring down at me.

He stood straight, shoulders back, and strange face void of expression. Two small feet stuck out from under the rough robes, the toes turned out, penguin style.

We stared at each other for a beat before he gave me a slight bow.

"Missis."

I glanced at Shane.

"It's a term of respect. He wants to speak to you about something he deems important."

"He probably wants to know what brand of dog food to get the flea hotel over there," Alina said. Nicht gave her a low growl. She chuckled at having gotten his goat.

I inclined my head. "Hello."

His folded hands came up, palms pressed flat together. "Missis. I...wish...convertation."

Instinct told me not to correct him. "Please," I motioned toward a bare spot next to me in the dirt. "Sit."

He sat. There was another beat of awkward silence while I waited for him to tell me what he wanted. Finally, I said. "Please, speak."

He bowed again, somehow making the movement graceful despite the fact that he was sitting on the ground. "You have..." He reached over and touched my hand, his skin cool and strangely rough, like coarse sandpaper. Then he lifted his hands, spreading his fingers. It looked like he was indicating an explosion.

Suddenly, I understood. "The energy? Yes, I siphon energy from the air." I pulled a bit of the magic out of my core that I'd drawn earlier. It emerged, rust-colored and agitated, to my fingertips and blossomed around them. With a thought, I formed the energy into petals and gave it a stem. Holding it between my fingertips, I handed it to him.

His eyes lit with inner fire, excitement clear in every line of his berobed form. He took the energy flower and stared at it in awe. Ever so slowly, his wide, fish-like mouth curved upward at the corners.

Another Brother joined the fire. He held his hands out and pushed them at me. I tugged more energy to my fingertips and created a balloon dog with it. He and his friend chortled happily, comparing their treasures.

Beside me, Shane said, "Nice trick."

I shrugged. "It's better than what I usually make with the magic."

"What's that?"

I looked at him. "Weapons."

"That would be an even cooler trick."

I laughed.

Soon we had five Brothers at our fire. And then eight. And then a dozen. Nicht's audience even abandoned him for a few minutes to beg magic toys from me.

By the time the last of them had wandered away, I was beyond exhausted. I trudged into our assigned hut, tugged a blanket from the pack I'd carried with me, and plopped onto the strangely spongy ground.

The floor in the hut was covered in some kind of moss that was surprisingly comfortable.

Despite being hungry, tired, and homesick, I think I fell asleep within seconds.

I awoke to something I couldn't identify. A noise, I think. One which didn't come again after I started listening for it. As I lay there, enveloped by the soft sounds of people sleeping around me, I realized I was thirsty.

When it became clear I wasn't going to be able to go back to sleep until I got some water, I climbed wearily to my feet and trudged toward the low door, taking care not to step on any of my companions.

I ducked my head to traverse the strange tunnel that led outside. As I emerged into a surprisingly cool night, a low, dark shape disengaged from the darkness and moved silently toward me.

I jumped, slapping my hand over my mouth as I realized who it was. "Nicht! You scared the stuffing out of me."

His low woof sounded too much like laughter for my comfort. I'd left my canteen inside the car, so I headed that way. Belle's heavy door creaked loudly when I opened it, and I stilled, hoping I didn't wake anybody.

The camp was still and silent, looking prehistoric in the silver light of the fat moon. Nicht bumped up against my leg.

"Okay, okay." I realized he was probably thirsty

too. "I think I have a dish in here somewhere." I had remembered to bring him a large bowl for food and water, but it had gotten buried in all the stuff we'd packed into the big car.

I found it, along with a bag of bread and dried meat, and grabbed them both.

Tipping my canteen back, I realized it was empty. Somebody had clearly finished it off without telling me. "It's gone," I told Nicht.

My voice must have held a note of panic because he rubbed his head against my thigh and jogged a few steps away, whining for me to follow.

Or, at least I think that was what he was trying to tell me. I followed, figuring the Brothers had to have a water source somewhere nearby. I'd find it and refill the canteen. There was no way I was going back to sleep until I got a drink.

Throwing the strap of the food bag over my shoulder, I jogged after the big hound. Unfortunately, he really needed a cowbell. I kept losing him in the darkness. He would come back when I called out to him though, and I could see the red glow of his eyes.

The ground beneath our feet was covered in the same spongy moss that carpeted the hut floor. It was easy on the feet and, with moonlight painting the area as we walked, it was almost pleasant.

Some kind of night bird called out high above our heads. I looked up but couldn't see it in the trees.

Like at Victoria, there were the usual strange, arrow-shaped trees that towered high into the sky. There were also some twisted trees with crooked trunks, bent branches, and long slender leaves that were torn and frayed along their edges.

It all seemed slightly surreal under the moon-light—like an odd children's movie directed by a madman.

Without warning, something in the air changed.

Something shivered and stilled.

I bumped up against Nicht before I saw him and realized he was standing very still, his gaze on a large oval with a glossy surface in front of us.

A lake.

"Good job," I told him.

His head whipped around on a soft snarl.

I clamped my lips closed, realizing the area was unnaturally quiet. Even the night bird had gone silent.

In the distance, I heard the soft swish of water against a harder surface.

Then I saw them.

Dark figures climbed from the water, their forms lithe and agile. They were covered in a midnight fabric that caught the moonlight and shimmered with latent energy. I knew that fabric. It was imper-meable to almost everything—bullets, laser energy, blades.

Just as I knew the shape of the enemy forming into loose ranks and jogging in our direction.

Nicht growled, the sound vibrating against my skin and raising gooseflesh along my arms. I reached over and touched his back in silent command. Then I spun on my heels and started running as fast as I could go.

Behind me, a shouted command told me we'd been spotted.

12

The ground slammed up against my feet, the spongy terrain as forgiving as it was disorienting in a full-on race toward the Brothers' camp. My mind raced like my feet until it all fell into place. Of course the Body would want to infiltrate the Brotherhood. The energy in that place was unlike anything I'd ever felt before.

In the hands of an unscrupulous user, that energy could do terrifying things. The Body must have found a way to portal into the middle of the encampment to avoid the warding around the perimeter. Or worse...maybe the Brothers were voluntarily working with the Body.

An arrow whistled past my head and I ducked, diving behind a tree as I pulled energy into my hands and formed it into a shield. Out of the corner of my eye, I saw a low, dark shape melting into the darkness. A moment later, two of the Body's soldiers went down amid pain-filled shrieking.

I changed my mind about using the energy for a shield. I needed to do two things at once. I needed to warn my companions that trouble was heading their way. And I needed to get Nicht and me out of trouble.

I needed noise—a lot of it.

So I yanked the Brotherhood's energy into my core so quickly that the sudden influx of energy hit me like a train, tipping me backward and making my eyes roll back in my head.

I slammed up against the trunk of the tree I was using for cover, and my senses came back to me. Still, I was disoriented and slow when a man dressed in the shimmery black body armor stepped around the tree and slipped the tip of a short sword beneath my chin.

I stilled, my breath heaving in my chest. Yanking the energy back, I raised my hands, trying to look harmless. A low whistle pierced the silence. The man standing over me turned his head toward the sound and whistled back.

Not willing to miss the chance, I yanked my energy forward and yelled, "Nicht, down!"

I threw everything I had toward the invaders in a wash of pure, unbalanced power.

The magic slammed against a dozen soldiers who'd accumulated within my sphere and lifted them off the ground with a concussive boom. They flew backward, mouths wide in silent screams, as the magic turned them into dust.

The atmosphere was thick with magic, cloying and sour. The sheer amount was suffocating as if the magic had sucked all available oxygen from the air. I fell to my knees, making a wheezing, gasping sound that did nothing to pull air into my lungs.

I clawed at my throat, panic making my eyes bulge, but nothing allowed my chest to rise or my lungs to fill.

A dark shape appeared from the shadows. Nicht bumped his big head against my shoulder. I shook my head, dropping to my hands and knees and still struggling to breathe.

He bumped me again. My oxygen-starved brain couldn't form a thought. There was no way I could absorb what he was trying to tell me.

Hard hands grasped my arms and I was flung into the air. I would have screamed if I'd had the breath to do it.

I landed hard on a broad shoulder and it knocked something loose in my chest. With tears skimming down my cheeks, I finally managed to draw a breath. And then another. But they were shallow and unsatisfactory gasps. So, as soon as I felt the protective warding of the Brothers' encampment snapping over us, I smacked Hawk on the back of the head and wheezed out, "Put me..." wheeze... "down."

He did as I asked but kept a hand on my arm to keep me from falling on my face as my knees buckled again.

"What happened out there?" he asked.

Nicht pressed against my thigh, supporting me as I wobbled. I dug my fingers into his thick fur for support. "Body soldiers," I wheezed out. "We took some of them down, but I have a feeling they'll keep coming."

If Hawk was surprised by my statement, he didn't show it. "Portal?" he asked.

I thought of the men walking out of the lake and nodded. "Has to be." Dragging welcome air into my lungs, I went on, "In the lake. We need to warn the Brothers."

Hawk nodded. "Come on."

Since Shane seemed to speak their language, he was the lucky one assigned to be our spokesman. He had no first-hand knowledge of the Body, but we filled him in enough to impress upon him the severity of having them appear in this area.

After a long and emphatic conversation in the Brotherhood's strange language, Shane's posture finally relaxed and he nodded, bowed, and returned to us. "They want us to leave."

I stared at him in disbelief. "*That's* what they took away from our information?"

Shane grimaced. "Yes. But it's not what you think. These guys can take care of themselves. But they don't want to be responsible for us. And..." he slid a look toward Nicht, who stood a distance from us, keeping vigil. "They don't want the Holy One to be harmed."

Alina snorted a laugh. "Holy One?"

Shane grimaced.

"Apparently, they haven't been subjected to the Holy One's farts after he eats too many wild berries," she said, laughing. "He could scour bark off a two-thousand-year-old tree."

She wasn't wrong.

"Regardless. They worship who and what they worship. For my part, if this Body you told me about are even half as bad as you've said, I support the idea of us moving on before they get here."

Since we all agreed with him, we gathered up our things and left.

Alina drove the next leg. It was probably no surprise to anybody in that car that she drove like the hounds of Hell were nipping at her heels. Initially, I whole-heartedly supported it, knowing the Body was probably looking for us. But as the hours passed, I started to grow weary of the constant fear of imminent, fiery death.

"Maybe we could slow down now," I suggested from the back seat.

She scanned me a disgusted look in the mirror and raced on.

I sighed.

An hour later, we passed a sign on the road. That fact was noteworthy because it was the first sign of any kind I'd seen since we started our journey. I'd grown to understand why Shane thought we couldn't find the auction without him. In fact, the sign was such a unique event that Alina actually slowed so we could read it.

Accipere Locum, it said.

Alina and I looked at Shane.

He shook his head, looking disgusted. "Don't people learn Latin in school anymore?"

"Place of Learning," Hawk said.

"That Professor I told you about?" Shane said.

We nodded.

"He's up the road a ways, at the University. If you want to speak to him, this is a good time to do it." He jerked his head toward an unmarked crossroad. "Otherwise, we should go that way."

We sat there for a beat, considering our options. I felt a sense of urgency about the auction that I couldn't explain. There was no reason for me to expect more trouble to find us from that place, or really a reason to expect any at all. David Bernes could have been killed for an entirely different reason than the auction.

Or really, for no reason at all. He could have just been in the wrong place at the wrong time.

But Shane had said he'd warned Bernes against messing with the auction. And Grams had warned me about Bernes' "guests" which, from everything I'd heard, were likely to have come from the auction. That made the auction the common denominator all the possible ways David Bernes could have died.

And then there was the wolfman and his cryptic but disturbing message.

Avenge him.

I looked at Shane. "Did David Bernes know this Professor Guwalt?"

"It's very likely. David worked at the university for a couple of years when he first came to Outvald. That's how he learned about the Auction."

That was enough for me. "Let's go see Guwalt." A quick side trip wouldn't hurt. And besides, I was starving. I'd had to abandon our food when Nicht and I were attacked.

Alina stomped on the gas pedal, and we were off.

The first time we passed another car on the road was also an event.

We all sat forward in our seats and stared at the passing truck, an ancient thing with gray primer for a finish instead of real paint. A small face with oversized eyes stared back at us as we gaped. The passenger, who looked older than the driver by a lot, cast us a wary glance, puckering a narrow mouth into a mass of wrinkles.

The truck bucked suddenly and farted a cloud of black smoke before puttering on down the road in the direction we'd just come.

"They didn't look happy to see us," Alina said.

"They were probably afraid our tailwind would blow them off the road," Hawk quipped in reference to Alina's hot rod ways.

We all chuckled.

"I'll bet they were shocked to see other people," I said.

"Learning is a population hub," Shane said. "Seeing civilization here isn't as much of a shock as you'd think." Then he thought about it and added, "But Belle was probably a bit of a shock. Most people who even have a car drive rust traps like that truck. He caressed the white leather of Belle's seat. "This beauty will stand out, I'm afraid."

"Great," I said. The last thing we needed was to stand out.

"We need to fuel up," Alina said.

"There are a lot of fueling stations along the next stretch of road," Shane said. "There's usually a place to get food nearby too."

"I'm surprised there are fueling stations, if not many Outvaldians drive cars," Hawk said.

"The settlement of Learning is kind of a cross-roads in Outvald. Besides, people use the fuel for other things. Heating and cooking, etc."

I grimaced. "Cooking?"

He nodded. "This isn't the kind of fuel you were used to in Render. Everything here is made from vegetation. For example, those tall trees with the straight trunks?"

"The ones that look like the goddess's arrows?" Alina said, grinning.

Shane laughed. "Those are the ones. Their pulp and leaves contain a potent component that can easily be made into fuel. It's non-poisonous, leaves no residue behind, and it's plentiful."

"Good to know," Hawk said.

"There!" I pointed to a sign that said, "Fuel," with some strange characters beneath it.

"I'm a little surprised you Outvaldians don't have your own language."

"Oh, we do. You heard it back there, with the Brothers. But we mostly speak an English dialect."

When I thought about it, I realized that made sense. Shane himself spoke just like we did. So did his granddaughter Kate. And Grams had always spoken English, albeit with a slight accent at times. It was almost like a Cajun patois, but not as thick.

Alina pulled Belle up to a tall cylinder standing in the center of a dirt field. It was bigger around than my arms would reach and looked to be ten feet tall.

The hose that ran from its base had a three-inch diameter and was draped along the ground rather than retractable, the nozzle on the end the only thing resting in a hook that kept it out of the dirt.

"How do we pay?" Alina asked.

Shane held up a coin, its surface a dull silver. There were symbols etched along the face of the coin. "I'll get it. We should fill up our cans too."

He climbed out of the front seat and pressed the coin against a round spot on the cylinder. Lights flared up and down the length of the tank, and I could hear liquid rushing toward the hose.

A beat later, the hose stiffened and shifted in the dirt as it filled.

Shane grabbed the nozzle and inserted it into the car. Hawk retrieved our fuel cans from the back.

I pointed to a small building at the back of the lot. "I'll go get us food."

Shane handed me the coin. I frowned, knowing he was spending too much on us.

"You can pay me back in cakes and cookies," he told me, his eyes alight at the thought.

I nodded, but I silently resolved to pay him in other things too. For one thing, he was going to get unlimited use of the car when he wanted her.

The building at the back of the lot was tiny, about the size of a food truck from back home. The girl who worked behind the counter had oversized dark eyes without eyebrows or lashes, a smooth wave of black hair that she wore swept straight back from a pale, unlined face and perfect cupid's bow lips.

She blinked those velvety eyes slowly, looking like something a caricature artist would create. "Help you?" Her voice was husky. The teeth she showed when she spoke were spaced apart rather than close together like a human's, and they were all cylindrical and sharp.

I eyed the shelves behind her, sniffing the air. "Food?"

The velvet eyes blinked ever so slowly. I was left wondering if she'd understood my request. But she moved away from the window and took several wrapped items out of a glass case, handing them to me.

Alina pointed to some bags on a tiered shelf behind the girl and some bottles, holding up her hand, fingers spread. "Five each."

The girl nodded and added the items to the wrapped food.

I handed her the coin and she pressed it against a small digital reader of some kind. Handing it back to me, she smiled, showing me those scary teeth. "Have a fine day."

We turned away, juggling our goodies.

"Nice car," she added.

I turned and gave her a grin. "Thank you."

"That went well," Alina said, breaking into one of the bags.

"What did we just buy?" I asked.

She shrugged. "I don't have any idea. But I'm starving. I'd eat just about anything right now."

I couldn't argue that.

The wrapped items turned out to be some kind of hot sandwich. They consisted of a thick, doughy bread that was stuffed with melted cheese and meat, with star-shaped red vegetables sliced along their length.

"Toffatelos," Shane said when he saw me looking at them funny. "Kind of sweet. They're good."

He wasn't wrong. All of it was good. And the little bags turned out to contain more of the toffatelos, red, green, and purple, sliced thin and fried to a crunch with salt and something that tasted like pepper on them. They were tasty too.

The drinks were too salty for my taste, but they quenched my thirst surprisingly well. Which reminded me... "I need to get a new canteen," I said.

Shane nodded. "There's a store at the edge of the University. We can stock up on food and water for the rest of the trip there."

The Learning University campus wasn't nearly as busy as the ones I'd visited at home, but it was a lot more populated than any other spot I'd seen in Outvald so far.

Most of the people we came across looked like the girl at the food stand, with variances in height, sex, and hair color.

They dressed much like you'd expect college kids to dress, though there was an unnatural look to the clothing as if it had been created to mimic something someone else had worn but didn't quite get there.

The campus consisted of one larger main building and two smaller structures which we quickly learned were administration buildings. All classes and teachers apparently inhabited the main building in the center.

Professor Guwalt's office was on the second floor. Despite my having seen some students entering a few of the classrooms on our trip upstairs, the place was deathly silent. Our footsteps sounded like claps of thunder as we moved across the gray, striated tile and climbed a narrow staircase to the second floor.

Shane knocked on Guwalt's door.

"Come," a cultured voice called out.

We filed inside, Alina and Hawk standing by the door and Shane and I stopping in front of the messiest desk I'd ever seen. Professor Guwalt was staring at a book in front of a wall-sized bookshelf, his attention riveted to the pages open in front of him. We stood there a long moment, watching him read with his back to us.

I looked at Shane and he rolled his eyes.

Guwalt turned another page in his book, seemingly content to keep reading while we waited.

I wasn't equally content to wait. "Excuse me, Professor."

The man jumped and the book flew out of his hands, slamming to the floor in front of him.

"Oh..." He placed a hand over his heart and stumbled to his chair. "Oh my." He looked at me and then Shane. "You startled me. When did you arrive?"

13

"We arrived when we knocked on the door a minute ago and you told us to come in," Shane said with a straight face.

Guwalt's eyes went wide. "Oh. Yes, of course." He smiled, showing us the same deadly sharp, cylindrical teeth most of the people in Learning seemed to have. "How can I help you?" He bent to pick his book up off the floor.

"Professor," I said, "I'm Glynn Forester. It's nice to meet you."

He held out a hand and I took it, barely biting back a grimace from the clammy feel of his moist flesh. "Pleasure. Are you from the Diabold Foresters? I knew your Uncle Tommy. He was a fine man. It's a shame about that plowing accident." Guwalt frowned, shaking his head.

"No...I..." Realizing it would serve no purpose to

correct him, I moved on. "I was wondering if we could get a map of all the portals in Outvald?"

He blinked at me, that same slow blink the girl at the food shack had. It was disconcerting and, along with the strange teeth, put me in mind of a large lizard. "Ah, the portals," he finally said. "Yes."

He turned away from us and looked back down at his book.

Shane and I shared a look and I sighed. "If you'll just point us in the right direction," I told the professor. "We'll get what we need and get out of your way."

Guwalt turned to me and gave a violent twitch, his overlarge eyes going wide. "Oh! My goodness. How did you get in here?"

Shane motioned toward a table near the window, which was covered in large sheets of paper that appeared to be some kind of blueprints. Then he moved around behind the professor's desk and engaged him in conversation. "Professor Guwalt, did you know David Bernes?"

"Bernes? Why, I'm not sure..."

I only half listened as the two men talked.

Hawk joined me at the table and we quickly rifled through the papers. "They look like star charts," he said in a soft voice.

"Or portals," I suggested in a whisper.

"David is dead?" the professor asked loudly. He sounded shocked. "Oh my. That is bad news."

"Do you know who might have wanted him dead?" Shane quickly asked, moving as Guwalt tried to see around him to what we were doing.

"If these are portals, there are a lot of them," Hawk said in a low tone. He picked up another sheet of paper and uncovered a small electronic device. It was about six inches by four inches and the screen was dark. Hawk tapped the glass and it lit up, showing us a scene that was heavily shaded as if the room it showed was dark.

It appeared to be a bunch of soldiers emerging from behind what looked like a big boiler or something.

"What are you doing?" Guwalt asked from just behind me.

It was my turn to jump. I swung around. "We're just looking for a map of the portals. We were told you have one."

He reached for the device and snatched it out of Hawk's hand. "Yes. I do." He stared at the men flooding into the shaded room, frowning. "I, um. We need to go."

He grabbed up the papers and turned toward his bookshelf just as the sound of shouting and a single, terrified scream split the silence. The sound appeared to be coming from the first floor.

I glanced at the door and, by the time I looked back at the professor, there was an opening in the shelving unit and he was disappearing into it.

Almost as soon as he entered the opening, it started to close behind him.

I looked from him toward the sound of shouting, torn.

Shane saved me from my indecision by grabbing Guwalt's desk chair and jamming it into the opening, stopping it from closing. "Go, help them. I'll keep this open."

I nodded and we ran for the door.

Alina was already gone. The thrum of her energy pistols joined the chaos on the lower level, and the tell-tale explosion that followed told me she'd found her target.

Deep-throated screams accompanied her energy blasts.

Hawk and I skimmed through the door and almost immediately ran up against a Body soldier. The woman was dressed in the usual black, form-fitting body armor that looked and felt like cloth. She swung a blade toward my throat, energy sparking along its lethal edge, and I ducked. Her blade clanged against a painted concrete wall, and she grunted with the impact.

Hawk lunged at another soldier, a man who was a head taller than the big guardian but not nearly as strong. The soldier was good with his dual blades, but Hawk was better. The two of them danced along the railing overlooking the floor below. I lost sight of them, needing to attend to my own attacker.

I yanked energy forward, pleased to discover that I still held the Brotherhood's powerful magic in my core. I formed it into a single, short sword that I thankfully managed to brandish in time to counter the woman's attack. Our blades clanked together loudly. She moved with lightness and agility, her movements showing great skill.

It did her no good.

As soon as her back was to the Professor's door, Shane popped out and smacked her over the head with an oversized book. She dropped like a stone. Shane grabbed her sword, winking.

"Thanks," I called out as I descended the stairs at a run. Interspersed with the sound of Alina's laser blasts was the terrified screaming of students who'd unwittingly gotten between the ruthless warrior and the Body soldiers attacking her.

I stepped off the bottom stair and stared in horror at the tableau in front of me.

Alina stood with both guns out, energy blasting from them in a constant stream as Body soldiers ducked and dodged and tried to make their way to her. Behind Alina, three students cowered beneath a counter that was covered with shredded, smoldering paper.

Somebody was going to have a great excuse not to turn in his or her homework.

As I ducked low and ran for the nearest pillar, a blast from one of the soldiers hit the top of the counter they were hiding behind. There was a blood-curdling scream as a chunk of the counter blew off, exploding into a hundred tiny projectiles.

Judging by the wild sobs, someone had been hit with the debris.

I spotted a Body soldier crouching behind a plant, sneaking up on Alina. Moving quickly, I lowered my center of gravity and ran, blade held close to my thighs to obscure its glow. The man didn't see me coming until I was on him. He looked up when I was three feet away. His blade came up to block my first blow, but he wasn't ready for the second.

I swung as hard as I could. My blade met flesh and severed it. He just had time to widen his eyes in surprise before sliding bonelessly to the ground.

I heard a soft scuff and ducked, spinning away as another soldier's blade sliced the air where I'd been. I shoved off my back foot and lunged, but my blade barely scraped across the flesh of his forearm.

He blocked my second strike and shoved me to the ground. I hit my head when I landed. Pain flared through my skull, and the world gained charcoal motes as dizziness swamped me.

The man stepped forward, an evil grin on his long, narrow face. "The magistrate will be happy to see you," he said, lifting the hilt of his sword.

I read the intent in his gaze a beat before he slammed the hilt toward my face.

The strike never landed.

The plant behind him erupted in a million tiny pieces and the soldier's body jerked, spun around, and slammed into the ground.

Alina was suddenly there. "Come on, Glynn. This is no time to take a nap. We need to get out of here before the rest of them come."

I let her lift me off the ground without comment. Shaking my head to clear it, I stumbled toward the stairs behind her. Several kids hit the steps in front of me, climbing fast. One big kid wrapped an arm around my waist and helped me climb.

By the time we hit the top step, more soldiers were pounding into the lobby below.

Hawk pounded toward us from somewhere down the hall. He shoved his knives into their sheathes and scooped me into his arms, jerking his head for the kid who'd been helping me to go ahead of us.

As soon as we were all in Guwalt's office, Alina and Shane shoved a desk in front of the door. The next thing I knew, we were diving into darkness, and, for a moment, I thought I'd gone blind.

"**D**id anybody bring a light?" a squeaky voice asked.

"I don't have one," Shane said.

"Nope," said Hawk. "Lina?"

She sighed, clearly disgusted with all of them. "It's not like I knew we were going to be jumping into some dark passageway."

A muffled crash told me they'd broken through our barrier in the office beyond. I slapped Hawk's arm, suddenly feeling stupid for letting him carry me around like a helpless damsel. "Put me down."

He complied, setting me down onto something squishy.

"Ouch!" said the squeaky voice. "That was my foot!"

"Sorry," I said quickly. I pulled energy into my hands and formed it into a light, shining it over some pretty rough-looking walls and ground. It appeared that somebody had built the passage from mud and rocks. "Does anybody have an idea where this goes?"

There was movement to my left. I skimmed my light in that direction in time to see three kids shaking their heads. The fourth kid was sagging against the wall, blood dripping down his forehead and into his eyes. He sank lower as I looked at him. "Hawk!"

The big man stepped around me and snagged

the kid around the middle before he hit the ground, then carefully laid him over one shoulder. Blood dripped slowly down Hawk's back, and the kid groaned softly. He needed medical help.

Beyond the wall we'd come through, crashing sounds told me the Body was tossing Guwalt's office. They knew we'd been in that room. They would keep searching until they found the passage. "We need to get out of here," I told my fellow travelers.

Alina pointed toward the ground. "It looks like the professor went that way."

She was right. There was a distinct footprint in the dust coating the rough floor. "Let's go."

The passage grew colder the longer we followed it. I had the distinct feeling that we were moving downhill the entire time, and I hoped we weren't going too far underground.

The passage gradually narrowed until we were forced to move in a single file. Those of us who were over five and a half feet tall had to duck in spots to clear the ceiling.

It wasn't a comfortable sensation, especially with the growing dampness of the space. The walls ran with water, the surface was slimy to the touch, and my shoes were wet from splashing through puddles.

The only good news was that the Body didn't come up on us while we were in the passage. But, my teeth were clattering together by the time we finally stepped outside into what looked like a park. The grounds were well cared for, the grass thick and short. Trees and manicured bushes dotted the area in tidy islands, and concrete benches were placed in strategic spots beneath the trees.

We looked around. "Where are we?"

The kids collapsed onto the grass beyond the opening. Squeaky voice pointed to a distant hill with a clam-shell-shaped backdrop. It reminded me of an outdoor concert location. "This is the Revelry. It's a park a few miles from University."

Hawk gently laid the injured kid on the ground. The big kid who'd helped me up the stairs rolled to his knees and crawled over to his friend.

"Do you have healing magic?" Hawk asked.

"Yeah," the kid said in a husky voice. He blinked like an owl and flushed with embarrassment.

Hawk nodded and motioned for the kid to do his thing. Then he joined us. "What now?"

Alina's gaze was locked onto the passage entrance. It was cleverly hidden behind a tall bush that sported fat, white flowers and prickles, discouraging anyone from looking too closely at the hillside in that area. "It's too quiet back there. You know they had to find a way into that passage."

"I agree," Shane said. "We need to move out of this area."

I thought of Belle and my spirits sagged. The car was miles away from our location, giving us no way to finish our journey or even get quickly away from the Body's reach. Then I looked at the kids. Two girls and two boys. The boy who'd been bleeding was looking better under his friend's care, but we wouldn't be doing them any favors by dragging them along with us. Still, we couldn't leave them there with the soldiers heading our way.

I chewed my lip, feeling unsure and not liking it.

"We can't take them with us," Shane said in a soft voice he probably hoped wouldn't carry. "If we could find Guwalt, he could take charge of them."

One of the girls lifted herself to her elbows and cocked her head at us. She didn't look like the others. She looked more human, except for the slightly scaly striations in her pale skin. "Are you serious?" she said in her high-pitched voice. "Have you met the professor?"

I fought a grin. "She has a point. He'd probably forget they were with him within two minutes and demand to know how they'd snuck up on him."

The girl nodded enthusiastically. "We don't need him." She pointed toward the stage. "We can just use the portal."

My eyes popped wide. "Portal?"

14

The ground blasted away ahead of us as we ran toward the stage in the distance.

The Body had found us. I looked on in horror as what looked like a dozen soldiers flooded out of the passageway.

Alina turned and ran backward, firing her weapons as she ran. I was impressed by her agility. I couldn't run as well as she did going forward, let alone backward.

Hawk peeled away from us as we neared the stage. "Get them out of here!" he shouted and then dove behind a tree, pulling his blades from their sheaths.

I looked at Shane. He gave me a cranky look. "Go. We'll be right behind you."

I stared at him for a beat. I couldn't leave him

there alone with what amounted to a death sentence pouring in our direction.

I shook my head. "I'm not leaving you."

He reached out and gave me a shove. "I promise, it will be okay. Just get the kids back and then come get us."

I shook my head again.

Shane turned his back to me and lifted his hands, fingers working the air in front of him. Amazingly, magic started to form before him—an intricate web of shimmering silver energy that took shape quickly. It fell from his dancing fingers like woven yarn from knitting needles and proceeded to creep along the grass, heading directly for the approaching soldiers.

I ran in a sideways jog as I watched him work, still not comfortable with leaving him behind.

His magic weave touched the feet of a charging soldier and yanked him into the air, head hanging as the web wound around his legs, coated his body, and then enveloped his head in an intractable prison.

The man's screams were cut off as the webbing closed over his face and his struggles ended quickly. I watched with a mixture of fascination and horror as the webbing compressed him into nothing.

Swallowing hard, I had to admit that was pretty effective. Apparently, Shane wasn't as helpless as I'd thought.

Gunfire and screams peppered the area as I turned and ran.

The kids waited for me in the shadow of the stage, their eyes wide with fear. "The portal...where is it?" I asked.

Squeaky pointed to a door at the base of the stage. "Are you sure it's okay to leave them here?"

I turned to look at my friends. Hawk was fighting a hand-to-hand blade battle with two Body soldiers at once. There was a growing pile of bodies at his feet. As I watched, he easily dispatched one soldier and concentrated all his power on the second.

He'd be fine.

Alina was well protected behind the enormous trunk of an arrow tree, and she was picking soldiers off with ease and regularity.

Shane...

Well, one of the Body's fighters finally recognized the source of his deadly magic and was turning to fire at him.

"Shane!" I screamed, but he didn't hear me.

My heart stopped. I took a step in his direction, but I was too far away to help. Distracted by Shane's plight, I didn't notice the woman in black armor who'd suddenly appeared in front of me until it was too late. She held a blade in each hand and had an expression of icy hatred on her stern face.

Without thinking, I yanked power from the air and formed it into a blade. "Get out of here!" I yelled at the kids. I didn't wait to see if they listened. I was too busy fighting for my life.

The woman in front of me was huge. Easily as tall and as big as Hawk, but with a lithe grace and agility that made it nearly impossible to keep up with her fluid strikes.

My hands were bloody after only a couple of minutes, my arms covered in shallow wounds that bled and stung more than they should.

She'd clearly coated her blades with something that enhanced blood loss. The excessive bleeding was starting to mess with me. My movements were becoming sluggish. My focus blurred.

Her impossibly fast strikes hit their target nearly every time. I was a sea of aching flesh, a bloody mess, and I imagined I could feel my heart slowing as the seconds ticked by.

Screams erupted across the battlefield—sounds of pain and terror that would have coated me in ice if I hadn't been in the process of dying.

I fell to my knees, unable to stop myself. The world swung dizzily around me. I was so cold. With glassy eyes, I stared up at the woman as her visage wavered and rippled in front of me, and I knew I was looking at my death.

She lifted her blade for the killing stroke, and then she was suddenly gone...shoved away by a huge, shaggy form with snapping white teeth and glowing red eyes.

Nicht! Where in the goddess's good night had he come from?

Screaming ensued. It was blood-curdling and rife with pain and fear. And then silence.

I wavered on my knees. Fighting to stay upright, losing the battle.

The ground smacked me between the eyes, and the impact nearly took me completely under. The only thing that kept me awake was the insistent whining of the big black hound and the rough scrape of a smelly tongue across my cheek.

Somebody grabbed me and we were suddenly moving. "Hold on, Glynn," said a sexy deep voice. I was deposited onto a furry pillow and somebody pressed my fingers into the fur. "Don't let go."

Time passed in a confusing whirlwind.

We were moving fast. It was dark, with flashes of multi-hued light that always engendered urgent conversation. Portal junctions? I smelled magic more than once. And heard screams. But beneath it all was a constant ba-bump, ba-bump, ba-bump that I finally recognized as a heartbeat.

My cheek lay against a soft pillow that occasionally whined and needed a good washing. But the heartbeat kept me focused...kept me aware of my surroundings on a level that was vague, slightly removed from reality, but constant.

At one point we stopped. Voices murmured

around me. Then there was heat, and my skin started to itch.

And we were off again.

I was tired and curious about where I was. But not curious enough to open my eyes. The journey was jarring. I was vaguely aware of my fingers clutching something in a death grip. And, occasionally, a low voice speaking my name, reminding me to breathe.

I breathed.

In. Out. In. Out...

Glynn!

Right. Breathe.

In. Out. In. Out...

Light flared, burning my eyes even through my closed lids.

"There!" someone yelled.

I mewled pitifully, burrowing my face deeper into the stinky pillow to escape the light. It burned me like fire.

The bumping movement stopped. A horrific creak jolted me into wakefulness. I tried to lift my head. "Where...?" My mouth was too dry to speak. My tongue stuck to the top of my mouth.

"We're okay," Hawk told me. "We're at Belle."

My eyes wouldn't open.

"So...thirsty."

"Yeah. I know. Let's get you in the car and we'll give you something to drink."

I think I nodded. I'm not entirely sure. But Hawk scooped me up off the stinky pillow without any apparent trouble and deposited me onto a hard, cool seat.

Something crunched beneath my feet.

My stinky pillow jumped up behind me and, after slathering my face with his stinky tongue, Nicht sprawled next to me, dropping his big head into my lap.

I dug my fingers into his fur as the world tilted beneath me. "Thanks, buddy. What took you so long?"

Nicht whined.

We'd left him in the car, figuring the school wouldn't welcome the presence of a hellhound around the students. I vaguely wondered how he'd gotten out. The air buffeting Hawk and me through a window with only the jagged remains of a little glass around the edges gave me the answer. Nicht had crashed right through the window to escape. I shifted at the thought and glass crunched under my shoe.

Hawk touched my hand. "Here. Take this. The kid gave you some healing, but you'll need to rehydrate and rest a bit before you feel like yourself."

I accepted the bottle, pressing it to my lips. The liquid was warm and slightly sweet, and I was pretty sure I could feel it reinflating my cells as it hit my system.

Belle's engine roared to life and we started to move. Cool air wafted over me.

"What happened?" I asked whoever would respond.

"She'd coated her blades with an anti-clotting agent. You nearly bled to death," Shane said, his tone rigid with anger. "Nasty bloaters."

I nodded stupidly. Then I remembered... My eyes flew open. "The kids?"

"Safe," Alina said from the front seat. She was driving, and I could tell by the dizzying flash of trees and buildings beyond the glass that she was moving at her usual speed.

I closed my eyes again when the dizzying movement made my stomach lurch.

"They were waiting for us inside the portal when we got in," Hawk told me. He took the bottle I hadn't realized I'd emptied and handed me another one. "We left them at the campus. They wasted no time getting out of there."

"Good," I murmured, feeling gradually better. "The Body?"

"We got most of them," Shane said. "But I have no doubt more are streaming in." He glanced back at me. "What we saw on that communicator..."

I nodded. "There's got to be a portal in the basement of the main building."

Shane nodded. "It makes sense. The University

tracks all the portals on Outvald. They'd want to have one of their own."

I sat up straighter in my seat. My brain was finally kicking in. "But a portal from Earth?" I shook my head. "I thought the Magistrate wanted Victoria's portal so he'd have access to Outvald. Why did he want it if he already had portals into this dimension?" I thought about the soldiers rising out of the lake near the Brotherhood's encampment. The one in the University's basement made two. I was certain there were more.

"There can be only one explanation," Hawk said, his gaze locked on mine. "They weren't after the portal. They were after you."

My stomach twisted painfully. I shook my head in instant denial. "That's crazy."

"Is it?" Hawk asked. "Think about it. They had Art, but his powers never really manifested. So rather than waste a resource, the Magistrate decided to use him to get to you. Don't you think it's likely Artur talked to the Body about you? About your powers?"

I frowned, instantly angry over his accusation.

Hawk lifted a hand to ward off my rage. "I'm not saying your brother betrayed you, Glynn. But it would be the most natural thing in the world to talk about his family. We know how cutthroat that group is. One of the other interns or assistants might have gone behind his back and shared what he'd told them in confidence."

I knew he was right. I'd even suggested the same thing to Art myself once. But something inside me refused to accept it. I couldn't. Because if I did...

"Why would they even want me?" I asked Hawk. "I don't have any natural magic. I have to borrow anything I use, like some kind of..." The word escaped me.

I caught Alina's gaze in the rear-view mirror and ice formed in my gut.

"Like a battery?" she said, her expression kind.

I swallowed hard. Good goddess! She was right. I was a magical battery. My ability to siphon magic was, for all practical purposes, infinite. For a group that had made a practice of scraping magic from other creatures, my skillset would be invaluable.

My very existance removed the magical middle man.

All the color ran from my face and I thought, for a moment, that I was going to pass out.

I shoved fear away so I could breathe, focusing on something equally terrifying. "Artur does have magic. He's bottled it away so deep that I'm not sure even he knows how to access it anymore. But both Grams and Sissy have told me he has it." I grabbed Hawk's hand. "We left him alone. We need to get back."

He stared at me for a long moment. Then he said. "Do you want to cut our current project short?"

He'd couched the question in neutral terms. But I knew what he was asking me. Did I want to abandon our attempt to get justice for David Bernes to protect my brother?

I closed my eyes, torn by indecision.

When I finally spoke, the single word was ripped from my torn and bleeding conscience. "No."

He inclined his head, something flashing through his gaze that looked like respect. "We'll get in and out. Find our answers and then get back home fast."

I nodded and sat back on the seat, resting my head against the leather that had been warmed by my body heat. I stared out the window and tried to still the fear raging through my middle.

I was terrified that I'd made a terrible mistake by leaving Art and everyone else behind at Victoria.

And I suddenly knew without a doubt that I was in grave danger of losing the only family I had because of that mistake.

15

"Pull off the road," Shane said.

Alina glanced around. "Why? Is something wrong?"

He pointed to a spot well off the road where several trees were clumped together. "Drive the car over there and park. We'll walk from here."

I frowned. "Walk? Why? How far is it?"

"About a mile. He scanned the sky. "It'll be dark in less than an hour. We'll go in under cover of darkness and on foot. It's the only safe way."

Hawk held up a hand. "Wait a minute. That's crazy. Are you telling me everybody who comes to this auction has to sneak inside?"

"Not everybody, no," Shane said, pointing again at the desired spot.

With a sigh, Alina did as he asked.

"But we're clearly not traders and we're not bidders." He eyed Nicht with a critical eye.

Hawk and I both said, "No!" even as the hellhound growled at Shane.

He held up his hands. "I was just thinking the dog could be our cover. It isn't every day you see a hellhound. He'd be a hot property in there. He might get us more answers than simple questions would."

"First of all," Hawk said, holding up a hand to stop Nicht from snarling. He *really* didn't like being called a dog. "We're not going to put Nicht into that position. It's too dangerous. And secondly, I have no intention of simply asking questions. I'll use lethal force if necessary."

Something in his tone made me turn to look at him. His face was hard, flushed with angry color. A muscle in his jaw jumped with rage. "The people who run this place deserve to be in the cages they put their victims into. I'm not interested in playing nice with them."

"Now, wait a minute, Guardian," Shane said, shaking his head. "That's not what I signed up for. Do you have any idea how many people you'll enrage if you overturn this particular apple cart? Lots of rich and powerful people in both dimensions make money from this auction. I thought we were just going to get information."

Alina climbed out of the car and strapped her

guns to her narrow hips. She yanked first one cartridge and then the other out of her weapons and checked the energy levels. "We'll get information, old man. Don't you worry about that."

Shane's scowl was a storm cloud in a turbulent sky. "I won't be a part of that." He leaned across the car as she bent down to look through the open door at him. "And if you call me 'Old Man' again, I'll give you a third eye in the center of your infuriatingly smooth forehead. Not that it will help you see things any clearer. But it will give me real satisfaction to uglify that pretty face of yours, so it matches your soul."

Alina laughed him off. "Sure thing, Old..." Something in Shane's face must have told her it wouldn't be wise to push her luck. She clamped her mouth shut and stepped back. "The hound and I will recon the area between this location and the auction."

Hawk nodded. "Be careful."

They took off at an easy run, leaving Hawk and me to deal with Shane.

I figured I'd better step in. Hawk's temper didn't seem to be tipping toward conciliation at the moment. "We'll do the minimum we have to do to get this done," I said. "I want to get in and out fast. Fast doesn't leave a lot of room for creative solution-ing." I gave Hawk a hard look, daring him to disagree.

He just shook his head.

"Maybe there won't be any creatures here," I said, hopefully. I wasn't excited at the prospect of witnessing a lot of suffering myself. And I knew, despite what I was telling Shane, if I saw creatures being mistreated, I'd be the first in line to get them out of there.

Despite who it annoyed.

He didn't look convinced, but he grabbed his stuff from the car and we started off.

Darkness clung to every surface, masking each footfall through the wilderness as we approached the edge of the auction compound. The sky was charcoal gray, clouds skidding thickly over a greatly-subdued moon.

It was as if even the atmosphere didn't approve of the Outvald auction.

The auction sign hung crookedly on a tall chain-link fence that had razor wire coiled along the top. The gate into the compound was reinforced with heavy-duty bars as well as a couple of stout locking mechanisms.

They seriously didn't want uninvited visitors getting inside. I had to wonder why.

We stopped at the fence and looked through the metal links at the cluster of low-slung buildings that comprised the compound. Several harsh yellow lights on tall poles lit up the area...an island of visibility in a sea of obscurity.

As we watched, a man with a long gun resting on his bent arms emerged from the shadows, stopped near the central door, and then proceeded on past it to the other end of the building. I noted two other guards, one on the roof of the largest building and one standing in front of a structure the size of a shed just beyond the edge of the light.

"I wonder what's in that building?" I asked, nodding toward the shed.

Shane grimaced. "I'm guessing that's where they put the influencers."

When Hawk and I looked a question at him, he clarified. "Beasts that can get into the heads of their prey. Generally, they're two-natured."

Two natured meant they could take human forms. I looked at him like he'd lost his mind. "You're serious?"

Hawk's expression transformed into an angry glower. "That can't be legal."

"Not where you come from, no. There's a reason these Neanderthal's set up shop in Outvald."

A small pebble skittered across the dirt. In the beat of a heart, Hawk had his blades in his hands, energy pulsed at my fingertips, and Shane had a gun trained into the darkness.

"I come in peace," Alina said, her voice carrying a note of amusement.

Without warning, a cold, wet nose goosed me. I yelped before I could stop myself, turning to glare at Nicht.

He gave me a wide, canine grin, his tongue lolling.

"Very funny."

Alina nodded toward the gate. "This isn't the best place to get in. I found a spot near the back where there's a blind spot. Guards have limited vision there because the light doesn't reach the fence."

We nodded and fell into a jog behind her, Nicht keeping pace at my hip. I glanced over at him. "It won't do you any good to try to suck up now, buddy. I'm holding a grudge."

He chuffed a sound like laughter.

We rounded the corner and ran along the fence line for several moments. Alina finally stopped, nodding toward the empty space between the fence and the nearest building. As she'd promised, it was dark. I watched the guards move through their paces from our new vantage point and noted they never even glanced in our direction.

"This doesn't make sense," I told her. "Why aren't they guarding this side? It feels like a trap."

"That's because it is." She pointed toward the ground on the other side of the fence, which appeared to be covered in what looked like a large mud puddle.

I frowned. "Mud? That's their trap?"

Shane leaned closer and sniffed. "That's not just mud. It's..."

"A magical residue pool," Hawk said.

Feeling like the odd man out, I was reluctant to ask what they were talking about. But I needed to know. "And that means...?"

"Nobody knows exactly," Shane explained. "That's the problem. It could be something harmless, or it could dissolve us into atoms with the slightest touch. Given the setup here...I'm guessing it's probably the latter."

"It is," Alina said. She leaned down and picked up a long stick, flinging it over the fence. It hit the muck with a sizzle rather than a splash and flashed into flames that disintegrated it in seconds, leaving behind a foul, sulfurous stench. "The pit runs the length of the sides and back of this fence."

"Smart," Hawk said. "They only need enough manpower to watch the front."

Nodding, Shane agreed. "And if anything escapes, it's forced to the front as well."

We stood in thoughtful silence for a beat. Finally, I had to ask. "So, how do we get past it?"

I didn't like the smile on Alina's face. Not at all.

"I have a plan for that. I just need the wizard to get us through the fence."

Shane threw her a glare. "Wizard? You're really begging for that third eye, aren't you?"

She gave him a sly look. "You can do this, right? I mean, it's a pretty basic spell."

His lips curled in a silent snarl that even Nicht would be proud of. "I swear, woman..."

Alina laughed brightly.

To my immense surprise, Shane's lips twitched with something that looked a lot like humor.

"Sometime tonight?" I urged.

Grumbling softly, Shane settled his bag on the ground and pulled out a small jar and a brush. He moved close to the fence and ran his palm over it, careful not to touch the metal. Then he nodded and unscrewed the jar. Dipping the brush into a thick black substance that smelled like tar, he painted a line from the dirt to the bottom edge of the razor wire, then over about two feet and down to the ground again.

He carefully repacked the jar. Then touched the tarry stuff clinging to the brush with the tip of a finger, sending the residue into the air in a light mist. Bristles clean again, he dropped the brush into the bag and slung the strap over his shoulder. "I'm ready."

Alina extended a hand, palm up and he sighed at her casual bossiness. Stepping close to the fence, Shane rubbed his hands together, then placed his palms over the space he'd marked and closed his eyes. A moment later, the metal links inside the tarry substance disappeared in a whoosh and a flare of silvery light.

We all stilled, our gazes sliding to the guards in the compound. There was no outcry, no movement in our direction. They hadn't seen Shane's magic.

"Clear," Hawk said in a husky whisper. He glanced at Alina. "Now what?"

There was that grin again. "Nicht?"

We all watched as the big hound stepped up to the opening in the fence and...

My eyes widened in horror. "Is this really a good time for that?"

Hawk barked out a laugh.

Shane's grizzled face took on a pleased expression. When he glanced at Alina, it was hard to miss the respect in his gaze. "Smart girl."

She took a little bow.

Frustration made me want to yell and stomp my foot. Why was I the only one who didn't have a clue what was going on? "Will somebody please tell me why Nicht is peeing on the magic trap?"

"Science is science," she told me smugly. "Even for magic. The pool is highly acidic. A Hellhound's urine is deeply basic. Therefore..."

A lightbulb flashed on in my brain. "Therefore, it neutralizes the magic residue."

"Precisely," Alina said, clearly very proud of herself.

"Yeah," Hawk said, grinning. "Don't look so

proud of yourself, soldier. We do have to walk through that pee now."

Alina's smile slid away. "Yeah. That part's not my favorite."

I took another step and my shoe made a loud squishing noise. I stopped, grimacing. When I looked up, everybody was staring at me. "What? I can't help it," I whispered angrily.

Alina made a soft noise, drawing my gaze to her. She quickly looked away, but not before I saw the suspicious gleam in her eyes.

Sure, she could think it was funny, she was wearing boots. She didn't have hellhound pee and goddess knew whatever else sloshing around inside her shoes.

"Try to keep the sloshing to a minimum," Hawk said, his own lips twitching.

"Ha," I told them crabbily. "It wasn't my idea to tromp through dog pee."

Behind me, Nicht growled.

"Sorry, buddy. I didn't mean..."

"Shhh!" Shane said. We looked in the direction he and Nicht were staring.

I saw nothing.

I was just about to ask them what was up when the shadows shifted and something leaped at us.

Nicht met the big lizard thing in mid-air, his teeth snapping down on the creature's throat before it could make a sound.

With a couple of sturdy shakes, Nicht dispatched the thing, flinging it away.

Too late, we realized the real danger the creature represented, as it detonated like a flash bomb in front of us.

Light and noise eviscerated the night, sending us to our knees on dual cries of pain and surprise. My ears rang and haloes shrouded my eyesight. The explosion had effectively blinded and deafened me in one efficient strike.

I was dimly aware of shouting. Nicht snarled and somebody cried out. I heard Hawk scream the hound's name and then hard hands were grabbing my arms, yanking me off my feet.

In desperation, I fought their grip with everything I had—punching, kicking, even biting hard into human flesh that unfortunately smelled like sour cabbage.

Pain sheared through my skull as one of the guards punched me hard enough to crack a tooth. I tasted blood and struck out again, but my reaction times suffered from the strike and my vision was still wonky.

The next thing I was able to concentrate on was a disconcerting return to light and warmth as the man dragging me along threw me against a wall and I slipped toward a hard, grimy floor as my knees gave out.

A large body landed next to me. My senses told me it was Hawk. I didn't like the way he was breathing. I reached for him and found a muscular arm. Clasping my icy fingers around his warm flesh, I held on as the world tried to dip and roll beneath me.

Voices sparred nearby. I recognized Shane's voice, arguing with somebody. The argument sliced off behind the sound of metal doors clanging shut.

Then I laid my head back and rested for a moment, willing the pain of a beastly headache to go away.

I woke up sometime later, disoriented and my head still killing me. Glancing around, I spotted Hawk lying on the ground next to me. Blood ran from a wound on his throat. It was an angry, puckered thing that looked like a bullethole. The livid red lines of healing wounds scoring his arms and back told me he'd also faced a blade at some point.

The guardian had been fighting while I'd been reduced to wrangling and biting like a girl. Shame filled me. Why hadn't I siphoned magic and used it? I had no excuse, except that the exploding lizard had left me disoriented.

Before I could stop myself, I snorted out a laugh. *Exploding lizard.* Those were two words I'd never thought I'd link together. I lifted an arm to shove hair out of my face, and there was a small twinge of pain on the inside of my arm. I looked down to find a puncture wound. A small amount of blood stained the area around the slightly swollen spot.

I looked away from Hawk and saw Shane sitting with his back to the wall on my other side. His eyes were closed, but I didn't think he was asleep. "Where are we?" I asked him.

His eyes didn't open. For a minute, I considered that I might have been wrong. Maybe he was asleep. Or...my pulse shot skyward and my gaze found his broad chest, rising and falling.

Relief hit me so hard it brought stars to my gaze.

"Shane?"

He expelled a breath, finally deigning to answer my question. "Isn't that obvious?"

"I meant, where in the compound did they take us?"

"Main building. Basement level. Stay away from the bars."

I glanced toward the cells on either side of us, seeing nothing. The only lightbulb was centered over our cell. The other cells were mostly cast into shadow.

A knifelike spike of pain sliced through my temple. I reached up and rubbed it with two fingertips. "Where'd they put Alina and Nicht?"

Shane's eyes opened and he turned to me, his gaze cold.

Looking into his eyes, I felt my world explode for a second time, sans lizard. I shook my head in mute denial. Tears sprang free and raked hot trails down my cheeks.

Shane's gaze rose to a small device high in the corner of the cell. A small yellow light blinked there. Then he rested his head back and closed his eyes again. "Forget about them. They're gone."

"No..." But his tone was filled with a finality I couldn't ignore. I slumped back again, letting tears drench my face and wet my shirt. I bit back the sobs that wanted to escape, knowing they wouldn't do anything except convince whoever was on the other side of that camera that they'd beaten me.

Hawk groaned, drawing me from my grief. He twitched and I was on him, helping him roll over and sit up. His face was colorless. Lines of pain etched his face. After he was sitting up, leaning against the wall, I caught his pain-filled gaze.

"Hey."

His lips tightened, and he stiffly turned his head. "Hey. How's things?"

I laughed wetly. "Oh, you know..." I closed my lips to keep from sobbing like a baby.

Hawk wrinkled his nose. "What is that terrible smell?"

I frowned. "I don't know. We're in some kind of dungeon."

He sniffed again. "No, it smells like...pee."

Smacking him on the arm, I felt like a jerk when he winced. "Oops. Sorry."

I watched him scan the space, find Shane, and then continue scanning. I reached up and touched his chin with my fingertip, giving him a quick negative shake when he looked into my eyes.

Pain swirled through the hazel depths, his jaw tightened, and angry color swept into his face.

Despite my own pain, seeing him gain strength of purpose made me feel better. We needed to fight. We needed to get out of there. And we needed to kill whoever had hurt our friends.

16

The outer door opened and a soldier walked inside. His fleshy face was battle-scarred, with deep pockmarks and a slash across the right side of his face that had taken out one eye. He walked with a limp, his corpulent form moving stiffly into the room. He stopped in the middle, his single-eyed gaze sour on us as if he could barely stand to be in our presence, and stood with his hands behind his back, his legs wide.

I stared at him a moment, wondering why he was there.

It didn't take long for me to find out. The door opened again and, to my surprise, a well-dressed woman walked into the room. She was tall, softly rounded, and had a thick crown of red hair. Freckles covered her lean face and her wide blue eyes were heavily made up in what I could only term as clownish colors.

Dressed in a black jumpsuit that cinched her narrow waist, she wore four-inch-high heels that were a vivid red. She carried a sparkly clutch in one perfectly manicured hand and diamonds sparkled from her ears, throat, and several of her long fingers. She looked like she was heading to a party, her posture and dress screaming of money and privilege. Not the type of character I'd have ever expected to see in a grungy dungeon.

Her wide mouth was painted a red that matched her heels. It spread in a hungry smile when she looked at Hawk. "My goddess. Such bounty for me tonight." She cast an approving look at the one-eyed soldier. "Good job, Maple."

The scarred man inclined his head.

"Is this all of them?"

The man shifted his feet. "There were two others. They didn't make it."

She watched him as if she knew there was more to the story. "Humans?"

The man's features tightened. "A woman, yes."

She lifted her brows, pinching her lips together with displeasure. "And?"

I got the impression he would have sighed if he thought he could get away with the insubordination. "A hellhound, ma'am."

She drew up another two inches, her painted

face going as hard as stone in the blink of an eye. "You killed a hellhound? Do you have any idea what that would have been worth to me?"

"Yes, Ma'am. I apologize. It couldn't be helped."

My stomach twisted with pain.

Inexplicably, the man turned a hate-filled look on Shane. I looked at the older man and saw that his eyes were open. He was staring at the woman with such hatred I was surprised she hadn't melted on the spot. One of his hands was fingering a metal bracelet I just noticed he was wearing. Was that bracelet the reason he hadn't performed some kind of magic to get us out of there?

I remembered the argument between Shane and someone when we'd first been brought in, but I couldn't place the other man's voice. It could have been Maple. I just didn't know.

"We'll talk about this later," she ground out. Her tone implied the discussion wouldn't be a pleasant one. Refocusing her gaze on our cell, she scanned a look over me, her expression momentarily speculative. She moved closer, but I noticed not close enough that we could grab her through the bars.

Not stupid then. Just breathtakingly evil. I filed that away.

"So this is her?"

I flinched. *Her?*

"Yes, Ma'am."

She walked back and forth in front of the cell,

her gaze skimming over Shane without interest before returning to me. She smiled. "Your siphoning power won't do you any good here, I'm afraid. The cells are impermeable to magical intervention. And you won't regain your energies for a while after your dosing outside tonight. I'll have you safely in the Magistrate's hands well before your magic returns."

I jerked in surprise. My feet were moving before I thought about it. I slammed my palms against the metal bars, gratified to see her blink.

Hawk was suddenly standing beside me, his expression murderous. "You can't give her to the Body."

"Can I not?" She laughed gaily. "On the contrary, Guardian, I definitely can. And I have every intention of doing so. Magistrate Martin is a good friend. And he pays very well for the toys he requests."

"Lady, you're more of a monster than any of the poor creatures you capture and sell," I growled out. "You're not going to get away with this."

"Oh! Mean words." She pretended to swoon. "I'm devastated." She spun on her heels and headed for the door. "They'll be here to collect her in one hour, Maple. Make sure she's here and ready for travel." The woman stopped at the door long enough to give the guard a final warning. "Do not disappoint me again."

The door slammed loudly closed, and Maple turned a sneer on us. "You lot have caused me trouble tonight. I'm not happy about that." He wandered closer, his hands still folded together behind him. He sneered at Shane. "You'll pay a price for that, sorcerer."

Shane shrugged. "Tell me something I don't know, troll."

The scarred man growled. I fought panic. We had one hour to find what we'd come to find and get out of there.

It wasn't nearly enough time. But we'd make it work. We had to.

I looked at Maple, giving him a tight smile. It wasn't friendly, but it was the best I could do. He probably wouldn't have trusted friendliness anyway. "So, Maple, are you the one who killed David Bernes?"

The man snorted. "Unfortunately, no. But the Misses was on a tear that day."

I let my brows lift in surprise. "She killed him? I don't believe it. She might have broken a nail."

Out of the corner of my eye, I saw Shane stand and move along the side of the cell. I wondered vaguely what he was up to.

"Don't be fooled by the fancy exterior, girl. Ma'am's a real killer, she is." His laughter was mean. He eyed Hawk. "Her playthings don't usually survive long."

His implication was clear. Hawk was going to be

one of those playthings. That knowledge was enough to bring out my own claws.

"I should have known you were too stupid to kill him yourself. But I'm surprised she'd lower herself to travel two days to take care of him."

The man's mouth twisted into an ugly grimace. "You're callin' me stupid? Who's inside that cage, girl? And who's outside of it?"

I shrugged, placing my hands on the bars and letting my rage show. "You killed David Bernes because he didn't like what you were doing here? Because he tried to help some of these poor creatures. Didn't you?"

"I told ya. I didn't kill him. And nobody cared if he took some of them away. We only gave him the duds. The ones nobody wanted."

"Then why?" I asked. "Why would you kill him?"

He scanned a look toward the door as if worried the woman would come back. Hawk and I shared a look. The man knew something. We just needed to find out what.

"Come on, man," Hawk said in a pleading tone. "We came all this way to find out what happened to him. You said it yourself. We're all dead. You might as well tell us how clever you've been."

Maple shook his head, his expression smug. "Nah. I don't think so."

When we didn't beg him to tell us, he relented. All he really wanted was to lord something over us.

He gave us a fake laugh. "Okay, okay, if you insist. I can tell you this. Old David was sticking his nose into things he shouldn't. He was planning to mess with the wrong person. Him and his dementia-riddled sidekick. And it didn't work out so well for him."

"Who?" Shane asked, moving to the front corner of the cell. "Who was he going after?"

Maple poked a finger toward Shane. "Nuh-uh-uh! You need to solve the riddle yourself." He glanced at his watch. "And you have about forty-five minutes to do it."

I fought a wave of despair, looking around the cell. There had to be a way to get out of there.

Shane gave a harsh laugh. "You don't know any more than we do," he told Maple with a sneer. "You're just a stupid grunt. Totally expendable."

Maple's face darkened with rage. "That's what you think."

"It is what I think," Shane said, nodding. "It's what everybody else thinks too. You're just trying to act important." Shane spit toward Maple. "Idiot."

Maple yanked a thick, black baton from his belt and stomped toward Shane. "I'll show you who's the idiot," he yelled.

Stabbing a hand through the cell, he grabbed Shane's shirt front and yanked him against the bars. His other hand came up and he tried to slam the baton into Shane's face.

I started to move, not sure what I would do, but feeling like I had to do something.

Hawk's hand found my shoulder and stopped me. I looked up at him and he nodded toward the two men.

Shane's face split in a wide smile. Faster almost than the eye could see, his hand came through the bars and grabbed Maple's baton. He smashed it hard into the guard's face and then leaned away as the shadows of the cell next door shifted. An enormous, dragon-like creature flashed forward and slashed through the bars at Maple. The creature's claws were as long as my fingers. They easily severed Maple's throat, sending his head bouncing along the floor like a grizzly kickball.

"Urp!" I said, covering my mouth as bile rose into my throat.

Shane wrenched the man's body closer and dug the keys out of his pocket, throwing them to Hawk. Then he looked at the dragon. "Thanks, darlin'. We'll have you out of here in a jiffy."

The dragon threw back her long, elegant head and gave a choked roar. Puffs of smoke emerged on the tail end of the roar, and the dragon coughed miserably.

I noticed she had a matching band of metal around her throat to the one Shane wore. Only a lot bigger.

Hawk threw the cell door open and motioned for

me to exit. He searched through the keyring for something to unlock the magic-nulling bands.

Shane took the ring from him. "It's this." He tugged a small vial off the ring, holding it up for us to see. The clear liquid in the glass vial swirled with amber filaments. My nerves fizzed with the need to move, but we were forced to wait while Shane unscrewed the lid, pressing a fingertip onto the top and tipping it. Then he touched the band on his wrist and it popped open.

To my surprise, he pocketed the band rather than flinging it away.

"Now it's your turn, Alice."

The dragon stomped her big feet, rattling the metal bars on the cells as Shane moved to unlock her cell door.

"Um," I said, taking an unplanned step toward the outside door. "Are you sure that's safe?"

Shane gave me an arch look. "Alice and I had a long talk while you two were drooling on your shirt-fronts. She promised to help us if I helped her. She'll keep her end of the bargain. Dragons are extremely trustworthy creatures."

Alice tossed her head and snorted, her jewel-hued eyes sparking in the dim light.

Hawk took my hand and tugged me toward the door. He lowered his head. "Just in case..."

"But..." We couldn't just leave Shane there alone with the giant beast. Could we?

Shane unlocked her cell and reached for the vial.

"You don't have access to your magic," Hawk whispered. "He does. And I don't have my blades. He's the best man for the job."

Shane tapped the collar around the beast's thick, muscular throat and the band fell off. The dragon gave a mighty roar, fire gushing from her throat in a thick, fiery column that scorched the wooden framing of the ceiling forty feet above our heads and turned the huge room into an instant sauna.

The giant creature flapped her wings and stomped toward the open cell door.

Hawk threw the exterior door open and tugged me quickly through. "He's on his own," he barked out as the dragon cleared the door and took off, sending fire along the auction's walls as she flew.

The last thing I heard as the door snapped shut behind us was Shane laughing like a maniac.

"We need to go help him," I told Hawk.

He shook his head. "Listen to him. He's having a ball in there."

"Until he's charbroiled," I mumbled back.

"There you are!"

I yelped, leaping off the ground as a woman stepped from the shadows.

"We've been looking all over for you."

I barely had time to take note of Alina jogging over to us before a giant black hound jumped up to lick me on the face with his stinky tongue. I nearly fell over from the impact of Nicht's snack-plate-sized paws on my chest.

I shoved him off, scrubbing dog spit off my face with my sleeve. "Ugh! You're alive." Tears of happiness burned behind my lids.

Alina frowned. "Of course we are. Why would you think we weren't?"

Why indeed? Shane was going to have some 'splainin' to do.

The door opened and himself came stumbling out. His face was flushed beet-red. Sweat stained his shirt and darkened his silver hair to gray. He was grinning and had a wild look in his eye. "Oh, hey," he said, nodding at Alina. "I see the band's back together again."

I glared at him.

He shrugged. "Maple didn't want his boss to know they got away. I extracted a promise that he wouldn't kill us for keeping my mouth shut about it. Win-win."

I think I might have growled.

He ignored me. "Alice and I are going to release the rest of the stock. I'll meet you back at the car in, say, about a half-hour."

"Alice?" Alina asked. "Who's that?"

Hawk gave her a wry grin. "Shane's new girlfriend. She's really hot."

"Okay," I said. "I have to ask. How do you know her name is Alice?"

Shane shrugged. "It actually sounded more like Alcepetuquintifec, or something like that. I gave her a nickname. Dragonish is a tough language. I did the best I could."

"You made a bargain with her without understanding the language?" I asked.

He shrugged. "It worked out. I either promised to set her free or vowed to give her five children. I'm not sure which. Either way, we're best buddies for now."

I snorted out a laugh. "A half-hour is cutting it short. That's about when the Body's expected."

Nicht growled. Beneath my scratching fingers, his fur stood on end.

Hawk turned to look across the grounds. "Yeah, about that timeline..."

I glanced where he was looking. The air was thickening, swirling, and a golden gash was opening where before only darkness had been. "Goddess in baggy bloomers!" I mumbled. Leave it to the Magistrate to lie about his arrival time.

"Looks like our priorities have changed," Shane said. "Hold them off until I release the cavalry. Then, my advice is to get the heck out of the way."

He disappeared back inside as we turned to face the flood of Body soldiers streaming from the portal.

"Hold them off," Hawk mumbled. "Right. Remind me to kick his wrinkly butt when this is over."

"You'll have to stand in line," Alina growled.

"It's going to be a long line," I agreed.

Nicht snarled his agreement.

I sighed, tentatively reaching for my siphoning energy.

And finding it still missing in action.

17

The black-clad soldiers poured out of the hole in the air, energy spitting at their fingertips as if they expected trouble the moment they entered Outvald. It made me wonder about their usual reception.

Nicht pressed against my leg, snarling, eyes glowing, and ruff standing on end. Hawk stood on my other side, and Alina took a position next to Nicht.

"I need a weapon," I said as the soldiers' heads snapped up and they spotted us.

Hawk handed me one of his blades.

"Thanks."

He already had another one in his hand. "You're welcome."

"How many of those things do you have on your

person, and where are you hiding them?" I asked, unable to keep from tweaking him a little.

He waggled his brows at me. "We'll discuss that later."

I laughed, despite the unfortunate situation we found ourselves in.

As if a switch had been flipped with my laughter, a roar went up among the enemy and they charged.

We started running, putting distance between us and what I hoped was the cavalry Shane was building. Alina broke to the right, Hawk to the left, and Nicht charged with me up the center.

I met the first soldier with a slash of my long knife, the blade slicing into the flesh of her wrist before she could fling the ball of spitting energy she was holding.

The woman screamed, buckling at the knees, and Nicht was on her.

I didn't stop to see her fate. I really didn't want to know.

I met another soldier, a big guy with hate-filled black eyes and a glowing shield of magic covering nearly his entire body. He wielded a smaller blade that was meant for close-contact fighting and held a long, leather whip in the other hand.

In the split second it took me to assess his weaponry, he snapped his arm forward and I found my knife-bearing arm entangled in the whip. Pain, like fire, sliced my skin as the whip bit into flesh. My fingers opened involuntarily and my weapon fell from them.

I saw stars from the agony, realizing the leather was imbued with tiny slivers of something along its length. The slivers bit into my skin, tearing it as I tried to rip my arm away.

My attacker yanked me closer, and I spun away from the blade he slashed toward my middle. As I dipped and danced to keep away from that blade, one tiny part of my brain followed the chaos around me.

Bodies were piling up around me and the whip-wielding demon as Nicht tore through anybody trying to come through our line on the battlefield.

The hellhound was...well...hellishly deadly. I was glad he was on our side.

The whip tightened again, and I suddenly found myself smacked up against my nemesis. I stared into those hostile eyes and realized too late that I was out of time.

With a cold, mirthless smile, The man lifted his knife arm and plunged downward, aiming for my heart.

I tried to jerk out of its path but I was well and truly caught. I couldn't move an inch.

Energy speared the dark, slashed across the man's lifted arm, and the flesh sliced clean away, falling to the ground as the man's face contorted in unimaginable pain. The whip loosened as he pulled away from me, holding the stump of his severed arm against his middle. I sent Alina a wave of thanks and grabbed my knife again.

Unfortunately, there was no break in the action. My next opponent was a woman. She was smaller than I was, petite actually, but she was fast and agile and impossible to catch with my blade. It was all I could do to stay away from her slashing blows, designed for maximum damage with the spiked, metal gloves she wore on her small hands.

I bent away from one punch, folded nearly in half to avoid a second, and sucked inward as a third nearly found my middle.

My heart was pounding, my lungs stung from breathing too hard and too fast, and the numbers of the Body's people weren't slowing down.

It looked like the Magistrate had brought his entire magical army to the battle, making me wonder what else besides me he'd been intending to take back with him.

Alice? That would certainly make sense. He could do a lot with a dragon in Magical Indy.

My distracted thoughts nearly did me in. I took a spiked punch from the woman right in the gut, the blow so hard it sent me to my knees, wheezing loudly in an effort to breathe. Sweat popped out on my brow as I struggled for air. I was unable to avoid a second blow to the chest that punched any chance of drawing a breath completely away.

I collapsed onto the ground, panicked and gasping, and waited for her to finish me off.

But no more blows found me.

Something exploded nearby. Fire flared into the night and hope surged. We had recruits. Dragon's breath lit up the night and set lines of the enemy ablaze.

Even as I struggled to breathe, I thanked the goddess for Shane's new bestie. Screams erupted as Alice sent her fiery breath into the hoards of Body warriors.

Finally...I managed to draw air. I gave myself a second to enjoy breathing and then forced my aching frame off the ground.

"Glynn!" Hawk screamed through the chaos. I looked up and saw him at the edge of the melee, using his blades only to keep the soldiers from escaping what I realized had become a creature army, with Shane standing at the rearguard, using his magic to incapacitate the soldiers so the formerly-trapped and abused creatures could take them out.

I saw one of those chameleon creatures flashing wildly from its bear to its lizard and then to its flying form as it tore through the black-clad bodies on the field. There was something that looked like the wolfman I'd seen at home, only smaller. A dozen of those exploding lizards slithered across the field, tearing into the fallen soldiers, exploding into debilitating light and sound when someone took offensive action against them. I took care to cover my ears and look away, managing to stumble out of the pandemonium toward where Hawk, Nicht, and Alina waited for me at the edge of the shadows.

I ducked as Alice flew by, claws outstretched, and snagged a soldier who'd been heading my way, ripping him off the ground and carrying him, screaming, high into the air.

I dodged a lizard thing and took off running, almost free of the battle.

My gaze was locked onto my friends, so I saw the moment their expressions charged, filling with horror and surprise.

I didn't even have time to wonder what was happening. A tall, dark figure stepped in front of me, and I recognized the Magistrate's hated face. "Hello, my dear," he said with a smug grin. His hand snapped out, clamping a metal band around my wrist before I could react. I was grabbed from behind by a man who had to be eight feet tall and nearly as wide. I screamed, struggling to get away, but it was no use. The portal was suddenly there. I turned my head to find Nicht and Hawk racing toward us.

They'd be too late.

I screamed Hawk's name, my voice raw and tight with fear.

The last thing I heard as the portal snapped shut

behind me was Nicht's mournful howl, slicing through the battlefield bedlam and tearing my heart to ribbons.

———

Hawk couldn't get there fast enough. Nicht tore past him, but even he couldn't make it before the portal closed. It about broke Hawk's heart listening to the big hound howling with pain. He dropped to a knee, breaths heaving in and out of his chest as waves of razor-edged emotions claimed his ability to breathe.

"What happened?" Alina asked, running up to them. "I smell sulfur."

"Portal," Hawk wheezed out. He forced himself to stand, putting a quelling hand on Nicht's ruff. "They took Glynn."

Alina went silent and still. Rage vibrated on the air between them. "We need to go after her."

Hawk nodded, his gaze locked on the space where the portal had been. He stared hard at the spot for a long moment, his body locked into immobility as rage robbed him of coherent thought.

"Hawk?" Alina said, impatience creating a deadly edge to her voice.

He jerked himself out of his emotional struggle and turned to her. "Find Shane. We're heading back to the car."

Her mouth fell open. "The car? No! We need to find Glynn and..."

He rounded on her, getting in her face. "And what?" he bellowed into her face. "Do you know how to reopen that portal? Do you know where it went?"

Alina finally lowered her gaze, expelling an angry breath. "No."

"No," he agreed. "I don't either. But I know someone who does."

Understanding lit her eyes. "Guwalt?"

He nodded. "Now, let's get Shane and get back to that campus. I'm going to dig that little cockroach out of his hidey-hole and force him to help us."

I yanked on the cuffs binding me to the hard wooden chair. They jangled noisily but didn't give. Frustration had been building in me for hours as I sat there, ignored and seemingly forgotten in a room that was only different from our cell at the auction by the lack of bars.

And the guard.

I stared at the enormous man standing perfectly still across the room. I'd never seen anything like him. He was enormous. My first guess at his height was off by a couple of feet. He had to be closer to ten feet tall. His shoulders looked to be a good three feet across, and his arms bulged with hard muscle. He wore only a tank top and a pair of rough pants that were tight around his dense thighs and didn't quite reach his ankles. His feet were bare, and the smallest of his toes were the width of my thumbs, with clean, tidy nails.

His whole person was tidy. Even the shoulder-length mop of brown hair, wavy and glossy, appeared to have been recently washed and brushed.

He wasn't slovenly, only big and mean.

As I stared at him, I decided I needed to rethink the mean thing too. He'd handled me firmly, without hesitation or remorse, but he hadn't been rough. He hadn't tried to harm me as he'd carried me through the portal and deposited me in what could only be the Body's dungeon.

"Hey," I said to him. "How's things?" The question brought me a flashback of Hawk saying the same thing to me mere hours earlier. My chest tightened.

The guard stared straight ahead and ignored me.

With nothing else to do, I scanned my surroundings again, looking for a weakness. A way out. I tried not to think about the fact that I was almost certainly back in the Earthly dimension.

Alone. And at the mercy of the Magistrate and his evil minions.

Not to mention the other twelve members of the Regnant Bench, the ruling elites of the city. If they decided I was useful to them, I'd never escape Magical Indy and get back to Boyle and the others.

If they thought I wasn't useful...well...

Tears burned my eyes, but I blinked them back. No crying. I had to figure out how to get out of there. Once I escaped that room, I'd need to find the portal they'd used to bring me there. If I could just get back to Outvald, I could find my way home.

If...

As panic swamped me, I tried again to talk to the giant across the room. "I'm Glynn. What's your name?"

A narrow brown gaze slid my way and held for a beat before skimming away again. He didn't move. Didn't speak. Barely acknowledged my presence in the room.

He was either extremely well-trained or terrified of his handlers.

My gaze slid to the bands encompassing his wrists and ankles. They'd slapped only one band on me. The fact that they thought he needed four was telling.

"So, I get that you're just as much of a prisoner here as I am."

The brown gaze slid to me again, holding with more interest than they'd shown to that point.

Progress.

"It wouldn't hurt to talk to me, right? I'm just

tired of being worried, and I'm trying to distract myself." I gave him a smile.

He looked away again.

"What's the deal with these bands, anyway?"

He shifted just a tiny bit on his feet.

"I figured they were to dampen our magic. I only have one. You must be pretty powerful since you have four."

Something like pride lit in his eyes.

Superior strength. Check.

"So, if you didn't have those bands on, how strong would you be?" I looked around the room, seeing a large wooden supply cabinet that looked like it might weigh a few hundred pounds. "Could you lift that cabinet over there?"

The giant scanned a look that way and a tiny smirk curved one corner of his mouth.

"Really?" I laughed. "That's got to weigh several hundred pounds."

He looked at me, his eyes alight. "Not so much," he finally said in a deep, ragged voice. I wondered if the torn quality of his voice was a natural trait for giants or if he'd been tortured. Ice climbed my spine because I was pretty sure I already knew the answer to that. "I miss my family," I said, tears burning my eyes again.

He stiffened, the tiny smile disappearing.

"Do you have a family?"

He wouldn't look at me. "You should be quiet now."

I thought it was just a general statement of irritation with my babbling. But a beat later, I heard footsteps hurrying along the corridor outside my door.

Exceptional hearing. Check.

Unfortunately, I recognized the man who came through the door. Cole Martin was tall—three or four inches over six feet—with graying black hair and piercing blue eyes. As he'd been the last time I'd met him, he was dressed unrelievedly in black. He wore a black shirt under a black coat, and his form-fitting black slacks were narrow, stopping at his ankles in typical elite fashion.

"We meet again, Miss Glynn. How's your brother? We've missed him here." Something cold... an ancient, unrelenting evil...slithered through his gaze. He knew exactly where Artur was. And he wasn't happy about it.

"Didn't you get his letter of resignation? He'll be so upset at the lapse in manners. But let me remedy that. He quit."

Though the Magistrate's cruel mouth tightened, he forced a laugh that scraped against my nerves. "Ah, yes. I suppose I should have taken the fact that he conspired with my enemies as his formal resignation."

"Enemies?" I couldn't help saying. "What have

my friends and I done to put ourselves in that category?"

He shrugged, choosing not to explain himself. Shocking. "Well, we have you with us now, don't we." He clapped his perfectly-manicured hands together with mock glee.

Seeing those pale hands, so unused to real and honest work, remorse stabbed through me for the loss of Hawk and my friends, who'd labored day and night to make our new home comfortable and safe.

At least they were secure. Hawk and the other cops. Shane. Boyle, Sissy, and Artur. They were all safe. Grams... Without me, would anyone see or hear her?

Despite my best intentions, tears bit the back of my lids. I blinked them determinedly away. "Why did you drag me here? If you're trying to get Artur back, you're going to be disappointed. He won't come after me. No one will."

I stiffened my spine because if I didn't, the truth of my statement might drop me into endless despair. They couldn't come after me because they couldn't work Victoria's portal. Artur wasn't trained because he hadn't wanted to be. And it would take him years to get up to speed. Even with Grams helping him.

"Oh no, my dear. You misunderstand. I don't want poor Artur at all. We found him entirely useless for our purposes." The Magistrate stepped closer and leaned down, placing a hand on each arm of the chair so he could invade my space.

His silky hair fell over his eyes, and his warm, mint-scented breath slid over my face. Revulsion rolled my gut into a knot. "We wanted *you*, lovely Glynn. Our very own magical repository. Endlessly refilling. Adaptable to any kind of magic. You are a dream come true, my dear."

I tried to claw him, but my hand lifted only a fraction of an inch and was jerked painfully back down by the cuff. "I'm not going to help you."

He sighed. "Maybe not at first, no. But you will. Eventually. Even if we have to use...incentives." He straightened and inclined his chin toward the giant.

I imagined I saw sorrow on the big man's face before the giant walked toward the door and opened it. He disappeared into the corridor and returned a beat later, dragging another man forward by the arm.

I gasped, my heart twisting. "Goddess," I whispered, my voice breaking in horror. "What have you done to him?"

18

Mitch's vibrant red hair was lank, stringy with grease, and peppered with a lot more strands of gray than I remembered. His eyes, once a bright brown and filled with hope and secrets, were dull and glassy. He stared through me like he wasn't even aware I was there.

His clothes were filthy and torn, a sour stench emanating from them that told me he hadn't bathed in a while. His bare feet were black with dirt.

"Oh, Mitch," I said, tears sliding down my cheeks. "What did they do to you?"

The Magistrate smiled cruelly. "We've honed him into something useful. Just as we've done for countless others. As we'll do for you."

For me. As if he was giving me a gift.

"I'll kill you," I said softly, my voice trembling with emotion.

"Now, Glynnie..."

"Shut up!" I screamed. "You aren't allowed to call me that. You're an evil, corrupt, dangerous man, and you need to die."

I knew as the words left my mouth they were a mistake. But I couldn't seem to help myself. "You need to die, and I'm going to be the one to kill you."

The Magistrate sighed. He was just so sad for me. I wanted to claw his face until even his mother, if any poor woman would admit to spawning him, wouldn't recognize him. He reached out and touched my forehead before I could jerk away.

It was just the merest touch of a fingertip. And the world exploded into agony.

The pain hit me in jagged waves, surging, ebbing, surging again. Horrible pictures played through my mind...familiar, savage, agonizing.

Every terrifying thing I'd ever experienced flooded through my thoughts, the edges of the memories sharp like blades. Fear pummeled my chest, making my heart pound too hard...too fast.

I couldn't breathe.

I couldn't see through the agony.

I couldn't stop the relentless punch of my heartbeat against my ribs.

I suddenly knew I was going to die. And it would be a slow, excruciating death.

The pain stopped.

I sagged against my restraints, head lolling.

Moisture dripped onto my jeans and I realized it was drool. I forced my lips closed and tried to concentrate on pulling one thready breath after another into my lungs.

My heart still beat too fast. My lungs ached from too-quick, panicked breathing.

A soft chuckle found my ears, barely heard above the throbbing in my head. "I hope that was the only lesson I'll ever have to teach you, Glynnie. It pains me to do it. But you need to learn."

His hand slid over my hair, like a father petting a child. I gave my head a half-hearted jerk and he sighed. "I'll give you time to think about your situation. When I come back, hopefully, we can make better progress."

He turned and addressed Mitch. "Come, Seer. You and I have work to do."

I lifted my head, my eyes crossing for a beat before I managed to focus them on Mitch. His gaze found mine, briefly, and for just a beat, I thought it sharpened.

Then he turned away and followed the Magistrate through the door.

I slumped in my chair, willing my body and brain to function normally. But the memory of that horrific experience coated me like blood. And I couldn't easily shake it off.

Silence throbbed in my ears. After what I'd just survived, it was a welcome thing.

"You shouldn't fight him," a rough voice said into the silence.

I twitched, my head coming up. I'd forgotten about the giant. Shaking my head, I didn't say anything.

I let the quiet soothe my nerves a bit longer, then I sat up straight in my chair, determined to find a way out of there. I needed a plan. I scanned as much of the room as I could see. The oversized cabinet dominated one long wall. There was a cot near the adjoining wall. A sink. And something that might have been facilities for bio needs.

I eyed the components of that metal device. "Maybe..."

"It's spelled," the giant told me.

I jerked my gaze back to him. I hadn't realized I'd spoken aloud. "There has to be something," I told him.

His gaze slipped to the camera high in the corner. *Oh. Yeah.* I'd forgotten about that. I tried to assess if there were any blank spots in the camera's reach and realized the giant was standing in the only possible blind spot. Was that a coincidence? The spot where he stood was too far from the door to do me any good, even if I could make use of it.

His gaze sharpened when I looked back his way. He gave me the tiniest nod.

Hope flared in my chest and then immediately died. I had little doubt the camera also had a mic on it. I couldn't speak, and I couldn't go anywhere useful without being seen.

But I needed to do something, I slid my gaze over the space again. I'd scanned right past a metal rectangle high in the wall before my brain recognized what it was.

A vent. Large enough, just barely, for me to shimmy through if I could find my way up there.

I looked at the giant. He stared back, not giving me anything.

Okay, at least it wasn't a negative head shake. I could work with that.

But I wasn't going anywhere unless I could get out of that chair. I looked at the camera again, realizing they'd see me working the cuffs. I could work the chair around, so my back was to the camera. I tugged on the restraints, searching for weaknesses. If I worked at breaking them, would the giant give me up?

I looked at him again. He stared back, his expression sad.

My tiny spark of hope died. My stomach twisted with dread.

But I had to try. I really had nothing to lose.

With that thought in mind, I jerked and pushed and wrenched my body against the chair, slowly but surely turning myself away from the camera.

The giant watched me, his gaze never leaving mine.

At least he didn't try to stop me.

W hen I'd exhausted myself trying to get loose from my cuffs, I lapsed into inactivity, eventually dozing off. I woke up when the door slammed behind someone. I whipped my head toward the sound, my body tensing for battle.

A young woman stood in front of me with a large tray. She looked at the blood coating my hands and frowned. "You're only hurting yourself," she said in a quiet voice. Shaking her head, she carried the tray over and set it down on the floor. A spicy scent teased my nostrils, and my stomach clenched hopefully.

She pulled a rag from a bowl filled with water, glancing at the giant. "You can go get something to eat," she told him, her tone kind.

He inclined his head and, with a final glance my way headed out of the room.

I watched the woman as she bathed my hands and spread ointment over my torn wrists. She looked up at me, her large brown eyes deep pools of unspoken emotion. "You should just do as he says." Her gaze flickered, and I imagined she'd glanced toward the camera.

I didn't respond.

When she'd finished with my wrists, she uncovered what looked like a burrito. Lifting it toward my mouth, she said, "Eat for strength."

I turned my head away.

She held it there for a moment, probably hoping the scent would entice me to eat.

I kept my gaze turned away.

Sighing, she stood. "You'll get hungry soon enough."

One soft hand fell to mine, pressing it against the chair arm.

I tried to jerk away. Her hand snapped up and slapped me on the face as her other hand grabbed mine. "Behave, leech!"

I was shocked by the abrupt change in her manner, but not for long.

She gathered her things and headed for the door, turning to look back at me before she left. "You'll do as expected eventually. You might as well save yourself some pain."

I closed my hand and frowned, watching her leave.

I waited several moments before opening the hand she'd pressed, carefully reading the message on the small slip of paper she'd passed to me.

· · ·

T *hey come.*
   M.

T *hey*? Was the Magistrate coming back to torment me?

I didn't know, but I knew I couldn't let the note be discovered, so I pretended to have a coughing fit, doubling over to shove the tiny slip of paper into my mouth. I mashed it as small as I could with my tongue and forced it down my throat.

Then I started trying to free myself from the cuffs again, finding the ointment the girl used on my wrists to be extremely helpful.

Was she an ally? Or had the ointment just been a tactical error on her part?

Time would tell.

The magistrate showed up sometime later, with me no further along on my grand plan to ditch my cuffs and shimmy through the vent to freedom.

The giant lumbered into the room behind him, his gaze sliding to my wrists and ankles as he took his usual spot against the wall.

"Well now, Glynnie," the Magistrate said in his smug, loud voice. "Are you feeling better?"

I stared at him, working hard not to allow any emotion to bleed into my expression.

He seemed not to notice. "I understand this is frustrating. Believe me, I do."

I ground my teeth together to keep from responding to that. He had no idea what it felt like to be abused and imprisoned since he was always the one doing the abusing and imprisoning.

"But believe me, life will be good for you if you just go along, my dear."

Okay, that was too much. "Yeah, I can see what you mean. Mitch certainly looks like he's living large," I growled.

He made a tsking sound. "That's an unfortunate case." He brightened. "Actually, it's a good case study for you to examine. Mitch wasn't cooperative when he joined us here. He forced me to be..." He sighed. "We'll just say I had to work harder to show him the right path. But now he's..." Even he couldn't come up with a positive spin on what Mitch was. "He's well on the road to a good life."

"Is he?" Despite my best intentions, I couldn't keep the acid out of my tone. "Funny, he didn't look the least bit prosperous or happy. In fact, he looks like a man who's been badly treated for a long time. I'm disgusted with myself for not getting here sooner to help him."

The well-fed, perfectly-coiffed monster in front of me looked delighted. "There, you see! You've found a good reason to be here already. You can help your friend Mitch fit in better."

"Dream on," I told him.

He pursed his lips, looking disappointed in me. "I see. Well…" he glanced at the giant. "I tried, Mike. You saw that I tried, didn't you?"

The giant's Adam's apple bobbed as he swallowed. "Yes, sir. You did all you could."

I looked from one to the other, my mouth hanging open. They were all insane.

"It looks like we're going to need more convincing arguments," the deranged Magistrate said. He leaned down, taking care to keep away from my clutching fingers as he whispered in my ear. "Maybe you'll be more cooperative if I bring that adorable little gargoyle pup into the room. Mike here would love to have a playmate." He playfully tugged a strand of my hair. "Giants like to play with their food. Did you know gargoyle is a delicacy for giants? I understand they can be quite tasty if prepared correctly. Isn't that right, Mike?"

My gaze slid to the giant's. He looked away, unable to meet my glare.

With a feral scream I barely recognized as coming from me, I lunged in the chair, trying to get to the Magistrate, but the restraints kept me from doing much more than launching myself an inch or two out of the chair and painfully wrenching my limbs. "You leave him alone! You monster. I'll kill you with my bare hands!"

The Magistrate laughed cruelly. Before I knew

what was coming, he extended a finger and touched me again.

Misery burst in my core, ripping outward to shred the nerve endings throughout my entire body. I shrieked in mindless agony as my brain seized, my muscles turned rigid, and every fear I'd ever embraced flooded through me, scalding me with fire from within. It went on forever, ripping at my sanity until my screams were more animal than human. Blood ran from my nose and ears. I slammed my head against the chair, trying to stop the images flashing past with relentless clarity.

I don't know when I finally knocked myself senseless. I only know it took far too long to accomplish.

And I was very afraid I wouldn't survive the Magistrate's special kind of magic even one more time.

19

Slamming. Screams. Explosions.

I jerked awake from my wild dreams and wrenched my head up, gasping at the dual pains in my head and neck. It's really not a good idea to fall asleep with your head on your chest. Especially after having your brain melted down by an evil magistrate.

The door opened and slammed shut, making me jump and tense. *Already*? I wasn't ready for another go-round with Dr. Doom. Then I remembered the Magistrate's threats about Boyle and my stomach twisted.

Had he found Victoria? Had he managed, somehow, to get Boyle away from the others? And, if he had, did that mean the others were...? I shook my head to dispel the disturbing questions. And immediately regretted the movement.

Heavy footsteps hurried toward me. I looked up to find Mike the giant moving purposefully in my direction, his expression fierce and his fists clenched.

Oh, oh.

I threw my weight into the chair, lifting with my legs at the same time, and the chair skimmed sideways. As he all but skidded to a stop next to me, I tried again, panic making my attempt clumsy, and before I realized what was happening, the chair was teetering on the outside edge of two legs, and I was going to fall.

I gave a little scream, still flinching despite my worry about falling, as he clamped one of his big hands around the arm of my chair. He jerked it around and dragged me across the room, all but throwing it at the wall where he usually stood when he guarded me.

I forced my spine straight, shoving the sleep from my tired brain, and forced a belligerent look onto my face. "So, you're just going to kill me now?"

He stared at me a minute and then reached for the cuffs on my wrists, giving them a twist that wrenched them open. I blinked as he did the same to the leg cuffs. The guy was seriously strong. He grabbed my hand and gently pulled me free of the chair. Leaning close, the giant spoke so softly I had to strain to hear. "Take me with you."

I stared up at him in confusion. "Huh?"

He picked up the chair. "When you leave. I'm coming with you."

The way he was looking at me, I assumed he was waiting for me to agree, so I nodded. "Okay."

Mike inclined his broad, dimpled chin and, without warning, flung the chair across the room. It smashed against the camera in the corner, turning it into a bunch of broken parts that dangled uselessly from the ceiling. Then he started for the big cabinet. "Come on."

I ran after him, forced to take three strides to every one of his. "What's happening right now?" I couldn't help asking. I didn't really expect him to answer, but he did. "You're getting out."

I jerked to a stop. "I can't leave without Mitch."

Mike fixed me with a long, intense glare and I thought he was going to argue. But all he said was, "That's what I'm counting on."

He reached out and grabbed the enormous cabinet, the muscles in his arms bulging as he slowly but steadily moved it away from the wall.

My eyes went wide as the wall behind the furniture was revealed. A broken archway of rock appeared as Mike moved the cabinet away. The archway's ragged perimeter reminded me of teeth in a gaping maw. It framed a black abyss of nothingness.

Mike motioned toward the opening. "Go."

I hesitated and he huffed. "Go! They'll be here soon."

In a very small corner of my very confused brain, I couldn't help wondering if that was the same *they* Mitch had warned me about in the note. Then I realized it didn't matter. He was giving me a chance to escape the Magistrate's control and I had to take it.

Worst case was that I'd be captured again. It was a risk I was willing to take. So I slid past him and into the hole in the wall.

Groaning with the effort, Mike pulled the heavy furniture back into position in front of the hole, cutting off every ounce of light.

I tried to siphon magic to create a light, but nothing came. Then I remembered the metal band on my wrist. "I can't see..." I started to say.

A light snapped on, and I squinted against its brightness. It was a flashlight. "Ah. Okay. That works," I said with a grin.

"Come," Mike said. Sliding past me, he and his small arc of light moved into the velvet blackness in front of us.

I learned very quickly that I needed to pay attention because the giant man in front of me kept stopping to shine his light over the wall every so often, clearly searching for something. I couldn't see anything beneath the glare of light except for the occasional marks scratched into the stone.

"What are you looking for?" I finally asked, tired of being in the dark, both literally and figuratively.

"An exit," he said.

I liked the sound of that. "What's the plan?"

He turned his head to look down at me. "Plan? To get out of here."

"That's a goal, not a plan."

He frowned at that. Apparently, he hadn't given thought to the differences between the two. In fairness to him, being a prisoner at the Body wasn't exactly conducive to long-range planning. "I'm trying to find the Seer's cell block. When we find it, we'll grab him and..." he scanned me another look. "And we'll use the hidden passageways to get out of here."

There was something in the middle of that sentence that he hadn't told me. "Doesn't the Magistrate know about these passages?"

"They haven't been in use for a decade, since before the Body made this its headquarters. I have no doubt someone has the blueprints showing these passageways, but I doubt anybody's made them known to the Magistrate."

That surprised me. "Really? I thought he ruled this place with an iron fist."

Mike stopped to scan the wall. Beneath the harsh white light, I saw a series of rough slashes carved into the stone. "That's precisely the problem," Mike said. He slid me another look. "Fear and hatred do not loyalty make."

Ah, profundity from the giant. Nice.

He nodded toward the wall. "This is it."

"Okay. How do we...?"

He placed a big hand on the wall and pushed, grunting softly as the wall moved slowly inward. When he'd created a gap of about two feet, he told me to wait there and slipped through. A beat later, curiosity got the best of me. I followed him past a chunk of wall that rested on heavy metal castors. I eyed the oddly-shaped edges and realized the lines of the moveable wall would melt into the stone when it was closed. Ingenious.

I glanced around, finding myself in a long, dark room that smelled of mildew and bodily functions. I grimaced, covering my nose, and then eyed the people cowering in the cells with shame and pity. They'd been forced to live in that filth. I could certainly stand to smell it for a few minutes. I stepped out, my pulse pounding in my chest. Suddenly, my wish to escape wasn't nearly as important as helping the people who were locked up down there.

I found Mike about halfway down the wide passage. He was using a circular object that glowed green in his hand to unlock a cell where a filthy creature lay on a cot.

As the door opened, the man on the cot sat up and I saw that it was Mitch. I hurried over. "I'll help him," I told Mike. "You open the rest of the cells."

His gaze held mine for a moment, surprise

lighting its depths. Then he nodded and moved to the next cell.

We'd gotten Mitch and two others inside the passageway before I heard the door opening. I panicked. "Mike!"

He gave me a gentle nudge. "Get inside. It will be okay."

I didn't believe him, but I let him push me into the passageway because I had the others to worry about. I started them moving forward, thinking there was no way we could possibly outrun the Body soldiers. The prisoners we'd rescued could barely walk, let alone run.

I pulled desperately at the band around my wrist, fighting to get it off so I could siphon magic to use in our defense.

It didn't budge.

I waited for an explosion of outrage or the sound of fighting. Neither came. A cold hand found my arm and I jumped, turning to find Mitch mere inches away. He was gaunt and filthy, but unlike before, his gaze was clear and focused. "They come."

I fought a frustrated response.

A shadow fell over the opening and I nearly leaped at it before recognizing the small woman who'd tended my wounds and given me Mitch's note. She slipped into the passage and gave me a small bow. "I've brought medical supplies."

"Good," I told her. "Thank you."

She reached into a cloth-covered basket and pulled out a hunk of bread, handing it to Mitch. He fell on it as if he hadn't eaten in days. Judging by his appearance, he probably hadn't. She readied some kind of syringe and jammed it against his arm.

Mitch gasped, his eyes going wide. But he seemed stronger and more alert afterward. "Thank you, Jessa," the Seer said, sounding more like his old self. He looked at me. "I won't say I'm not glad you're here, Glynn, but it's too dangerous. What were you thinking?"

"I didn't think I'd be grabbed up by the Body," I told him, frowning. "But since I have, I thought I might as well bust you out too."

He chuckled softly.

A soft cry brought my head around to find one of the prisoners folding to the ground. The woman next to him dropped to the ground too, draping herself over him and wailing with despair.

Jessa looked on, her expression tight with anger.

I grabbed her arm and jerked her around. "What happened?"

She turned a glare on me and yanked her arm from my grip. Quick panic flared. Was she with the Body after all?

"He was a spy," she said, shaking her head.

The woman on the floor lifted her head. "He weren't no spy, girl!" Beneath the filth on her skin, the woman's face flushed with anger.

But with Jessa's words, I noticed the full flesh beneath the filth covering the man's limbs. He wasn't malnourished like the others. Jessa was right.

"I'm sorry, Polly," Jessa said, not sounding sorry at all. "The serum doesn't lie."

Mike appeared next to me. "We need to get moving. They're coming."

Again, I wondered who *they* were.

I grabbed Mitch's hand. "The note you sent me. Who did you mean? Who are *They*?"

He shook his head. "It's murky, like everything else in this accursed place. They've mangled my magic until I can barely see yesterday, let alone the future." He bit off the words, filled with anger.

I couldn't blame him.

"What *can* you see?" I urged.

Mike nearly vibrated with the need to move. It took a force of will, but I ignored him.

Mitch closed his eyes. "Sky, clouds, pounding wings. Passage where passage shouldn't be. Burning trees."

He gasped, clutching his head. "I'm sorry, Glynn. That's all I've got."

"It's okay," I told him, patting his back.

"We need to go," Mike repeated. He grabbed for the woman still wailing over her downed friend, but she jerked away. "I ain't goin' with you people."

"He's not dead, Polly," Jessa said. "But if you don't

come, he'll turn you in to the Magistrate. I can promise you that."

Polly shook her head. "Go. I won't tell them nothin'."

I knelt down in front of the woman. "Are you sure? Don't you want to get out of here?"

The woman's face softened. She placed a filthy, calloused hand on my cheek. "I don't know nothin' else, child." Her eyes melted to pure, cold black, making me jerk in surprise. "It ain't so bad."

Mike and Jessa shared a look. Without a word, she gave the woman another shot. The female prisoner collapsed over the already unconscious man, going limp.

Mike took off down the passage. "Hurry. We're taking too long. We'll be lucky if they're not already gathered at the entrance when we get there."

"Is it possible they already know we're gone?" I asked.

"Likely," Mike said. "You were a prize to the Magistrate. And that one..." he jerked his head toward Mitch. "He doesn't have any other Seers."

We ran. And ran. Mitch stumbled too many times to count, nearly breaking his head open before Mike grabbed him up and threw him over one shoulder like a sack of flour.

I don't know how much time passed, but I realized the passage was growing lighter. "Where's the light coming from?" I asked.

"The entrance," Jessa said.

We slowed to a walk. Mike and Jessa seemed to move more carefully, their gazes alert.

"Have you been in these passages before?" I asked them.

Jessa shook her head. "No. But I've heard stories from those who have."

"Most thought it was an urban legend," Mike added. "But then I discovered the hole behind the cabinet."

"And you put it together?" I asked.

He nodded. "I did some exploring before you came...working on a plan."

"So you do know the difference between a goal and a plan."

He chuckled.

"Why didn't you leave sooner then?" I asked.

Mike looked at Jessa. Something warm passed between them.

Ah. That explained why he'd hoped I'd get Mitch. She must have been in the same cell block. But Mike could have busted her out without Mitch or me.

Jessa fixed an earnest look on me. "We know of your guardians. The great Protector and his Hound of Hell. They will come for you. They will protect us too."

My spirits sank. They'd been hoping Hawk and Nicht would find and protect me. I wished they were right. I was torn between letting them continue to believe a lie or breaking their spirits with the truth. In the end, I knew I had no choice.

"They're in another dimension," I told Mike and Jessa. "Trapped there. They can't come for me."

"Confused words," Mitch mumbled. "Empty spaces in the mind. These will guide them."

He'd descended into complete gibberish. My heart broke for my friend. If I managed to get him out of Magical Indy and back to Render, would it matter? Would he ever be sane again?

Mike stopped suddenly and held up a hand.

He was large enough to block my view ahead, so I concentrated on trying to hear whatever he was focusing on.

There was a sizzling sound, sibilant and hungry, on the air. My nose twitched as I realized I was smelling smoke. I glanced at Mitch, frowning. What had he said?

Sky, clouds, pounding wings. Passage where passage shouldn't be. Burning trees.

"What's burning?" I asked Mike, my gaze never leaving Mitch. He looked to be unconscious, but for all I knew he could be lost in another vision.

"The woods are on fire," he said, seeming perplexed. "I don't see anybody around."

"Wouldn't it make sense for them to be trying to put it out?" Jessa asked.

Mike nodded wordlessly. He turned to us. "Stay

here. I'll go see what I can find." He settled Mitch onto the dirt and slipped out of the entrance, his big form surrounded by an aura of flames and smoke in the distance.

Then, without warning, he shimmered and disappeared.

I blinked. "Ah!" I looked at Jessa. "What just happened?"

She smiled. "They can't keep his magic down. Every month or so, they add another cuff. But he breaks through it within a few weeks."

"He went invisible!" I said, impressed.

But she shook her head. "Not invisible, not really. Look closer."

I moved closer to the entrance and did as she said. There were trees, branches ablaze, and smoke spreading above and around them, but I didn't see him.

I squinted and then twitched in surprise. "There!" I pointed toward a spot on the air that looked slightly pixilated, like a digital image under-going interference.

"Mike's a basin giant. They live in places where there aren't a lot of natural protections. No trees or buildings to hide behind. Over the generations, they've formed a natural protection that has some-thing to do with fracturing light." She shrugged. "I have no idea how it works. I only know it does."

"So the bands aren't working on him anymore?"

"To an extent, they are. If he was at full strength, you wouldn't be able to see, hear, or smell him."

"So cool," I said, momentarily forgetting how dire our situation was.

"Yeah." She infected the word with such sadness, it pulled me away from observing Mike.

"What?"

She sighed. "It's very special magic with important wartime applications. Especially when added to his size and strength."

"Yes. I can see that."

She finally looked me in the eye, her gaze haunted. "They want to create an army of them. Unfortunately, they don't have the numbers for that. There aren't many of Mike's people around anymore. They were sold at the auction and many died fighting for their freedom. But the Body has a few. And those are expected to..."

I waited for her to finish that sentence. When she didn't, I realized why. "Oh. Yuck."

She grimaced. "Yeah. He's managed to mostly avoid it so far. Mainly because the female they chose for him wasn't any more on board with it than he was. But they were running out of time. If they didn't get pregnant soon..."

"The Magistrate would know something was wrong."

Jessa nodded, her pretty blue gaze following Mike across the open land and into the trees.

"What about the others?" I asked her. "How many giants do they have imprisoned here?"

"Four. Mike was going to come back for them after getting me free." She blinked back tears. "He'll probably be killed trying. But he can't leave them here. They're his people."

I promised myself I wouldn't let that happen. He was helping me. I would help him. "We'll do something," I promised her. "I'll come back with my people."

She nodded but didn't look very hopeful.

Mike suddenly appeared in the doorway, his big body reforming in chunks of color and light. "There's nobody. It's strange. But we need to get off the Body's land before they decide to send a force out to douse the fire." He scooped Mitch out of the dirt and trotted out the door.

Jessa and I had to run to keep up with his extra-long strides.

20

The world was bathed in fire, doused in smoke.

Hawk glanced around the grounds, taking in the once-pristine hedges that had been carefully crafted into images of the thirteen elites. They were smoldering bits of blackened branches and sparking leaves.

The enormous brick and stone building, more like a castle than a headquarters for a tyrannical ruling body, was pocked from explosions, painted in gore, and belching smoke from every window and door. Hawk didn't see its former glory when he looked at it. Instead, he saw the stark, uncomfortable cells filled with filthy, starving prisoners. He saw the empty gazes, devoid of hope. The remnants of a fear that had first focused on promised pain and then turned, inevitably, to a craving for an end to the horror their lives had become.

He saw what he'd been forced to serve. What he'd eventually rebelled against.

But not soon enough. To his eternal shame.

And knowing that Glynn had been in that place...

His lips curled on a silent snarl. Beside him, Nicht lifted his head and whined.

Hawk's hand found the hellhound's scruff and sank into it. It calmed him, reminded him that his job wasn't done.

They hadn't found Glynn inside the Body's head-quarters. She wasn't in any of the cells or on any of the upper levels, where the pampered elite tried to pretend they weren't monsters.

Hawk needed to find the Magistrate. He'd get her location out of the man if he had to peel Martin's pale, unblemished flesh away from him an inch at a time.

Nicht snarled as if reading his thoughts.

A roar went up, and Hawk watched Alice dive toward the fleeing soldiers infesting the grounds like cockroaches. They shrieked in terror as she swooped low into them, snatching and tearing and rising into the smoky sky to fling them to their deaths. The soldiers' vaunted black armor didn't do them much good against the dragon's fire or her relentless claws.

An answering roar had Hawk's gaze rising again to the big building. A huge creature slithered through the door. With fangs as long as Hawk's hand and a muscular body as big around as Hawk's torso, the giant snake slithered out into the chaos, its eyes, a deep, red-gold like the dragon's flames, flashed with interest as it spotted the fleeing soldiers. The snake recognized its jailers and clearly wanted a little payback.

Hawk had no pity for the Body's people. He'd once been drawn into the Body's web. He'd settled there happily for a time, filled with a sense of doing something good for the magical community, which had suffered torture, imprisonment and death at the hands of the non-magical for decades. But the dream had soured under a stark dose of reality.

Power, as it always did, had corrupted the fantasy. And the Body's special type of tyranny had been born.

Hawk had pulled away. And, with a few like-minded people that included Alina and the men currently protecting Victoria in Outvald, he'd formed an underground and worked to save as many of the Body's victims as he could. He didn't regret a minute of that effort. Especially since it had brought Glynn and Boyle into his life.

He stared at the building and wondered where the Magistrate would have gone. Somewhere behind all that former opulence, he knew Shane and Alina were leading prisoners away from their prison toward the portal, or releasing them into the city if they preferred to make their own way from there.

"Mr. Hawk?" He turned to find Professor Guwalt blinking owlishly at him. "The man you're looking for has stepped into a portal."

"Show me." Hawk glanced at the device Guwalt held in his hands. It was the gadget they'd found in the professor's office and had assumed was a simple monitoring appliance. Like the tricky professor himself, the device was way more than it had seemed.

Guwalt slid a finger over the screen and waited, then used the thumb and forefinger of his left hand to expand the image on the screen. "Here." He pointed to a familiar flashing rectangle among dozens of similar rectangles. Except only one was flashing. The Magistrate was on the move. "Where will that portal take him?"

Guwalt's overlarge eyes widened. "Oh. Well. I'll have to..." He wandered away without finishing that sentence, his head bowed over the device.

Hawk sighed, jerking his head toward the professor. Nicht spun around and walked with him, running interference with a dozen fleeing creatures when Guwalt inadvertently wandered into their paths as they rushed to escape.

Hawk stared at the chaos around him and felt the sense of urgency he'd been nursing since watching Glynn get yanked into that portal turn into a fist-sized rock in the center of his chest.

He couldn't shake the feeling that he was running out of time.

And that Glynn would be the one to suffer if he didn't catch up. Fast.

We walked all night. We hadn't dared go in a straight line to our destination. Every time we neared the road, I saw the big, dark cars the Body soldiers drove moving purposefully along the road, searchlights scouring the darkness. I couldn't believe they'd go to that much trouble looking for me. Maybe it was because of Mitch. Or the giant.

Or they had some other reason entirely for searching the area. It didn't matter. We needed to avoid them no matter what their purpose there was. I just prayed to the goddess that they wouldn't keep up the search all the way to our destination.

By the time we entered Render, I was so tired I could barely move one foot in front of the other. I hadn't realized how much two days of imprisonment, and a lack of enough food and water, had debilitated me.

All I wanted to do was lie down in the soft grass and go to sleep. But I couldn't. First, we needed to find a safe spot to hide. Then we had to find food and water. And, we wouldn't last very long if we didn't get out of sight soon.

Mike stopped walking and looked at me. Mitch hung over his shoulder. We'd found a lake a few miles away from the Body Headquarters and drunk deeply from it. After we'd gotten some water into Mitch, and Jessa had fed him some more of the bread she'd smuggled out in her bag, the Seer had walked as long as he could, but he had no resources to tap into, having been half-starved for a long time. He'd dropped a few miles outside of Render, and Mike had carried him from there.

"Where do you recommend we settle for the night?" Mike asked me.

I'd been giving it a lot of thought as we got closer to Render. I'd considered and ruled out a lot of places. Any place that the Body had raided during our final standoff with them was immediately marked off the list. That left out Sissy's place, Mitch's little shed, Hawk's place, and several other neighbors' homes.

Victoria was off the list for obvious reasons. As I looked down the empty, broken streets of Render, a deep sadness turned my muscles to lead.

There was really only one option. And it had the added benefit of allowing me to check on a friend we'd left behind. "The fairy's house," I told him. "Next door to where I used to live." Della's home had been raided, but there was a passage inside the house that led to an underground cavern. If the Body showed up, we would be safe in that cavern.

I thought about what I now realized had been a fairy portal in that underground cave. Della, the Earth fairy who'd lived in the house had used it to send me, Boyle, and Nicht back to Victoria when the house was under siege from the Body.

If we were lucky, we could use it to get somewhere safe.

We moved quickly and quietly through the night, listening to the soft whir of the night bugs. I jumped with nerves when an owl hooted high above our heads and laughed at myself. The night air was cool, and the familiar scent of Render, never sweet or welcoming, nevertheless made me long for the simplicity of my old life in the small town.

I was making a home in Outvald. I was finding new friends, forging new levels of strength and perseverance in myself that I never knew I had. Every day was a challenge. Every challenge was a chance to grow and learn. But Render was a part of me. It had been my life for as long as I could remember And I missed its siren call like I missed food or air.

"Which house?" Jessa asked softly.

I blinked and turned to her, realizing I'd totally zoned out. "That ranch right there. The one with the darker brick."

My gaze slid past Della's home to the spot where

Victoria had lived, and my heart skipped a beat. For just an instant, the length of a single breath, I thought I saw her regal, well-worn form rising up out of the ground. It was like her spirit, appearing in the darkness to welcome me back to Render.

"Are you okay?" Jessa asked, still speaking in a near whisper.

I blinked, looking at her. "What?"

"You look like you've seen a ghost."

I let her words sink deep and then I laughed, the sound totally devoid of mirth. "Something like that." I forced myself to look back to the spot where my house had been, just so I'd understand, once and for all, that she was really gone.

"This door has been broken into," Mike said. He was standing in front of Della's home. It was dark and silent, no more welcoming than any of the other places on the street.

"Yeah," I said. "It's okay. Hopefully, we won't be staying in the house anyway."

He gave me a strange look, but I pushed past him and held the door open so he could slide inside with his load.

Jessa followed him, then I closed the door and tried the lock. There was a deadbolt higher on the frame that apparently hadn't been locked when the Body broke inside. I managed to get it to slide into its track by leaning heavily against the door.

A cool breeze skimmed over me, reminding me

that I couldn't do anything about the big front window Nicht had shattered the night we'd rescued Della from soul suckers.

I grimaced at that memory.

I sent Mike and Jessa down the hall to the bedroom at the end. "Put Mitch down on the bed, and I'll see what I can find us to eat."

It didn't take long for me to realize my mistake.

The cupboards were bare. The refrigerator wasn't even plugged in. It was apparently just there for show.

I sighed. "Of course," I murmured. "Fairy spirits don't need to eat."

I'd always known Della was a fairy spirit. She'd explained once that she'd died in her early forties, and in the way of her people, her body should have been given over to the rich soil of her fae homeland so she could be reborn. For reasons she'd never explained, she hadn't wanted to return to Fairy, where, according to her, she'd have been reborn into another life.

Instead, she'd become a fairy spirit. Which meant she was mostly a prisoner of her home, where fairy soil helped her spirit thrive, and fairy wood and stone gave her form corporeal properties. She could leave the home, of course, but only for short periods of time. After a while, her body would lose its corporeal state and become truly the spirit she projected.

That was the story she'd given me. And I wasn't

sure how much of it was the truth. I'd later seen her body, pale and weak but solid and real, in the cavern beneath the house.

The cavern I planned to visit once I'd gotten us some food to give us the necessary strength for travel and, potentially, battle.

I filled several glasses with water at the kitchen sink and carried them to the bedroom where my traveling companions waited.

Mitch was awake on the bed, but his color wasn't good and his chest rose and fell way too quickly.

Jessa sat on the edge of the bed and had one hand on Mitch's chest. She looked up when I came into the room. "He's too weak to go on. We need to get him food and water."

I handed her a glass. "I need to go out for a few minutes. Hawk's place will have food."

"I'll go with you," Mike said, taking his glass when I offered it.

I shook my head. "No. You stay here, protect them. Just in case."

He held my gaze, knowing what I was telling him. If the Body rolled up to the house, he'd be their only protection. Unless Jessa had powers she hadn't yet shown. Mitch could do nothing defensively, even if he weren't knocking on death's door.

"You don't have your magic," he reminded me.

I glanced down at the accursed band on my wrist, wanting to swear. "I know this area. I can keep out of sight. And I'm sure Hawk has weapons in the house."

I wasn't sure. I'd never seen any weapons there. But the man never seemed to go anywhere without several blades on his person. He surely had a stash of the things somewhere.

"I'll be back in five minutes."

He nodded, downing his water in one long pull.

I handed Jessa her glass and started down the hall, drinking mine as I hurried through the kitchen and unlocked the back door. Sticking my head outside, I hesitated, listening carefully.

The wind had picked up, rustling the branches of the oversized trees lining Della's yard in a series of silken sighs. The sound made me hesitate. It sounded almost like someone murmuring deadly secrets.

Finally, I slipped outside, quietly closing the door and sliding along the back of the house to the corner. My view of the street was abbreviated there, but I saw nothing to indicate that anyone was sneaking around Render except for me.

I took off running, diving into the line of tall evergreens along the property line and coming out behind where Victoria would have been. I ran quickly from tree to tree, using their thick, aged trunks as a barrier between me and the rest of the world.

When I moved too close to where Victoria had

been, magic danced along my nerve endings, familiar and sweet. My heart twisted at the touch, feeling as if Victoria were there with me, giving me encouragement.

I ran to the big oak at the corner of the front yard, only five yards from the street, and scanned the road in both directions as far as I could see.

Nothing.

Feeling calmer, I hurried across the street, memories of my battle there with a giant reptilian creature from Outvald making me shudder. Nicht and Hawk had nearly been killed during that battle, and I'd almost lost myself to the thing's acidic magic.

I was moving so quickly that, when I neared Hawk's house, I stepped down into a hole in the yard and twisted my ankle.

Agony speared up my leg, and I bit down on a surprised yelp of pain.

"Goddess in garters!" I cursed quietly. Why hadn't I been more careful?

I sat up and felt the ankle, gasping as I gently probed it. It didn't feel broken. But it was definitely tender. Sighing, I hoped Hawk had a first aid kit in his home too. And prayed nothing tried to attack us while we were in Render.

Because I'd just made myself worse than useless.

21

I hobbled over to the door in the low-slung brick building attached to the enormous garage. The building had once housed the Render fire department. Two of the bays still held shiny red fire engines that looked as if they might have been polished up only a few days previous.

The door into the house was locked. With a small sound of frustration, I hobbled around the building and tested the sliding door in the back. To my supreme relief, it was unlocked.

I slipped inside, locking the door behind me. As I turned toward the kitchen, I brushed against the dusty curtains, dislodging a cloud of dust that assailed my nostrils. I sneezed three times in quick succession, realizing any hope I'd had of sneaking around in case something lurked inside the house was squashed.

Sighing, I limped into the kitchen.

I found a goldmine of goodies there—bottles of water, protein bars, and even some jerky. I made a big pile in the center of the table and went looking for a bag to put it all in.

There were four bedrooms down a long hallway that likely ran along the back of the garage bays. The first three were stripped of everything except a simple wooden dresser and a single bed sporting a stained mattress and box spring. The closets were empty except for a few hangars and some trash on the floor.

The last bedroom was Hawk's. I knew this because it still carried his delicious, clean male scent that I suddenly missed almost as much as I'd miss breathing. I leaned against the wall and closed my eyes, inhaling him deep into my lungs.

Tears burned my eyes. I might never see him again. I might never see Boyle again. Or Sissy...or Grams.

I let the tears fall, giving myself a minute to mourn. Then I scrubbed angrily at the tears and pushed away from the wall. The pity party was over. I needed to get back to Mitch and my new friends.

I searched the closet for a bag, noting the clean jeans and tee-shirts hanging on the rod and the shoes settled neatly on the floor. Hawk would probably love to get his hands on the spare clothing. He and the guys had been making do in

Outvald with minimal clothing and really no spares.

We needed to fix that. Somehow.

The closet shelf finally yielded what I was looking for in the form of a canvas bag with straps. It would be perfect. I spotted a small metal box with a cross painted on it in red. Curious, I opened it and found a first-aid kit. It was old and simple, with some bandages, wraps, and clean gauze pads. There was also a bottle of pain killers, two small jars of what I guessed were probably topical antiseptics, and a small sewing kit. I took a moment to wrap my ankle tightly and swallow a couple of the pain pills before throwing the kit into the bag. Standing in the middle of the room, I looked for a likely spot for Hawk to hide his weapons.

They weren't in the closet. I searched the dresser and found only socks and underwear. I dropped to my knees and searched through the shoes on the closet floor in the hopes there'd be a hidden niche there. Then I felt my way along the back wall of the closet.

Nothing.

I briefly considered and then rejected the idea that he might hide his weapons in the garage. He'd want them close at hand.

My gaze fell on the bed and narrowed.

The twin-sized bed had plain white sheets, two pillows stacked in front of a scarred maple headboard, and two thin blankets. Apparently, Hawk was a hot sleeper.

My cheeks heated at the thought.

Bad Glynn. Drag your brain out of the gutter!

I slid my fingers under the mattress, lifted it...and smiled.

Bingo!

A wide array of knives in leather sheaths and a single gun covered the top of the box spring. I threw the mattress off and dragged the bag over, throwing the knives inside. Slipping the gun into the waistband of my jeans, I wondered where he kept the bullets?

I didn't find any bullets in his underwear drawer, but the bottom drawer had two neat piles of folded white tee shirts and a box of bullets. I threw the box into the canvas bag.

Grunting under the weight, I slung the straps of the bag over my shoulders and headed back to the kitchen.

At least the wrap and pain killers were helping my ankle. It still ached, but I could put all my weight on it again.

As I entered the kitchen, a shadow slid past outside the sliding door. Jolting to a stop, I ducked, using the small island in the center to hide my movements until I reached the table. I watched the door for several minutes, my heart pounding against my ribs.

Nothing moved. There was no sound other than the wind whistling through the soffits of the elderly building.

I quickly slid the food and water into the bag and then, struggling under its weight, slipped the straps over my shoulders and headed for the door into the garage. Just in case something was out back, I'd avoid going out the way I'd come in.

I unlocked the dividing door and reached for the handle, pulling it open just as the sliding glass door exploded inward in a wash of flying glass.

"Render!" Professor Guwalt screamed above the din. "He's gone to Render." The professor shook his head, looking perplexed. "I hadn't even known there was a portal into Render." He flapped his hand and jerked his head downward several times as if agreeing with some unheard statement. "Yes, except for the Forester portal, of course. But that was a natural portal, built on a lei line. That portal is hundreds of years old. This..." He flipped his fingers toward his device, curling his lip in disgust. "This is like the shadow of a portal. Man-made no doubt." He frowned. "It's just what David and I were afraid of. The Body has learned to create second-rate portals."

Hawk was only half-listening to the man. His

mind was spinning. *Render!* Did the Magistrate know something they didn't? Had Glynn returned home? Suddenly it made perfect sense. Of course, she'd go there. He spun on his heel, screaming into the chaos of fleeing magical humans and creatures. "Shane! Alina!"

Nobody responded to his elegant summons. He swore, glancing at Nicht and then back to Guwalt. "Can we use the same portal?"

Guwalt's fingers danced over the device, his expressions changing with each jab and punch of a digit onto the screen. Watching him work was like viewing a video of an insane person descending into complete madness. But, having spent a couple of days with the man, Hawk knew Guwalt wasn't as mad as he appeared. He was eccentric in the extreme. But insane? Not even a little. To the uneducated eye, supreme genius could sometimes look like madness.

"Yes. But it will only carry one at a time." He glanced at Nicht. "Maybe two with the dog…"

Nicht snarled wetly and the man rolled his eyes. "Sorry, sorry. Hellhound."

Nicht chuffed softly.

Alina jogged up to them, looking ragged and battle-worn. She was covered in blood but looked far from tired. She was in her element. Chaos was her drug of choice. "I heard you bellow. What's going on?"

"Where's Shane?"

She rolled her eyes. "I don't know. Probably playing with his dragon." She waggled her brows. "That sounded dirty, didn't it?"

Hawk ignored her. He grabbed Guwalt's arm. "Get Nicht and me into that portal. Then, as soon as Shane shows up, send these two through."

"What about me?" the professor asked, looking stunned.

Hawk fought the urge to tell the man he could do whatever he wanted. He realized that, by requesting Guwalt's help, he'd put the professor into an untenable situation. "Can you show us how to get back to Outvald?"

Guwalt's gaze was haunted. He shook his head. "These manmade portals are volatile. Unlike the gateways that were created naturally over time, they aren't fixed. I must constantly monitor them to determine which ones will take us where we need to go."

Hawk tamped down on the fist of urgency that was making it hard for him to breathe and thought through their options. "But you *can* find the right one? When we're ready?"

He nodded, his slow blink seemingly at odds with his agitated state. "Yes. Take me with you." His wide mouth turned down in the corners. "I do not wish to end up like my friend David."

Hawk nodded. "Send Nicht and me. Then send

Alina through. And when Shane shows up, send him and follow."

Relief softened the worry lines between Guwalt's overlarge eyes. "Yes. I can do that."

"Okay, let's go."

I was aware only of a massive amount of teeth, very large teeth, and then a leathery snout with enormous, oversized nostrils. I sucked back with a scream as those teeth snapped mere inches away from my face and flung the door open on the snapping jaws of something that looked like an enormous crocodile.

I dove through the door, tripping over the threshold and stumbling ungracefully into the garage.

I caught myself on a shiny fender and turned toward the exterior door, hoping the thing in pursuit was slower than its first charge at me would seem to indicate.

It wasn't.

By the time I was within reach of the door handle, the croc was snapping at my ankles, its muscular tail propelling it forward as if its belly was greased.

I yelped and jumped to the side as the thing smashed snout-first into the heavy wooden door.

The entire wall seemed to rattle from the impact. I turned away and ran blindly toward the other end of the oversized garage.

Maybe there was another door on the other side.

There wasn't. Except for the oversized doors that allowed the fire engines to be driven in and out of the garage. I eyed the huge doors and knew I wouldn't be able to lift them.

The monster flew my way again, trailing a black miasma of foul magic in its wake that fully explained its speed. I wasn't dealing with a regular old crocodile.

Not that Indiana generally sported crocodiles, except for in the Magical Indy zoo.

Those thoughts spun through my mind, irrational in the midst of a lethal attack, but who can explain the way the mind works in a crisis? Seeing no other place where I'd be safe, I chose to climb onto the fire engine at my back, scurrying quickly up a ladder on the side. Squatting on top, among the fire hoses, dials, and gadgets that probably come standard with such vehicles, I trying to regain my breath.

I took quick stock of my condition and situation.

My shoulders ached from hauling around the canvas bag. It probably weighed a good fifteen or twenty pounds with all the hardware and water inside. I shrugged it off, rubbing at the indentations in my skin.

I was winded, but there wasn't much I could do about that since adrenaline was coursing through my system in buckets.

But that same adrenaline had hidden my ankle pain for the moment, so that was good.

I was safe. Relatively. But unless that thing down there decided to wander back through the house, I was stuck for the foreseeable future. No. That wouldn't do.

The others were depending on me to bring them food and get them to Outvald.

I had to get out. I scanned the area, assessing my options.

Below on the concrete floor, the creature paced around the truck, its snout open and nostrils flaring wetly as if scenting me.

Then I saw something that turned my spine to ice.

Something flapped on the creature's long, knobby back.

Wings.

Goddess, no!

My options were suddenly reduced by one. Staying where I was, was no longer an alternative.

I left the pack where it was and clambered up to the cab of the truck. It was a solid piece of metal with large, fixed windows. I wouldn't be opening a window and climbing inside from up there. I climbed to the side and looked around, wondering if

I could clamber down to the running board, open the door and get inside before that thing was on me.

Teeth snapped mere inches from my elbow before I could jerk backward again.

Nope.

I paced the available, cluttered space carefully to keep from tripping over something and falling right into the monster's copious jaws.

The thing lunged upward again and then hung in the air, its wings whirring above it.

The jaws snapped together, making a clunking sound from the force of the snap that had me just about peeing myself.

Without thinking, I reached back and grabbed the gun. As the creature lunged on a terrifying hiss, I pulled the trigger.

The bullet smacked into the creature's leathery leg and punched it backward, spinning it in the air and slamming it into the second fire engine. It slid down with a roar of pain and hit the concrete floor with a meaty thud. I didn't waste any time. I clambered down, flung the door open, and dove inside.

I barely got the door closed again before finger-sized claws scraped over the glass and down the metal door.

Like an idiot, I slammed my palm onto the door lock as if the monster could open it. I laid my head back on the seat and closed my eyes, my heart pounding. My breaths came out in fear-induced wheezing. Sweat ran down my face and neck, soaking my shirt. I tried to siphon magic from the air and got nothing. Screaming in frustration, I gave the band around my wrist a brutal yank.

The monster slammed into the other side of the truck, its wings pulling it up to window height. It slammed into the window, and I thought I heard something crack.

I couldn't just sit there and wait for the thing to break the window.

My gaze landed on the keys dangling in the ignition.

The monster slammed into the glass again. A prolonged splintering sound followed the attack. I watched as a large crack bisected the big window.

It would only take one or two more strikes and he'd be in. I had run out of time to dither. Sliding across the seats, I quickly turned the key. The engine choked, sputtered, and died.

Oh, goddess, no! "Come on!" I screamed, pumping the pedal I could barely reach.

Slam! Craaaaaacccccckkkkkkkkkk

I turned the key again. The engine spluttered. Died.

Again.

Slam! Slam! Slam!

Glass shattered inward, peppering me with jagged shards that sliced through my cheek and neck and coated the seat and floor.

The monster rose until it was staring through the splintered glass at me.

I stared into its cold black eyes, unable to look away, as I pumped the pedal and turned the key in a final effort to get the truck to start. The engine caught, held, and roared as I jammed my foot down on the brake and yanked the truck into Drive. The monster struck again and I slammed the gas to the floor. The big truck jerked forward, crashing into the glass and metal door with an explosion of sound and a structure-jarring concussion.

22

T he big door disintegrated in a shower of glass and splintered wood, oversized chunks slamming down onto the cab as I gunned it through the door. I had no plans for where to go or even how to drive the massive vehicle. My only thought was to get away from the crocomonster in the garage.

Unfortunately, I didn't make it very far. The big tree I'd hidden behind before crossing the street loomed up in front of me. I yanked the wheel to the side in a too-sharp, too-fast turn and the truck spun around, the back skidding out from under my control and smashed into the tree.

I pulled my foot off the gas and hit the brake, the tires screeching and smoke rising up around me as the truck shimmied, wobbled, and leaned to one side in a real attempt to roll over onto its side.

I whipped the wheel the other way and let up on

the brake. Somehow, by the goddess's everlasting mercy, all the tires slammed back onto the road.

I eased my foot back onto the brake, finally easing the truck to a stop. Shockingly, I wasn't too far from Della's house.

Slam!

I screamed with rage as the crocomonster crashed against the opposite door, rattling it in its frame.

I was soooo done with that stupid thing.

Slam!

Mumbling to myself, I grabbed the gun off the floor where it had landed in my ill-thought-out escape from the garage and shoved the door open. I stared down at the creature as it ambled around the front of the truck, mouth open and hissing.

"I'm sick of you," I yelled.

The thing hissed again, its wings coming up as it prepared to fly up and eat me.

"I don't think so," I yelled, firing bullets into the creature as fast as I could pull the trigger.

It twitched, jolted, and shuddered with each impact, slowly backing away but not nearly as injured by the bullets as I'd hoped.

The gun clicked on an empty chamber.

I didn't hesitate. Throwing it into the other seat, I climbed behind the wheel, turned the key, and threw the truck in reverse.

As the creature started its ascent for another

attack, I stomped on the brake, flung it into Drive, and gunned it.

The sound of the big tires rolling over the huge carcass was very satisfying, but the bump from the impact threw me out of the seat and slapped my skull against the ceiling. Rubbing my head, I stopped the truck, put it in reverse, and gunned it.

The truck bounced hard over the monster again. My head slammed into the ceiling.

"Ouch!"

I stomped on the brake. The fire engine screeched to a stop, leaning slightly to one side. Killing the engine, I opened the door to examine my handiwork.

All I could see of the crocodile was its muscular tail, still thrashing in an attempt to wrench itself free. The rest of the body was pinned under a huge tire, the weight of the fire engine holding it in place.

"You deserved that," I told the monster. Climbing out of the cab, I hurried up the ladder to retrieve the bag and then started toward Della's house.

I really needed a shower and a nap.

I was so tired I nearly missed the sizzling, whooshing sound of magic behind me. I barely restrained a groan as I turned. "What now...?" The question died on my lips as my world spun around me like a top and then settled back into place.

I stared at the gorgeous man striding toward me

across the lawn, something that had felt broken inside of me aligning itself again. "Hawk?"

His smile melted all the stuff his arrival had fixed. "Glynn." He didn't slow as he approached me. Didn't take his gaze from mine. We didn't so much hug as slam together into a single, fused and heated column of desperate flesh. His arms went around me. His lips found mine. And magic of a totally different kind flared between us.

My thoughts turned to mist in my head. My body heated and softened. And I let myself fall into the delicious oblivion of that kiss.

Just for a moment.

I needed the comfort and promise his presence provided.

A sharp woof tore us from the kiss, and Hawk stepped away as the big black hound leaped off the ground and slammed into me, taking us both to the ground.

I was dimly aware of Hawk's scolding as a wet tongue bathed my sweaty face in kisses.

I laughed and then snapped my mouth closed as the wide pink tongue slathered over my lips. "Ugh!" I said, shoving at him and trying to hide my face behind an arm. "Okay! I get it. You missed me."

Hawk smacked the big hound on the haunches. "Get off her, you beast. We just found her and you're trying to slobber her to death."

Whining around a doggy grin, Nicht backed off

and, tail wagging, fixed an adoring if slightly feral red gaze on me. Hawk helped me to my feet. "Sorry about that."

I ran a sleeve over my wet face, laughing. "No. It's fine. I'm glad to see him too." When Nicht made a move to come at me again, I held up a hand. "No! You're good where you are."

He dropped to his haunches.

The portal dissected the air behind Hawk and Nicht and spat out another familiar form. Without missing a step, Alina strode toward us, her unhurried gait proclaiming her the baddest hombre in town.

I grinned to see her. "Hey! What took you so long?"

Her answering chuckle was deep and sexy. Totally wasted on me. She pulled me into a hug that just about broke my ribs. "Hey yourself. I'm happy to see you in one piece." She scanned a look at the lopsided fire engine and the still-thrashing crocomonster. "What's happening there?"

I grimaced. "Long story. And the trauma's still too great to go into it right now."

She chuckled again.

The portal contracted and spit Shane out. He waved at me, grinning.

He gave me the once-over as he approached. "You're looking a little the worse for wear, girl."

I sighed, holding up my banded wrist. "This is making my life harder than it needs to be."

His expression brightened. "Oh! I brought this." He showed me the glass vial he'd used to remove his and Alice's bands.

The portal wheezed, expanded, and regurgitated a funny-looking man with oversized eyes. He wore a long robe that was torn and filthy, and he seemed vaguely familiar. His identity slowly formed in my battered brain. It was Guwalt. The professor from Learning.

Suddenly, Mitch's vision made sense. *Confused words. Empty spaces in the mind. These will guide them.*

He'd perfectly described Guwalt.

Shane grasped my wrist. A beat later, the band fell away. A sense of relief unlike anything I'd ever felt filled me as magic swelled again in my core. I closed my eyes and let the feeling expand beneath my skin. "Much better."

Shane patted my shoulder.

My eyes popped open. "I need to get inside!" I pointed toward the house. "I have friends in there who need help."

Guwalt joined us. He was holding the device we'd found in his office. He waved. "Hello again."

"Professor." I inclined my chin and turned away. "They need food and water." I glanced at Hawk as he fell in beside me. "I found Mitch. He's in rough shape."

"Why are you here? At the fairy's house?" He asked.

"There's a..." I thought about the cavern below and guilt slid over me at the idea of invading Della's long protected sanctuary with so many people. I shook my head. "I'll explain it later."

Thankfully, Hawk didn't press. His fingers touched mine as we walked, and I found myself pressing closer to him, enjoying his solid warmth. Until his next words chilled the world again.

"Have you seen the Magistrate?"

I took them around to the back door. "No. I'm hoping we're out of here before he shows up." I reached for the doorknob on the kitchen door. "Why?"

"I'm pretty sure he took a portal to Render a couple of hours ago."

I blinked, thinking of the monster in the street. Had that been one of the Magistrate's pets? "I haven't seen him. If he's here, he's keeping a really low profile."

Hawk held the door for Alina, and they shared a look. She nodded and melted away into the darkness of the huge backyard. Nicht went with her.

Shane and Guwalt came inside.

I looked at Shane. "Do you have any healing capabilities?"

"Who are these people?" a harsh, uncertain voice asked from a shadowed corner of the room.

I spun around to find Jessa, eyes glowing softly yellow through the darkness.

"My friends," I told her. "We got separated when the Body kidnapped me. They just found me."

She kept a hostile glare on Hawk for a long moment, clearly pegging him as the most dangerous of the bunch. Finally, the glow in her eyes dimmed and she inclined her head toward the canvas bag. "Did you bring food?"

I nodded, holding it out to her. "There's water and a first aid kit in here too." Then I remembered the weapons and jerked it back. "I'll carry it. The bag's heavy."

She inclined her chin. "The Seer is not going to make it. Holding up her wrist, I saw the band I hadn't noticed before. "If I could reach my magic, I might be able to save him."

Shane looked at me and I nodded. "I can help you with that," he told her.

Relief filled her pretty face when she saw the key. "Bless the goddess."

I left them to it and tugged Hawk into the hallway with me. Speaking in a whisper, I warned him about the giant. "Let me give him a heads up before you barge..."

The air in front of us thickened. Something big and heavy slammed into Hawk, sending him flying backward away from me.

I was struck in the shoulder and thrown sideways, crashing into the wall. I went down under the weight of the bag, my weariness finally turning my legs to pudding beneath me.

Hawk and his invisible attacker were flying around the living room, overturning furniture and smashing lamps and other small items on the tables.

I shoved myself off the floor and tried yelling. Nobody heard me over the chaos. In desperation, I dug into the bag and found the box of bullets. Jamming one into the gun, I ratcheted it into the chamber and lifted my arm above my head. "Mike!" I yelled, and then, when that didn't work, I pulled the trigger.

Sound exploded through the small house, plaster and shards of wood filtered down on my head. And Hawk, on his back on the floor with both hands pushing something away from his chest, looked over at me.

The invisible attacker slowly formed into Mike, a bit and a section at a time.

"He's a friendly," I told the giant.

Hawk's gaze widened at the size of the man pressing him into the dusty carpet.

"Mike," I said in a warning voice. Slowly, the big man pushed himself to his feet and took a couple of steps back. "This is Hawk," I said in measured, clearly enunciated words, in case his brain was still compromised by adrenaline. "He and the others..." I took a deep breath to calm my pounding heart. "They're my friends. They came looking for me."

Mike slid a glance toward Shane and Guwalt, who was peeking around Shane's shoulder, blinking owlishly.

The giant's expression softened from rage to reluctant acceptance. He offered Hawk a hand and the guardian took it, allowing himself to be tugged off the floor.

The two men glared at each other. I reached for the box of bullets. "Do I need to reload this thing?"

Mike expelled air and turned his back on Hawk. He cut the distance between us in very few steps. "Did you bring food?"

I reached into the bag and tugged a handful of bars out, along with two bottles of water, handing them to him.

Shane offered Mike a hand. "Shane."

The giant took it. "Mike."

Shane held up the vial. "Would you like me to get rid of those bands for you?"

Mike's only response was a slow, delighted grin.

23

We sat in front of the broken picture window in the living room. Hawk had offered to find some lumber to cover it, but I told him not to bother. I didn't plan to sleep. Since I had my magic back, I'd keep watch through the night, and then we'd use Professor Guwalt's device to figure out where the nearest portal was.

In the interim, I enjoyed watching the play of stars across the night sky and listening to the crickets singing in the tall grass as if nothing had changed in the world.

I wished it was true.

But everything had changed. And I doubted my life would ever find its way back to what I'd once thought of as normal.

At one point during the night, I'd heard the creak of metal and a loud thud that probably represented the fire engine tire hitting the street. Somehow, that goddess-forsaken crocomonster had escaped its thirty thousand pound shackle. I sighed, hoping it moved on down the line and left us alone. But if it decided to attack, I wasn't overly worried. Everybody had their magic back, and we had a lot of firepower in the house.

A soft groaning sound from the back room mingled with a whistling snore that I recognized as Guwalt's. I grimaced at the groan, knowing Mitch was still struggling to survive. His fate was in Shane and Jessa's hands. It was going to be a long night for all of us.

Alina had checked in an hour previous, declaring that she would spend the night in the uncomfortable embrace of the big oak tree on the corner. I'd warned her not to fall asleep and topple out of it. With her luck she'd land right on top of that flying crocodile thing. She'd just rolled her eyes with disgust, giving me a look that had proclaimed me stupid.

I smiled at the memory. It was good to have them back.

"Protein bar for your thoughts," Hawk said.

I glanced at the bar he held between us and lifted my gaze to his. Taking the food, I said, "I was just wondering how long it would be before Alina bumped up against that crocomonster out there."

He chuckled darkly. "I wouldn't be surprised if

she was the one who released it from under that tire so she could play."

I bit into the sweet-salty bar and allowed it to melt over my tongue before chewing and swallowing. I'd had a bar earlier, but my body was tired and the calories helped. I took the bottle of water Hawk offered me. We settled back onto the couch in companionable silence.

Despite my best intentions, my mind wandered back to the knee-melting kiss we'd shared earlier. I licked my lips, remembering how delicious it had been. Hot and sweet and full of promise. Realizing my thoughts were probably written all over my face, I flushed with embarrassment, not sure if I wanted him to know. It was all I could do not to glance his way to see if he was thinking about the kiss too.

A moment later, Hawk stirred. I used the excuse to look at him. "What?"

He shook his head. "I was just thinking about the Magistrate. Guwalt had been sure he was coming here. It seemed logical. Especially since you were here."

"But he's not here, and you're wondering where he went." I said.

He nodded. "It's a concern."

"Could he have gone back to Magical Indy?"

"I suppose so. But why? And, if he had, I would have thought he'd use the portal we used. We entered it not too long after he did. I didn't see him."

"Maybe he went somewhere else?"

"Guwalt was sure he came here." He turned to me, his hazel eyes dark pools in the night. "Have you been well hidden the whole time?"

My face heated as I thought about all the noise and commotion I'd made trying to escape the crocomonster. "Not really," I answered, wincing.

We were quiet again for a few minutes. I finished my bar and took a sip of the water. My eyes tried to close. I shifted on the couch to keep from falling asleep.

"Go ahead. Take a nap. I'll keep watch for a couple of hours, and then you can spell me."

"No. I'm good." But sleep kept tugging at me. I started talking just to keep awake. "What happened after I was taken? How'd you end up with Guwalt?"

"As soon as we figured out we couldn't access the portal they used to take you, we went back to the University. We found Guwalt in his office, gathering up a box of stuff. It looked like he was going into hiding." He fell silent for a beat as if remembering the scene. "I insisted that he tell us where the local portals to Earth were."

"Did he fight you on it?"

"Not really," Hawk said. "He's scared he'll end up like his buddy Bernes."

I nodded. "I've been thinking about that. He and David Bernes were trying to stop the Body from bringing magical creatures to the Earthly dimension, weren't they?"

Hawk nodded. "They started by trying to barter or buy creatures from that terrible woman at the auction. They promised information on portals in exchange for as many of them as she could be talked out of. Then, they decided to go right to the source. They'd been in the process of enticing a Body representative into working with them when the Magistrate found out. Bernes was killed and Guwalt was next. That's what we were unfortunate enough to walk into the day we went to speak to the professor. Now, he's afraid to go back without us."

I grimaced. "So, are we joined at the hip to him now?"

"Maybe?" Hawk said, a grin in his voice.

"Ugh! I guess we'll have to squeeze another room out of the Annex for him."

Hawk shrugged. "Maybe he could stay in Bernes' home?"

"Not unless we can come up with a way to secure it." I gave that some thought, coming up with some potential ideas. "I'll talk to Grams about it when we get back." Saying the words made me sad and ecstatic at the same time. I couldn't wait to see Boyle and Grams. Sissy. And the rest. But we still had to figure out how to get there.

Sometime in the course of my musings, I made the mistake of closing my eyes. I woke up hours later to the sound of voices and the smell of coffee coming from the kitchen.

Pushing off the couch, I stretched, barely stifling a groan as my muscles lamented the movement in the most painful way.

A cup appeared in front of me. Looking up into Hawk's weary face, I smiled at him and took the steaming mug. "Hey."

He smiled back. "Hey. You look rested."

I couldn't help reaching out and placing a hand on his bristly cheek. His whiskers made scratchy noises against my palm. "You look exhausted. You didn't sleep?"

"A little." He grabbed my hand and gave it a squeeze before pointing toward the kitchen. "Come on. Breakfast is on."

He pulled me along behind him. "Omelets? Biscuits?" I joked.

Jessa looked up as I came through the door. "Not omelets."

My eyes went wide when I saw the eggs and sausage on the plate. "How?"

Hawk handed me a fork. "The eggs are a frozen substitute. But they're not bad. My freezer still has some surprises in it."

I dropped into a chair and tucked into the food. It tasted delicious. My plate was empty in seconds. When I looked up to find Hawk and Jessa watching me with amused expressions, heat flared in my cheeks.

"More?" Jessa asked.

"I don't want to eat somebody else's share."

She took my plate and heaped it with more food. "Everybody else has already eaten."

I ate my second helping more slowly. "How's Mitch," I asked after a moment, feeling guilty for not thinking about him before my stomach.

"He slept well," Jessa said, sitting down across from me. "Ate two plates of food." She grinned, sipping coffee. "And Shane's babysitting him in the shower. Just in case his legs give out on him. He's still a little shaky."

I thanked the goddess, sipping my coffee and sitting back in the chair. My hand dropped onto a comfortably full belly. I hadn't experienced the feeling of being sated since leaving Victoria days earlier. "That's really good news."

"He wants to go back to his shed," Hawk said. When I looked my horror at him, he nodded. "I think I've talked him out of that. But I had to promise we'd somehow get his chair to Outvald."

I laughed. "Yeah, that chair has almost as much of his magic in it as he does." I would certainly know since I'd used the chair when he was taken to try to find him and to stop the Body from overtaking Render. When Mitch had lived in his little shed behind a once-wealthy magic user's home that had been abandoned in the Disruption, he'd envisioned most of his prophecies, spent most of his days, and had slept most of his nights in the comfortable recliner as well.

He loved that chair more than anything he had.

"We'll figure it out. With Guwalt's help, we should be able to come back and grab it and anything else we need." I was thinking about Hawk's clothes and other stuff, some of which he might want to bring to Outvald, and maybe some building supplies or foodstuffs we didn't have access to in Outvald.

The thought made me smile. Having a portal that went both ways between dimensions would be very handy.

"I wonder if we could bring that fire engine through," Shane said, walking into the kitchen. He grinned. "That would really come in handy there."

I laughed. "I'm not sure they make portals big enough for that."

He shrugged. "We need to find a big one anyway." He lifted his eyes to the ceiling, a slow smile spreading over his grizzled face. "Because Alice is here."

A roar split the quickly-lightening sky.

From the backyard, where she no doubt prowled, Alina called for Shane and he headed outside. Hawk and I followed.

I turned to Hawk. "I can't believe he brought Alice."

Sighing, he nodded. "I'm afraid he won't go back without her."

"Goddess in garters," I mumbled. "My life is a circus and I'm the ringmaster."

Hawk dropped an arm around my shoulders, leading me outside. "Dibs on borrowing your whip since I'm the one who's in charge of wrangling the clowns and tigers."

My laugh was sliced off as I caught sight of the gorgeous creature circling the backyard.

With the rising sun glinting off her midnight black body and the graceful sweep of her massive, crenated wings, she was stunning and terrifying, even without the thick column of fire and smoke billing from her roaring maw.

I turned back to the house.

"Where are you going?" Hawk asked.

"To find Guwalt. We're going to have our hands full finding a portal that's big enough to admit Alice."

H awk, Alina, and I leaned over the table, watching Guwalt work his device with a studied doggedness that I would never have assumed he was capable of when I'd met him the first time.

He kept mumbling and shaking his head as if something was perplexing him. Finally, I couldn't stand the suspense anymore. "What's wrong?" I asked the nutty professor.

He shook his head again. "It's not there. But it is."

I glanced at Hawk, my eyes widening.

He smiled.

The back door opened and Mike and Jessa came inside. They'd been checking the dragon out with Shane.

"Is she okay?" Alina asked.

Mike nodded. "A few scratches along her sides. It looks like somebody got her with a jolt of energy. And one of her foreclaws was ripped off."

I grimaced. "Ouch."

He nodded. "The wizard's doing what he can to help her."

My eyes went wide. "Wizard?" I looked at Alina. She was laughing silently, her whole body shaking. "You didn't."

"I did," she said. "He's too full of himself. He needs an attitude adjustment once in a while. It's good for him."

Hawk raised a brow. "Pot. Kettle."

She snorted out a laugh. "Whatever."

"What?" Mike asked, his expression telling me he realized he'd been had.

"Shane is a sorcerer. A very powerful one, from what I can see. He worked with my Grams and she was known as one of the most powerful in the Earthly dimension."

Mike narrowed his gaze on Alina.

She shrugged. "What? He likes it when you call him wizard. It's like a pet name."

"You're going to get that third eye any day now," Hawk muttered.

She laughed again.

The door slammed open, and we all jumped. Shane came into the room looking worried. "Has anybody been tromping around next door?"

I frowned. "At my house? No. Why?"

Rather than answering me, he glanced at Guwalt. "Professor, are you getting an anomaly on that thing?"

The professor looked up, blinking slowly. "I am. It's darn frustrating too."

Shane closed his eyes and scrubbed his hands over his face. He looked tired and frustrated and something else. "Glynn, have you tested the portal next door?" he asked.

"No, I..." I realized I should have gone over there. I was a coward, but I knew that seeing the empty lot would rip a hole in my heart. "It's gone, so I didn't see the point."

Shane looked at Guwalt.

The professor slowly slid his gaze to mine. "He's

right. I've been seeing a shadow there. A portal that isn't a portal. I keep adjusting the sensitivity of my tracker, but it won't go away."

Hawk straightened away from the table. "Shane, what's going on. Stop being mysterious and just come out with it."

"I was walking Alice around, checking her gaits since she lost the claw." He scratched his head. "She's got a tiny limp. I think I can regrow the claw, but..."

"Shane!" Hawk, Alina, and I all yelled at once.

He raised his hands to ward us off. "Okay, don't get your bloomers in a bunch. "I saw footprints in the basement of the old place." He eyed me. "I've been in that old house enough times to recognize the basement. The stairs and one stone wall are still there."

I stood up so fast my chair crashed to the floor behind me. "The portal wall?"

He shrugged. "I've never been down there when the portal was open..."

I didn't wait for him to finish. I ran past him and out the door. As I ran, the significance of those footsteps suddenly became clear.

And horror almost stopped my lungs from working.

Hawk had said the Magistrate came here. But we hadn't seen him. If he'd looked for us, he'd have found us. Which meant he hadn't come for us. He likely had no idea we were here. It had been a miracle we'd missed seeing him.

Fear ripped holes in my insides and I faltered, dizziness nearly making me fall down the rough wooden steps that led into a muddy hole in the ground that used to be Victoria's basement. Just as Shane had said, the hole was familiar, even without the walls.

But there was *one* wall. The stone gave off a familiar energy even as I jumped off the bottom step and ran to it.

I pressed my palm against the stone and it warmed. I felt the moment the energy boiling behind it recognized my touch and started to heat. The atoms in the stone began to swirl, growing more frantic by the second. I knew what would happen if I didn't step away. If I didn't remove my hand.

Tears filled my eyes. Happy tears, of course. We could get back to Outvald. To my family. To my friends. They were also tears of terror and guilt.

We wouldn't get there in time to save them all.

Because clearly, the Magistrate had gotten to them first.

Footsteps pounded toward me. Hawk yelled my name as he ran, worry clear in his voice.

I stood staring at the pinprick on the inside of my arm. Blood. He'd taken my blood. I hadn't been able to access the magic at the time. But it had been there, in my blood. In my DNA. And he'd taken it.

As long as he had my blood, the Magistrate could use Victoria's portal.

With a terrified cry, I slapped my palm back on the wall. I was going back and I'd stop him from hurting my family.

And I'd kill him as I'd promised.

24

A big hand wrapped around my wrist and tugged my palm away from the wall. The heat that had begun to build beneath my touch wavered and started to drift away. I spun on my heel, rage heating my face. I struck out blindly at the person trying to keep me from Boyle and my home.

"Let me go! I need to get back there. He's going to kill them!"

Hawk's narrowed gaze was filled with determination. "We'll go, Glynn. But we need to take a few minutes to plan. You can't just fly off by yourself. It will only add you to his list of conquests. Is that what you want?"

A soft growl rumbled at the back of my throat. I blinked in surprise and sliced it off, realizing I might have spent too much time siphoning feral creatures' magic. Even as I opened my mouth to argue, I recognized that he was right. I'd be no good to the people in Outvald if I flew into danger and left my backup behind.

I slammed my lips together. "Ten minutes. That's all I'm willing to wait."

He inclined his chin. "Alina and Shane are prepping now. We can't assume the Magistrate went to Outvald alone. Or that he hasn't bullied or coerced others to join him once there. If we've learned anything about the guy, it's that he's been busy in Outvald."

I nodded and began to pace in front of the portal wall, finding it impossible to stay still. "Tomas and Grodan would have gotten everyone into Victoria and battened down the hatches. Grams is powerful there. She can keep them safe for a while." I just didn't know how long. From what we could tell, the Body had arrived there sometime the night before. He had several hours head start on us.

I mentally cursed myself for taking the time to rest. While I'd been lazing around Della's home, they'd probably been fighting for their lives.

"He'll think he's got the element of surprise on his side. He won't rush, knowing the prize Victoria represents." Hawk skimmed me a look, guilt and worry thick in his gaze.

I knew what he was thinking. The house was a goldmine of powerful magic. The portal alone was priceless. Adding the leverage factor for pulling me and possibly my brother into his sphere...

My stomach twisted painfully and, for a moment, I thought I might throw up. I stopped pacing and bent double, fighting the nausea that had bloomed in my middle.

Hawk's warm hand found my back and rubbed it in soothing circles. "Breathe, Glynn. We're going to fix this."

I knew he was just trying to calm me down, but it still worked. The surety in his tone and his touch did soothe me enough to allow me to breathe through the terror. I straightened, taking a deep breath. "We need to prepare for the worst." I leaned against the wall and looked him in the eye. "Let's talk assets."

I n the end, my ten minutes turned into a couple of hours. Once I calmed down, I realized that Hawk had been right. I couldn't rush in at the expense of planning.

So we planned. And planned. And all of us wished we had more resources to pull from, though nobody said the words aloud.

We stood in Della's kitchen and talked over what we might find when we stepped out of the portal and how we could best address it.

Guwalt had left an hour previous. He'd used the

portal the Magistrate had used to get to Render from Indy to return to the Body's headquarters. From there, he'd return through the portal he and the others had traveled to come from Outvald to Earth. His job was to gather as much help as he could and bring it to us at Victoria.

Mike went with him, but Jessa stayed with us. "I have medical experience," she told us. She didn't elaborate and I didn't push. Whatever magical skills she harbored, they were welcome. Her medical expertise would be worth its weight in gold.

Mitch insisted he was healthy enough to work. Alina took him down the street to his recliner and promised to return as soon as Mitch had cast his energies out to the Universe and pulled in anything he could see.

Hawk, Shane, Jessa, Nicht, and I...and Alice... waited for Alina to return. Then we were going through the portal.

If Mitch didn't get anything when he sent out his feelers, we decided, since we knew the grounds around Victoria better than the Body ever could. We'd enter Outvald in stealth mode and spread out to maximize our forces.

My first job was to break the warding. I had a feeling there might be help available next door at David Bernes' place, and I wanted them to have access to my land in case they wanted to join the party.

I was going to try to bring Alice through the portal with us. I had no idea if I could do it, but if I was truly the master of the portal as Grams had told me I was, I should be able to make it as big or small as I wanted.

Nicht would be our eyes at Victoria. He was good at making himself invisible, and he could work around the outside perimeter, taking out Body soldiers quickly and quietly, giving us an edge.

Hawk's job was to get to the Annex. We were counting on the Body not knowing about the tunnel we'd dug between the house and the big outbuilding that would allow Hawk to get into the house to confer with his soldiers and share the plan with them.

Then if we had time, we'd stay on the outside edge of their forces, working our way quietly through them until reinforcements came.

That was where things got murky. I had no idea what to expect in reinforcements. If Guwalt and Mike were successful, we'd have some help. But we didn't know what or how many.

We'd just have to make do with what we had.

The front door of the house opened. We all stilled, listening for the signal that it was a friendly.

A low whistle sounded and we relaxed. A beat later, Alina strode into the kitchen. "I've got our intel. And you're not gonna like it."

My friends were arrayed behind me. Some were down in the shell of a basement left behind after Victoria was sucked back into Outvald. Some of them paced along the higher ground above. Alice lifted her massive wings and gave a smoky chirp of impatience. I resisted looking up at her, knowing that Shane had her under control.

After some discussion, we'd decided to leave Mitch in Render for the moment. He was in no condition for what was ahead in Outvald, and with the Magistrate's gaze set on Victoria, he should be safe enough in his little shack for a while.

Placing my palm against the rock wall, I closed my eyes and reached for the portal's energy, tugging it free to dance against my metaphysical touch. Victoria's energy throbbed against my skin like the beat of a heart. Too fast. As I concentrated, the heartbeat beneath my fingers strengthened, grew more frantic. I felt Grams in the magic. She was infused into Victoria's energy. Her magic...*our* magic...kept it alive and strong.

Grams was upset and the magic transmitted that to me. I fought the spread of panic that knowledge gave me and tried to focus on the connection that would open the gateway.

The portal began to open beneath my touch,

glowing an eye-searing amber as the magic grew. The stones along the wall shimmered and softened under the onslaught of the magic's impossible heat. A heat that my inherent energy blocked and turned outward, so it wouldn't burn those who'd be passing through the magical gateway.

I stepped backward as the mouth of the portal spread, pulling my hands apart to stretch it beyond the space it usually required for passage.

Hawk and Nicht moved aside to give me room to back away, my arms spreading wider and wider as I went. By the time I hit the wall at the back of the basement, my arms were stretched as wide as they would go and an enormous tunnel pulsed with amber magic in front of us.

"Go!" I said, and Jessa, Alina, and Nicht entered the shimmering gateway I'd created. Hawk stayed at my side. I threw him a look and he shook his head. "I'm staying with you."

I sighed. "Shane!" I called, my voice throbbing beneath the magic. "Get her in there." The magic pounded against me, throbbing like an oversized heart inside my chest and against my skull. My skin felt too tight, the energy stretching me taut in every way.

I was relieved to hear wings throbbing on the air. A heartbeat later, the big dragon drifted gracefully to the ground in front of me, her enormous frame forming a vacuum in the energy that nearly pulled me to my knees.

Wordlessly, Hawk wrapped his arms around my waist. He'd had to do this once before when an over-charged portal tried to pull Sissy into a fiery gateway that threatened to burn her alive.

"Get her inside, Shane!" I screamed.

He jumped down into the basement and hurried forward, placing a hand on the dragon's slender neck and walking forward. To my relief, she followed him docilely into the gateway.

I gritted my teeth against the magic's manic pull, my knees scraping painfully along the ground as the dragon stepped through the interface and into the portal.

I screamed at the effort not to be dragged inside with her. Hawk's legs came around me and he dug the heels of his boots into the hardpack dirt and rock floor, buying us a little distance as Shane stepped in behind Alice.

The energy yanked hard on my core. Pain blossomed through me, the magic tearing little pieces out of my insides as it fought to accommodate the enormous creature passing through.

Then, suddenly, the pressure stopped as if sliced off with a blade. And Hawk and I shot backward to slam against the wall.

Or, more accurately, Hawk hit the wall. I smacked up against his comparatively forgiving chest.

"Umph!" he grunted.

"You okay?" I asked.

"I'll live. Can you let it go?"

I sent my senses along the portal, feeling for the energies of the people passing through its length. I'd created a short gateway, making their journey quick. I felt only two energies still inside the portal. And as I had the thought, Alice stepped out of the portal. I gave Shane a second to clear it before I expelled a breath and let the energy seep away from my palms.

The gateway slammed down to its normal size, still held open through my intentions, but no longer stretched beyond its normal limits.

I pushed to my feet and offered Hawk my hand. "Ready?"

He nodded, letting me pull him to his feet. But as we stepped into the shimmering portal, I noted the glistening spot of blood on his shirt where the sharp edge of a rock must have pierced him when he slammed into the wall.

I'd heal him after I'd returned to the magical embrace of Victoria and Grams. When I regained the full use of my hereditary magic.

By the time Hawk and I stepped out of the portal, everyone else had dispersed per our plan. I'd planned for the portal to let us out in the valley near the cemetery. Our people were to disperse to their assigned locations from there. Trusting that they were all in place as planned, I let the portal go.

I turned to Hawk, and all the blood ran out of my face at his expression.

Following his line of sight, I got a punch in the gut from what I saw.

Hundreds of Body soldiers surrounded Victoria up on the hill.

Hundreds.

We'd known the Magistrate had an army at Victoria from Mitch's seeing, but knowing it and observing it were two very different things.

My heart twisted painfully in my chest.

Two walls of the big old house were in flames, the black smoke barely visible in the night sky as it flowed upward in a thick column.

As we watched, energy blasted from the windows of the house and was answered by a fourfold response from the invaders on the ground.

The Annex was alive with activity. Lights were on inside, and the sounds of crashing and splintering told me the Magistrate's forces were tearing the place apart. I thought of the closet filled with Grams' potions, powders, and spell-books. My heart broke. Had they found and destroyed that too?

Rage rose like a poisonous cloud inside me, turning my muscles to stone. I opened my core and pulled magic into it as fast as I could, taking in far more than was comfortable because I was fully planning to use it as fast and in as deadly a way as I could manage.

Hawk took one look at my face and said. "Open the ward first. Then fight."

I growled, the sound no longer surprising. Then I gave him a stiff nod. "Go. See if you can get into the house."

He reached out, touched my lips with a fingertip, and then he was gone, his running footsteps fast and light.

I took off running in the opposite direction. It was all I could do not to run toward the house. To try to save her from the vicious attack currently being waged against her. But I knew I'd quickly be overwhelmed. And it would do no one any good for me to throw my life away because my emotions were getting the best of me.

Locating the perimeter of the ward, I threaded my fingers through the vibrant strands of defensive energy. I reached out to Victoria, tugging on her defensive magics until I got an answering pull in response. "Break it," I told her. "Friends are coming to help."

A feeling of relief, followed by a jolt of pure joy, bled through the magic to me. I sent what I hoped was a reassuring pulse and started to turn away. I had a thought and stopped, reclaiming my grasp on the house's magic. "Show me where my friends are?" One by one, I fed her the images of my battle partners and she shot me back a snapshot of their locations.

Hawk had somehow gotten past the soldiers inside the annex and was making his way quickly through the tunnel toward the house.

Alina was sneaking up on a man who'd made the unfortunate decision to walk into the woods to pee. She had a small knife clutched between her teeth and two guns shoved into holsters at her narrow hips.

Nicht was chewing on a Body soldier, and there was a pile of them on the ground behind him.

Shane was running up the wooden stairs to his farmhouse. The door opened and Sissy looked out at him, magic dancing on her fingers. Micah shoved his way past her, holding a rifle and wearing a look of deadly intent.

Shane shook his head and started to speak. I couldn't hear his words, but Sissy gave a small cry and grabbed the older man into a hug. Then she started firing questions at him. Boyle appeared behind her, his big turquoise eyes filled with fear and worry.

Tears slid down my cheeks. Sissy and Boyle were at Shane's place. They should be safe there. I doubted the Body knew about it.

Shane had to force his way inside as the other non-combat members of my group flooded out onto the porch with questions.

I blinked the vision away. They were safe, and I had to help Victoria and whoever was fighting from inside her walls.

But before I released her, I asked about Mike.

There was nothing.

He wasn't within Victoria's perimeters. I hadn't really expected him to be. But it would have been nice to have him with us.

Fighting a dogged sense of the uselessness of trying to battle so many, I cut the connection between Victoria and me and took off running.

The Body wasn't taking it as slow as we'd hoped. Their forces had apparently been close by. I realized the Magistrate must have set the plan to overtake Victoria into motion much sooner than we'd suspected. They were already at full force and clearly had the advantage. We were going to have our hands full.

I knew what I needed to do. I ruthlessly pushed back on the fear engendered by my plan. Carefully skirting the field of soldiers, I took off running toward the front of my property.

Hopefully, I'd find what I needed there.

25

Hawk pulled himself the last three feet through the tunnel and fell out into the basement beneath the stairs. He tried to brush some of the dirt from his clothes and hair, but the tunnel had been wet and it was really more mud than dust.

Giving up, he hurried to the stairs and climbed them quickly, taking two steps at a time. At the top, he stopped and listened to make sure the house hadn't already been breached.

He heard several familiar male voices.

Hawk opened the door a crack and called out to warn them he was there. It would be beyond embarrassing to get shot by his own men after managing to evade capture by a dozen Body soldiers around and inside the Annex.

Rian Pierce was the first one to greet Hawk. The other cop embraced him, patting him hard on the back. Rian had lost some weight from his recent poisoning, but he had good color and seemed strong enough, if a little tired. "I'm glad you're back," he told Hawk.

Grodan clasped Hawk's hand. "Glad to see you. Alina?"

"She's here." He jerked his head toward the front of the house. "Out there, doing her thing."

Grodan laughed. "I wouldn't expect anything less. Nicht with her?"

"He is. They're working the perimeters, quietly reducing the enemy's numbers."

The men nodded.

Tomas Fowler stood near a window, a laser rifle in his hands. He didn't speak to Hawk, merely returning to his work of laying down a line of fire along the front of the house. He quickly stepped back as return fire splintered the wall around the window.

Hawk thought Fowler looked ticked, probably because they'd been gone so long. Hawk moved closer and the man's first words verified what Hawk had suspected. "So, you finally decided to come back."

Hawk kept his expression neutral. The men had been under a lot of pressure. He decided he'd cut Tomas some slack. "Things got a little dicey, but yes, we all made it back. Plus some."

"What do you mean?" another voice asked.

Hawk turned to find Artur Forester standing in the kitchen. His brown hair stood in tufts at the top of his head. His eyes were wild. Dark circles stained the skin beneath his brown eyes. As Hawk stared at him, something flared in the depths of those eyes. And he wondered if the Magistrate was looking back at him instead of Glynn's brother. "Is he safe?" Hawk asked the others, making Art's mouth tighten with pique.

"Grams has my invisible friend under lock and key," Art said, his voice tight. "But he's messing with me. I'll hold up. I'm motivated."

They stared across the space at each other for a long moment and then Hawk inclined his head. "You'll tell us if that changes?"

Art clearly didn't like the question, but he nodded.

"It means we brought extra recruits back with us," Hawk said, answering Art's question.

"Good," Rian responded. "We can use all the help we can get."

"Where is everybody?" Hawk asked.

"We got Boyle, the Krafts, and Sissy out at the first sign of trouble," Rian said. "Micah went with them as protection, and it turns out the Tellsons were in the human army, so they're serving protection duty too."

"Good. Shane's granddaughter?"

"Kate's there," Grodan said with a smile. "Girl's fearless. And she's a fine shot."

Hawk did a mental headcount and glanced toward the stairs. "Ms. Blanchette?"

The men exchanged a look.

"What?" Hawk said, already thinking about heading upstairs to check on her.

"Kara's..." Tomas began. He stopped and shook his head.

"What he's trying to say is that she's barricaded herself in her room and refuses to leave," Art said. "We don't know what's going on up there, but the last time we went up, the whole second floor was filled with an icy mist, and she was talking to someone we couldn't see."

Hawk nodded. The woman seemed to have a connection with the dead. He was pretty sure she talked to Glynn's Grams. He suspected he knew what she was but intended to respect her need for privacy. She'd share when she wanted to. "I don't want to march in here and step on any toes," He said, frowning. "But has anybody noticed the house is on fire?"

As Hawk said the words, he jerked his head toward the flames he could see outside the window in the living room. But there was no smoke and no heat inside the house.

"Magical flame," Art told him. "It keeps the Body from scaling the house. With limited resources, it saves us from having to protect all sides. We can focus on just the front and one side."

Clever. Hawk filed that one away in case he ever needed to defend a magical house with a sorceress as its soul with limited manpower against unimaginable odds. "Why not infuse the whole house?" he asked.

"No visibility," Tomas answered in a cold voice. "We need to know what they're up to out there."

"Good. Okay, here's the plan..." Hawk's words died away as a roar rattled the windows of the old house.

I slipped quietly into David Bernes' yard, cognizant of the unnatural silence that covered the dark, heavily-treed property like a blanket. My gaze assessed the night for the telltale sign of glowing eyes I'd seen there before.

It had been a while. Maybe David's old friends had finally drifted away.

"Hello?" I said softly into the silence.

Nothing and no one responded.

I forced my feet to move forward. "Is anybody here?"

A scent wafted past and I jolted to a stop, recognizing it. The odor was a mix of wolf and something unnatural. Panic flared, kickstarting my heart into a frantic rhythm in my chest. I really hoped I didn't have to convince some wild animal that I wasn't a Scooby snack.

"I'm not here to hurt you," I said as gently as I could. "I thought you might want to help us get some justice for David?"

The shadows near the trees shifted. A tall, dark creature stepped free of them.

I stared at the eight-foot-tall beast in front of me. My lizard brain screamed at me to flee.

Run. Danger. Escape!

I slammed down on that instinctive response and forced my mind to consider what I was seeing.

The wolfman.

A low growl throbbed on the air.

I held my ground, though I was starting to wish I'd taken time to pee before just diving into the battle. Pressing my thighs together, I tried to look harmless. "Hi. We met before."

Good goddess in a girdle! Had I lost my mind? Next, I'd be asking him if he wanted to join me for a nightcap.

I barely kept from rolling my eyes.

The wolfman had spoken to me before. Surely, he wouldn't try to eat me now...especially after I did the very thing he's asked me to do. Unfortunately, I had no idea how feral he was. It was unlikely he thought like a human. But he *had* once asked me to get justice for David Bernes. I was trying to do that, among other things.

The growling stopped and I heard sniffing.

He was scenting me.

"You asked me to avenge David. Remember?"

The creature dropped into a crouch and sniffed again, his wide nostrils flaring.

Seeing my plan being ground to dust at my feet, I willed him to turn and walk away. Instead, he moved closer and sniffed again. Then he tilted his head. The wide muzzle opened. And he said, "David?"

Relief swept through me. "Yes."

He stared at me a moment longer and then straightened to his full height. Pointing toward Victoria's grounds, he asked, "Man who killed him?"

Goddess, I loved a man of few words in a crisis. "Yes. He's come back. Will you help us?"

He stared at me for another long moment and then nodded. "Come then," he said. He took off running toward Victoria. I took a deep breath and started after him, mentally preparing to engage.

Sending my senses into the air, I tasted the available magic. It was a smorgasbord of vibrant energies —a magical buffet.

And I was suddenly feeling very hungry.

We hit the battlefield just as a roar sent the waiting soldiers into frantic motion.

I stumbled in surprise at the sound. Glancing

upward, I felt my eyes widening at the unexpected sight.

Several bursts of fire pierced the cloudy sky in a dense red and gold spray. I grinned, realizing that the dragons had arrived. Leaving them to their work, I yanked magic into my core and waded into battle.

Bodies flew around me. I suddenly realized there was more than just the dragons and the wolfman at work.

The night pixilated beside me and a female Body soldier flew into the air, arms and legs thrashing. She crashed hard into the grass.

A broad face appeared for just a moment and winked at me.

Mike was plowing through the soldiers, an unseen force they couldn't hope to overcome.

A dark shape with glowing red eyes melted out of the night and deadly jaws closed over the downed woman's broken form. Her screams followed me through the battle.

Dragons shot out of the sky and painted the surging soldiers with fire.

Flailing figures, bathed in flames, stumbled across the field, smacking into their fellow combatants and transferring the magical fire to them. Blood-curdling screams nearly drowned out the dragons' roars.

I spotted Alina a few yards away, taller than most

of the women fighting and some of the men. She fought with balletic grace, fierce and agile.

Shane stood in the center of a patch of empty ground, his hands glowing with magic death and his body straight and strong as power pulsed around him, creating an impermeable magic wall. A group of Body soldiers decided to attack Shane at once, but they didn't get far. The sorcerer threw up his hands and a shimmering curtain of power blew away from him, sending them flying to crash against their fellow invaders. Another man dodged forward, energy dancing at his fingertips, and Shane took him down with a single slash of his hand. Deadly energy cut into the soldier like a blade. Several more ran forward, splashing potent magic at Shane and screaming as he cut them down without apparent effort.

A woman charged me, face twisted with hate. Energy sizzled on her fingertips, and she clearly intended to hit me with whatever magical demise she wielded. She never had a chance to send that energy my way. The ground beneath her split in a wide black crevice and she dropped into it, shrieking as it folded back over her.

Across the battlefield, I noted several other assailants dropping away, pulled beneath the land before they even had time to scream.

"Thanks!" I yelled to Victoria, receiving her response as a warmth that infused my senses.

Nicht's passage through the crowd was marked by the terrified screams of his victims as they dropped into the roiling crowd and disappeared from sight.

The wolfman fought with simple grace, claws slashing and teeth snapping as soldiers encircled him with determined faces. He threw back his head and bellowed a warning, and one soldier forgot the thrust she was making, eyes blanking as the wolfman swung an arm and cut her down. A man sliced toward the big creature's legs, the blade somehow stopping just short of its target. Magic glowed in the wolfman's eyes and it somehow dulled the will of his opponents, leaving them open to his deadly attacks. Bodies were piled up around him.

I realized in that moment that the impressive creature was an influencer.

I grinned. "Nice work getting him out of there, David," I whispered.

A man dove at me, his blade slicing past my head with near-lethal accuracy. I threw off my contemplations and focused on the job at hand.

Twisting the energy at my core into a long, slender whip, I set my stance and snapped the air with it. The magic was very effective in keeping Body warriors at bay, cutting them down as they risked the snapping energy and tried to attack. A sorcerer rose up in front of me and I danced away from his twin magical jolts. His energy speared the spot where I'd been and cut down one of the man's fellow soldiers.

I ducked the swing of a knife, danced away from an energy bolt, and leaped over another surge of sulfurous black power, spinning elegantly while slashing an energy blade across another's middle.

The whip found a target and I yanked the man into my blade, watching death take the light from his eyes before releasing him and moving on.

I feasted on Victoria's energy, embracing the power that had seeped into the earth and saturated every living thing on my land.

Covered in blood and non-lethal wounds, I nevertheless battled on with continually renewing energy. I felt like I could take all comers.

A shout went up near the house. I spared a glance in that direction and gave a startled gasp as the entire structure seemed to explode into flames, smoke rising into the clouds above. "No!"

I took a step toward the house, and agony slashed through me, burning with its own kind of fire as a Body soldier sliced me across the back with a razor-sharp blade. I took two more steps, desperate to get to Victoria, and then went down from a blow to the back of my knees. I crashed down hard into the grass, tasting dirt as I struck.

There was a roar of pain, and the people around me scattered. Fire burst on the air above my head. Strong arms snatched me off the ground and yanked me away as a dragon, writhing in pain and spitting uncontrolled flame, hit the ground and skidded several yards, taking out a dozen people as she went.

I turned my head, fighting to get away from whoever had me in a restraining hold. "Alice!" I punched the arm around my waist. "Let. Me. Go!"

"Glynn! Leave her. We need to get to the house."

Even through my despair and frustration, I recognized Hawk's voice and gave up fighting him. He released me and we started to run, slashing blindly at anybody who tried to stop us. My legs screamed with every step. My back bellowed its pain. But ahead of me, Victoria was dying. I could feel her agony with every pulse of the consuming flames.

Screams erupted on the night as a dozen Body soldiers formed a pile on the ground. Mike flickered into existence beneath their punching fists and slashing blades.

His magic sputtered away as he succumbed to the concentrated violence of their blows.

Tears burned in my eyes.

A soldier danced forward with a sword. Nicht suddenly appeared and took him down under a chorus of screams.

Several men fired weapons at the attackers. I recognized our security team—Rian, Tomas, and Grodan.

My mind blocked everything. Every cell in my body was attuned to Victoria's silent screams. Her magical heartbeat slowed and stuttered. I felt every faltering beat in my core. "Victoria!" I screamed, desperate to make it stop. But the flames ate away at her. They consumed her bones and melted her flesh.

Inside the big old house a phantom shrieking had begun. It tore at my senses, ripping a matching shriek from my chest and breaking my mind as I leaped onto the porch and into the inferno that threatened to consume her.

To the basement child, a disembodied voice said. *You know what you need to do.*

The third floor crumpled and crashed down onto the second. I sobbed as memories of Boyle's attic room slipped through my mind. His bed, his toys, his cute little form perched on the windowsill staring out into the night.

He'd be so upset without his things.

Flames licked up around me. Flesh-melting heat burrowed closer. I faltered, stumbled, and had to push myself forward toward the basement stairs. A fire-enveloped hunk of ceiling smashed down in front of me. I tried to leap over it and fell, my ankle twisting. It was still weak from its prior wrenching outside of Hawk's house.

Hands pulled me back to my feet, supporting me to the open doorway. Hawk's scent filled my nostrils as he wrapped an arm around my shoulders, all but carrying me through the conflagration.

You know what to do, Glynn, Grams assured me one more time.

But, did I? It didn't matter. I would do as she said. "Grams!" I screamed, the word coming out in a violent cough as smoke scraped my throat raw.

Hawk and I stumbled down the steps. I blinked, coughing violently as my brain tried to take in the sight before me.

The portal blazed, opening wide, and Artur stood before it, arms raised, palms up and head thrown back as his lips moved over a spell.

I faltered for a beat, unsure at first what I was seeing. "Art?"

The figure in front of the portal turned slowly, eyes glowing with an evil he hadn't been able to dispel.

The Magistrate was in control again.

26

"Art, no!" I said, tears blinding me. "Don't let him win."

"Don't blame him," a hated voice said. "The boy couldn't help himself," The Magistrate stepped forward from the shadows, a smug smile playing across his cold face. "But I am glad you've decided to join us, Glynnie. I thought I was going to have to use the little gargoyle beast to draw you in. Now, maybe I'll just keep him for a pet."

Hawk moved lightning fast, settling a blade against the other man's throat. "You aren't going to touch that boy or anyone else."

"Guardian. It's a pleasure to see you again," Martin snarled.

Hawk pressed the blade closer, drawing a thin line of blood along the other man's throat. The Magistrate's expression tightened, but he smiled.

I saw his intention in the coldness of that gaze. "Hawk, don't let him touch you!"

I was too late.

The Magistrate reached out and touched Hawk's shoulder with a fingertip.

The big guardian went rigid, his eyes rolling back but his lids staying open in an eerie parody of death. He convulsed violently, slamming to the ground before I could grab him. Blood-tinged foam coated his rigid lips.

The Magistrate stared down at him, a pleased expression on his face.

"Hawk!" I screamed, dropping to my knees beside him.

Do what needs to be done, child, Grams said again, more urgency in her voice than before.

I tried to pull Hawk into my lap, but I couldn't wrap my arms around him. He was too stiff, his body violent in its reaction to the Magistrate's ugly magic.

"Artur Forester!" I screamed. "Don't let him do this to us."

The floor above our heads creaked, groaned, and then split apart, spilling fire down onto the dirt floor of the basement. I bent protectively over Hawk. An ember landed on my brother and burned its way into the flesh of his outstretched arm.

He didn't react. More fiery embers shot toward his legs, burning tiny holes into his clothing. Art finally twitched, gave a violent jerk, then spun around, the glow gone from his gaze. He looked at me, horror filling his eyes.

Behind him, the portal started to close.

I knew I couldn't let it close. There wouldn't be time to open it again. The house was quickly succumbing to a fiery death, and we'd all die right along with it.

"I need your help," I screamed to my brother.

The Magistrate seemed to realize he'd lost control of Artur, and his magical control over Hawk slipped away.

"Hawk!" I yelled, trying to wake him up. I needed to get him out of that inferno before the whole house fell down around our shoulders. There was no way I was strong enough to move him by myself.

Glynneth Forester! Grams yelled in my head. *Do it. Now!*

Sobbing, I forced myself away from Hawk and stumbled to the portal. I whispered the words of a spell I never thought I'd use once, let alone twice.

As the final word left my lips, I stepped into the portal and it began to close behind me.

I took two steps before my legs gave out and I landed hard. Biting back a cough from dust and smoke, I dug my hands into the ground.

"You are mine!" I told the magic of the portal. "You belong to me. And you will do as I command." I had no idea where the words had come from. They emerged from a deep well of ancient magic I hadn't known I possessed.

The portal began to spin, a violent revolution that made me so dizzy I had to close my eyes. I pictured Render and the Earthly realm. I pictured my old life, my simple ways, and Victoria whole and healthy.

I held the vision in my mind until I felt the portal stop its dizzying rotation. And then I opened my eyes.

I could immediately feel the difference. I smelled Earth's unique scents. I felt the loss of energy that leaving Outvald had precipitated.

I dropped my head back and looked at the solid wood that formed the ceiling above my head. I noted the lack of smoke.

But my stomach twisted when I felt the emptiness in the house above me—the emptiness of the street outside.

I was alone. I'd left everyone I loved behind.

Victoria was no longer a home. It was a shadow of itself. An empty promise.

I was in an in-between of some kind. An *unplace*. Where the house was whole again but devoid of everything that had always given it life.

Had I messed up the spell?

More importantly, how did I fix it? The sheer terror of being in an unplace took me to my knees. I folded to the ground on a barrage of sobs. And let the horror of the last hours take me over.

But time pushed at me. I needed to do something. I just didn't know what. I pushed to my feet. Scrubbing tears from my face, I stood before the portal and tried to open it again. It didn't comply. I stood looking at the cold stone wall, fear a razor-sharp agony in my chest.

I threw back my head and screamed.

Overcome with desperation, I ran up the stairs and burst through the door, finding the Victoria I'd expected to find. But it was a colorless version of the one I'd grown to love.

Like a retro black and white television show.

I kept climbing until I'd reached the attic level. I stood in the doorway to Boyle's room, my chest heaving as I took it all in. His little pjs still lay discarded on the floor alongside his favorite toy truck. A chunk of bread sat on the table beside his bed, crumbs littering the wooden surface. His window was open to let the cool night air inside, but he wasn't there. I couldn't feel his presence anywhere in or near the house.

A soft sound by my feet brought my gaze downward. The little black cat wound itself around my ankles, its bright gaze lifting to mine. I bent to scoop it up, pressing my face into its sweet-smelling fur. "Why are you here, little one?" I murmured against the silky fur.

Purring vibrated against my skin. The little cat's tail smacked gently against my arm. It wriggled to be released and I set it down on top of Boyle's messy bed. Reaching down, I ran my fingers over the tangled covers and smiled sadly. "He never makes his bed."

Pain sliced through my heart. I looked around and realized what I'd always known but hadn't really understood.

Without the people I loved, Victoria was just a house.

The boards and rugs and windows were simple manifestations of a life that wouldn't exist without the people who'd passed through it. Love had built the old Victorian. Love sustained its walls and fed its soul. Grams was its magic. Boyle was its soul. And I was its heart. Artur...

My heart clenched in pain as I thought of my brother. Artur was an imperfect creature like I was. Like everyone was. He was as much a part of Victoria as I was. As Grams was. He deserved to be within her walls no matter his flaws.

The truth made my chest tight. Had I pushed Art away since he'd come home? Depriving him of a way to become his complete self?

Meow! the little cat mewled.

Back in Outvald, Victoria was gone. But not Grams. Not Artur. Not Boyle. Not... "Hawk!" I'd left him in that basement to die. I had to get back.

As I ran toward the stairs, plunging down them at a dangerous speed, I prayed I wouldn't be too late.

The house would burn. It would be gone.

But by the grace of the goddess, the people who lived there would go on. We'd live to fight our battles and love each other. We'd struggle, we'd thrive, we'd crash, we'd rise.

It had never been about the house, I realized. It had just been a random bit of luck that rested an old house within the fiery embrace of a lei line.

But the real magic was about my family and our indomitable will to forge our place within the lives we'd been handed.

It didn't matter if that was in Outvald or on Earth. As long as it wasn't in this cold, loveless unplace.

We could build new walls. A new roof. New memories. Victoria would live on in our hearts. And we'd be all the stronger for it.

With these things spinning through my mind, I jerked to a halt before the stone wall and placed my palms over its cool surface. I didn't bother with a spell. I didn't try to craft the perfect words. Instead, I simply said, "Take me home."

And the magic swirled beneath my touch.

A moment later, I stepped out into a smoke-filled basement.

Artur stood over the Magistrate's lifeless form, a bloody knife clutched in his hand.

Hawk was stirring, his eyes opening as I dropped to a knee beside him. "Glynn?" He frowned with confusion.

I grabbed his arm. "Come on. We need to get out of here."

I looked at my brother. "Art! Let's go."

He turned slowly, and I reveled in the human brown of his eyes. The evidence of his unwelcome visitor was gone from his gaze. "He's dead."

And apparently his spell died with him.

Hawk came to his feet and I jerked my head toward the bulkhead door in the back wall. It was deep in the shadows. I'd nearly forgotten it was there. "Can you get that open? It's probably rusted. We haven't used it in years."

Hawk didn't hesitate. He nodded and headed that way. His strides were slightly uneven but grew stronger with every step.

I went over to my brother. Feeling his confusion and pain, I said to him, "You had to do it. He gave you no choice."

Art shook his head. He stared at the blade in his hand and then opened his fingers to let it fall. His voice was soft, filled with sorrow. "He wasn't always evil. He was good to me at first. I...thought of him like a father once."

I wrapped my arms around my brother and held him tight.

His body shook beneath a violent, emotional tremor for a moment. Then he stilled.

"Come on, big brother. We aren't done yet," I told him. "We have people who need us."

He nodded, slid his gaze determinedly away from the Magistrate, and followed me to the metal doors Hawk had thrown open to the night air.

Smoke sifted past the door as we climbed up out of the basement. Behind us, the ceiling collapsed inward, ravaged by the flames. But there was no more fire. My trip through the portal had somehow arrested it.

We hurried around the house and stopped, staring at an incredible sight.

The battlefield was quiet. Dozens of people still stood, their faces pointed toward the house, contorted in terror. But they seemed unable to move. To run away.

I looked toward the porch and saw Kara Blanchette standing there, arms outstretched, eyes closed, and head back. Her lips were moving, and a pale white fog emerged from between them. As the fog drifted into the night, spectral forms emerged from it, their empty gazes locked on the remaining soldiers on Victoria's grounds.

Ghosts!

I blinked, looking at Hawk. "She's a necromancer."

He nodded. "A powerful one, it looks like."

When I turned my attention back to Kara, I realized Grams was standing next to her. As if feeling my gaze on her, the spirit of my Grams turned to Art and me and smiled.

Beside me, Art gasped, tears filling his brown eyes. "I can see her, Glynn," he breathed.

I nodded. At that moment, Grams' slight form was as clear and solid as she'd been before her death.

Kara's ghosts drifted across the field, reaching for each remaining Body soldier and touching their chests before moving on to the next. As they moved on, the person they'd touched folded silently to the ground, unmoving.

The spirits moved past the members of our army, never touching Shane, whose back was bowed with great weariness and probably sadness as he stood looking down on the fallen dragon.

Not reaching for Alina, who was covered in blood but stood ready to battle the specters if necessary.

They glided past Grodan, and Tomas, and Rian, the three men bleeding and bent with pain but alive.

The spirits split and moved around the young Tellsons, who were leaning on each other and watching Kara's progeny with haunted eyes. They ignored Nicht's defiant snarl. They didn't touch the giants clustered around Mike, who was still stretched out on the ground but seemed to be alive.

And they passed the Wolfman and a dozen other creatures who stood with him, jaws and fur covered in blood.

By the time the specters had passed over the entire battlefield, only our people still stood.

My gaze caught on Alice and my heart broke. Then I noticed movement behind the enormous body. The sun lifted an inch higher in the sky. Pale light fell across a large, snowy white bird with a long yellow beak and beautiful plumage adorning her head and tail. The white bird sat on Alice's heaving belly and pierced her with a sharp beak, lifting and lowering her wings in a rhythm not unlike a natural heartbeat.

"No!" I said, starting forward to stop the bird.

Hawk snagged my wrist, stopping me. "It's okay. It's Jessa. She's healing the dragon."

I frowned. "Healing? What is she?"

"A Caladrius," Grams said, walking toward me with the small black cat in her arms. "Very rare." She patted my arm. "It is a statement of great influence that she attached herself to you. The creature is a powerful healer. She'll put your dragon to rights."

I squinted accusingly at the cat. It ignored me as it bathed its pristine paws. Then her words sank in, and relief softened some of the tightness in my chest.

Art moved forward in awe, reaching for Grams. "It's you, isn't it?"

She laughed. "Yes, child. I'm happy to see you've finally embraced your legacy." She frowned. "Your sister could use the help. She's been doing everything herself for years."

His cheeks flushed guiltily and he nodded.

Grams turned toward the house, sighing. "Well, all things come to an end eventually."

We stepped back and looked up at the smoldering remains of Victoria. The two walls where Grams had engaged magical fire were intact, nearly unblemished. But the real fire, origin unknown, had taken the rest of the house nearly to the ground.

A deep sadness filled me. I'd miss the familiar quirks and flaws as much as the old girl's innate elegance.

"I've got lumber and roofing materials," Shane said. "And I'm pretty handy with a hammer."

I turned to him, seeing the weariness creasing his face. "You okay?"

He nodded. "I am now that Alice will be okay. But, I could use a nap and some of that cake you brought us."

I laughed. "Good luck with that. Boyle's been at your house for hours."

Shane swore softly.

"We've been testing flours," said a soft, feminine voice behind us. Allison Tellson smiled at Shane. "We've got everything we need in the Annex. I'd be happy to make you some cakes."

His arm around his wife's waist, Dillon Tellson nodded. "We've perfected a recipe for donuts too." He cocked his head. "Have you ever had a donut?"

Shane's eyes lit. "Bless the goddess. I'd just about give my left arm for a couple of those right now."

Rian, Tomas, and Grodan agreed enthusiastically.

They all wandered away toward the Annex, talking animatedly about food.

I knew it was their way of coping and envied them that release from the horrors of the night.

I glanced at Kara, finding her still standing on the porch, eyes cast toward the disappearing shadows of night.

I followed her gaze. The other dragons had melted away with the light. They would no doubt stay nearby to help Alice when she regained her wings.

The giants and Mike were gone. I'd have to ask someone later how he was. I really hoped he'd be okay.

Out of my peripheral vision, I saw a tall black shape moving near the tree line. When I glanced his way, the wolfman's eyes shone with golden light through the last of the darkness.

I lifted a hand to him. He nodded, then turned and melted into the trees, followed by a small army of other creatures, many of whom I suspected had been David Bernes' "guests."

Hawk put an arm around me. "We should make plans for temporary lodgings for everybody."

Artur stepped up on my other side. "I have some ideas about that."

I sighed, glad for his help. "Good. Because I'm too tired to think right now."

"Let's see how bad the Annex is," Hawk told him.

I watched as the two men headed in that direction, hoping the Body hadn't destroyed too much of the big building. If they had, the task of creating a place to sleep was going to be daunting.

I had a sudden, overwhelming need to see and hold Boyle. But the idea of walking all that way was daunting. I sat on the porch and stared out at the grounds, blinking as I realized there were fewer bodies draped over the grass.

The Caladrius rose into the sky with a long, shrill cry and flew toward me, dipping its wings in greeting as it took off toward the trees.

I waved at Jessa, searching my memory of mythological studies for details about the healing bird. I remembered something about the Caladrius drawing a patient's sickness and injury into itself and then flying away to disperse the illness over a large, open space.

A handy trick.

As I watched, Alice grunted in a failed attempt to roll to her feet. She finally managed it on her third try and then stood with her sides heaving for a moment before taking off. As her elegant form speared the sky, the other dragons set a flight path to intersect with hers, roaring their greetings.

I watched them until they were out of sight and then pushed wearily to my feet.

Another look at the field showed fewer bodies still. Victoria's magic was taking them away, probably pulling them under the soil.

"Glynnie, Glynnie, Glynnie!" a welcome, adorable voice called out.

My head snapped up to find the enormous Bessie trotting toward me with Boyle, Emma, and Shane's granddaughter Kate sitting astride her wide back.

I waved, feeling a grin spreading across my face at the baby gargoyle's antics.

Boyle's gaze slipped over the burned house, and I saw him go very still. My grin slid away. I wondered if the baby would take the loss hard.

Kate's gaze was kind as she stopped Bessie in front of me. "Oh, Glynn. I'm so sorry."

I helped Emma and Boyle down from the horse. Keeping hold of Boyle for a few extra minutes, I set him on the ground when he started to squiggle.

"Glynnie! What happened?" he asked, his tone hushed.

"It's just temporary," I told him. "We're going to make the house as good as new again."

His round, turquoise eyes widened at the sight before him. "My room..."

I ruffled the little tuft of orange hair between his big ears. "It will be okay, sweet boy."

He stared at it a minute longer and then sighed. "Can we make my room really high in the sky?" he asked, an excited spark finding his expressive eyes.

His resiliency touched my heart. "Absolutely. I'll tell Uncle Art to add that to the plans."

He bounced up and down a few times. "Can me and Emma go to the 'Nex?"

"Yes. But don't get in the way."

They took off running...or, in Boyle's case... loping toward the Annex. As they left, I heard him tell Emma, "It's juss tempwy, Emma. Don't worry."

Kate and I chuckled.

She climbed down from Bessie. "He's such a cutie."

I nodded, my throat clogged with emotion.

"I wanted to tell you we cooked a big meal at the house. And I've set up cots for everybody. The Krafts are taking inventory of the building supplies Gramps has in his work shed."

Tears burned my eyes, and I blinked them back.

Her words reminded me of the revelations I'd had in the unplace.

We'd all lost things in the battle. Some of us had lost blood. But we hadn't lost our will to thrive. And in the end, we would all come out stronger for it.

The Body was beaten back, at least temporarily.

Tomorrow, we'd start to rebuild. And then we'd shore up our defenses so the Body couldn't sneak up on us again.

And one day, we'd return to the Earthly plane and do what we could to extinguish the Body's poisonous form of control.

Because everyone had a right to live as they pleased.

And nobody had the right to try and stop them.

EPILOGUE

Summer had been a busy season in Outvald. The days were much hotter there than they'd been in Render. And the nights barely cooled off. But, for the most part, we were too busy to notice. We'd managed to rescue the two rocking chairs from Victoria's porch after the fire. They were slightly singed but mostly fine. Grams and I had made a habit of sitting in them every evening as the sun slipped from the sky, making way for a fat, silvery moon.

The chairs were on the Annex porch, under a newly constructed roof that allowed us to stay out of the sun and avoid the rain.

As usual, the black cat was sitting in Gram's lap. I could hear him purring from where I sat a few feet away.

Boyle and Emma were playing in the pool the

guys had made for them. They'd brought a big old metal trough from David Bernes' home for the purpose. It was big enough for the two kids to float their boats and safely pretend to swim.

David's home was no longer empty. We'd encompassed it with our warding and Mitch was comfortably ensconced in the place, his recliner holding a position of prominence in the center of the main living space. To his credit, he'd cleaned the place up nicely and we no longer dreaded going inside. If any of David Bernes' relatives ever showed up and wanted the place, we'd happily move Mitch back to Victoria. But, in the interim, it gave him a private place where he could live his best life and protected the home from squatters, who'd probably destroy it.

From what I could tell, the creatures David had rescued still lived on his land in safety and peace. I hadn't known David, but I had a feeling their continued presence would have made him happy.

With the Body an ever-present danger, Professor Guwalt had decided to leave the University. He'd stopped by our place on his way across Outvald, dropping Belle off and staying a few days to visit. He'd been vague about his future plans, but I'd gotten the impression that he hadn't given up on helping the creatures of Outvald against unscrupulous magic users in other dimensions.

We'd assured him we'd support him in those efforts whenever he needed us.

Before he left, he told us they'd discovered the woman who'd owned the auction, apparently some kind of shifter, had indeed been the one to kill poor David Bernes as the unfortunate Maple had told us. It seemed she'd since succumbed to the poison of the "feral flu" and had died a horrific death. The best part of that was that the live auction was no more.

We'd celebrated the news with a huge dinner of roasted meat, baked toffatelos, homemade bread, and cake. Then we gathered by the road to give the professor an enthusiastic sendoff, and watched him ride his three-wheeled bicycle down the road.

The smell of freshly cut lumber had been a constant since the fire, and it had begun to represent home to me. Behind us, in the Annex, voices rose and fell, interspersed with bursts of laughter. I rocked contentedly as the pleasant aroma of something sweet and doughy wafted out from the oversized oven Art and Dillon Tellson had built.

Shane had gained a potbelly since the Tellsons discovered he was an eager taste tester. Baked goods increasingly found their way to the adjoining property and into Shane's growing belly. We saw the older man a lot. He seemed to take special pride in helping us recreate Victoria after the fire.

I stared at the renovations across the grass, eyeing the tall tower at the back where Boyle's bedroom would be. The room was circular, with windows in the north, south, east, and west. A catwalk encircled the outside of the structure, with steps that led to the rest of the roof so he could do his nightly wandering.

Boyle loved his new room and couldn't wait to move in. For my part, I wasn't looking forward to climbing the fifty stairs leading to his lodgings in the sky and planned to turn over a new leaf and only visit every couple of days to nag him about cleaning his room.

A man and a woman walked up the hill arm and arm. I poked Grams, pointing at Kate and Grodan. The two had become something of an item over the months. It made me happy to see them together. Grams made a soft noise of pleasure. "It's good to see you young people happy."

I deliberately avoided her gaze. I knew she was really talking about Hawk and me. She wasn't wrong. Hawk and I had definitely been whispering about the future and sharing heated kisses in the moonlight. It was a new situation for me. A delicious and promising future that brightened more with every day. I found myself smiling more than frowning lately, despite the challenges we continued to encounter.

Artur and Alina had also been spending a lot of time together. That had been a constant source of fun for all of us as we watched the shapely blonde tigress tame my hopeless nerd of a brother.

And of course, there were Sissy and Micah. I'd

seen that one coming a mile away. But it still made me smile to see them with their heads together, giggling like teens.

Kara Blanchette had been friendlier since the battle. It was as if she was relieved to have her secret finally known and accepted by everyone. Still, she was a private person and, when she'd asked for help building a simple little home down by the cemetery, I was proud of the guys for jumping in to construct a cute little cottage for her. She'd become the mistress of the cemetery, and she'd made it into a pleasant respite where the living could stay connected to the dead.

Grams and I rocked in silence for a while, both of us staring at the unfinished lumber covering the framing of the new house like flesh over bones. I was looking forward to the new, larger kitchen with room for more people so we could all gather together for special times. Hawk would have his own security room, with adjoining quarters so he could be near the new monitors he and Art had planned for the room.

To my everlasting relief, Victoria had managed to protect the library from the fire, so all the books had been saved. We'd lost most of our furniture, which had necessitated several trips through the portal to gather more.

The big abandoned house on the property where Mitch's shed was, had been filled with a bounty of furniture the owners had left behind. We'd happily scavenged the place, adding it to Mitch's recliner in the truck we'd borrowed from Hawk's old garage.

In the end, I hadn't tackled bringing the truck through the portal, despite the men all nagging at me to try it. You might say I lacked motivation for the task.

Grams had been stoic about losing Victoria, which surprised me a little. For as long as I could remember, she and Victoria had been like a single entity. Even more so after Grams had died.

But she seemed to take pride in the changes we had planned. And had been reluctant to interject when asked for her opinions, saying, "This house belongs to you and Art, child. You should create exactly what you want."

After some initial resistance on my part, we happily embraced that philosophy.

I looked at the black cat in Grams' lap and asked her the question I'd wanted to ask since the night of the fire. "What's up with that cat, anyway?"

She turned to me, appearing surprised. "What do you mean?"

I narrowed my gaze on her. "There's something odd about him."

She shrugged, a secret smile on her lips.

"Is he..." I struggled for the right word. I finally settled for one that didn't exactly capture the essence of what I wanted to know, hoping she'd understand my question. "Alive?"

Her laughter was bright, cheerful. "Of course he's alive, child."

There went my theory that he was a ghost cat.

I frowned. "But he shows up everywhere." He'd been in a vision once. And in the unplace. He'd been in Render, and he'd come with us to Outvald. "I get the feeling he's always sending me a message."

Her brows lifted. The cat rolled over and offered Grams his fat belly. "Really? How fascinating? Do you understand the message?"

Yes, I realized. I did.

I laughed. "I'm just saying, that cat's not normal. He doesn't even have a name."

"Probably not," Grams agreed with that same secret smile. "But he is what he is meant to be."

I shook my head. I certainly couldn't argue with that.

"And he does have a name," she went on, her eyes sparkling. "It's Merlin."

I barked out a short laugh. "Of course it is."

The End

DON'T MISS OUT

Sam doesn't give away a lot of books. But she values her readers and, to show it, she's gifting you a copy of a fun book just for signing up for her newsletter!

SIGN UP FOR SAM'S NEWSLETTER!

https://samcheever.com/newsletter/

ALSO BY SAM CHEEVER

If you enjoyed **Auctus,** you might also enjoy these other fun mystery series by Sam. To find out more, visit the **BOOKS** page at www.samcheever.com:

Enhanced Magic - **For more fun with Glynn, Hawk, and Boyle**
Enchanting Inquiries Paranormal Mysteries
Reluctant Familiar Paranormal Mysteries
Yesterday's Paranormal Mysteries
Gainfully Employed Mysteries
Silver Hills Cozy Mysteries
Country Cousin Mysteries

ABOUT THE AUTHOR

USA Today and WSJ Bestselling Author Sam Cheever writes contemporary and paranormal mystery and suspense, creating stories that draw you in and keep you eagerly turning pages. Known for writing great characters, snappy dialogue, and unique and exhilarating stories, Sam is the award-winning author of 80+ books.

To learn more about Sam and her work, visit her at one of her online hotspots·
www.samcheever.com
samcheever@samcheever.com